Rabbis
of the
Garden State

DANIEL MELTZ

RATTLING GOOD YARNS
PRESS

Copyright © 2025 Daniel Meltz

All rights reserved.

No part of this publication may be reproduced, distributed, or transmitted in any form or by any means, including photocopying, recording, or other electronic or mechanical methods, without the prior written permission of the publisher, except in the case of brief quotations embodied in critical reviews and certain other noncommercial uses permitted by copyright law. For permission requests, write to the publisher, addressed "Attention: Permissions Coordinator," at the address below.

This is a work of fiction. Names, characters, businesses, places, events, locales, and incidents are either the products of the author's imagination or used in a fictitious manner. Any resemblance to actual persons, living or dead, or actual events is purely coincidental.

Rattling Good Yarns Press
33490 Date Palm Drive 3065
Cathedral City CA 92235
USA
www.rattlinggoodyarns.com

Cover Design: Rattling Good Yarns Press

Library of Congress Control Number: 2024951358
ISBN: 978-1-955826-83-9

First Edition

For Amy, Betsy, Dave, Mitch and Steve Ackerman

"If a slave says to thee, I will not go out from thee, because he loveth thee and thy household and because he is contented with thee, then thou shalt take an awl and pierce it through his ear into the door, and he shall be thy slave forever."
~Deuteronomy 15:16-17

"Thou shalt do the same in the case of thy female slave."
~Deuteronomy 15:17

Ninety Miles an Hour
1966

1

"What am I going to do with you?" she said.

She was driving like a nut again, so crazy I pictured our seatbeltless carcasses flying through the windshield. She had her elbow out the window, resting on the ledge, and her other hand off the steering wheel—completely off the steering wheel!—digging into the seat for one of her cigarettes. "Crap." Her fingers couldn't find one.

"What are you doing?" I said.

"My emerald bracelet slipped off my wrist—what do you think?" She shoved her hand in her broken-down pocketbook and slid it all around. "The one Prince Charming bought me." We almost hit a tree.

I said, "I wish you would drive like a normal person for once."

"I have no idea what to do with you, Andy. Honestly? I'm shocked. Oh look. My mahjong card. I've been looking for that for weeks. I never had any faults when I was your age. I was always tops in my class."

I said, "What do you mean? I got an excellent report card, except for the. Well. Put your hands on the wheel!"

"That's not the point, honey. Do you even know what deportment *means*?"

"I am not a dope."

"Of course you're not. You're my son."

"Being your son has nothing to do with it, Jesus. Why do you always say things like that?"

"There! See? That's your F in deportment talking."

She had no good reason to be snappy with me. It's not like my teacher gave me F's in every subject. Maybe it was just fun for her to put me down. Her very own child.

3

"I got A's in everything else," I said.

She continued to hunt for a cigarette. "Immaterial, buster." Her bag was as orange as a candy-corn pumpkin. "An F is an F. You're always yakking it up in class and you're a know-it-all on top of it. Now where are those—here they are—oop, goddamn it!"

"What about you?" I said. "You'd never get an A in deportment, I'm sure of it. Not in any school in the country."

It was clear she wasn't listening, but really she was terrible. Always so impatient and ready to holler. No faults when she was my age, right.

We almost whammed a pickup truck.

My hand grabbed the dashboard but there was nothing to grab onto. I said, "Why aren't you looking? Step on the brake!" I imagined the worst. Slam, splat, ambulance, funeral. I didn't want to die.

Her fingers found a cigarette. "Ah." She stuck it in her mouth and jabbed at the lighter. "I mean, I wasn't a perfect angel. I once read Shakespeare with a 'lithp.' In front of the whole thophomore clath." Oh boy. Here it came. She'd told me this story a hundred million times already. *"Friendth, Romanth, countrymen. Lend me your eerth."* She laughed too long. "Ha-ha-ha-ha!" It wasn't that funny.

What if she crashed for real one day when I wasn't around? What if it was *her own stupid head* that went flying through the windshield? Just think of the attention I'd get. All the grownups concerned for my future and happiness. Poor orphan. What a darling. Let's adopt him. Yes, let's.

But she wasn't that bad, come on now, was she? She could crack you up singing silly songs like "Mairzy Doats" and "Your Feet's Too Big." She loved the messy paintings at the modern museum and the black-and-white photos of greasy-haired teens in Washington Square who looked like they could rob you. She liked those record-your-own-voice booths and artichokes with ketchup-and-mayonnaise and "Doctor Zhivago" (the movie) and "Another Country" (the book) by that Negro writer with the bulging eyes, and the smell when you walked into Ohrbach's department store. Plus everyone got along with her. At temple and in the neighborhood. Well, just about everyone. And how would we survive if she died in an accident anyway?

Vroom.

Screech.

1

"What am I going to do with you?" she said.

She was driving like a nut again, so crazy I pictured our seatbeltless carcasses flying through the windshield. She had her elbow out the window, resting on the ledge, and her other hand off the steering wheel—completely off the steering wheel!—digging into the seat for one of her cigarettes. "Crap." Her fingers couldn't find one.

"What are you doing?" I said.

"My emerald bracelet slipped off my wrist—what do you think?" She shoved her hand in her broken-down pocketbook and slid it all around. "The one Prince Charming bought me." We almost hit a tree.

I said, "I wish you would drive like a normal person for once."

"I have no idea what to do with you, Andy. Honestly? I'm shocked. Oh look. My mahjong card. I've been looking for that for weeks. I never had any faults when I was your age. I was always tops in my class."

I said, "What do you mean? I got an excellent report card, except for the. Well. Put your hands on the wheel!"

"That's not the point, honey. Do you even know what deportment *means*?"

"I am not a dope."

"Of course you're not. You're my son."

"Being your son has nothing to do with it, Jesus. Why do you always say things like that?"

"There! See? That's your F in deportment talking."

She had no good reason to be snappy with me. It's not like my teacher gave me F's in every subject. Maybe it was just fun for her to put me down. Her very own child.

"I got A's in everything else," I said.

She continued to hunt for a cigarette. "Immaterial, buster." Her bag was as orange as a candy-corn pumpkin. "An F is an F. You're always yakking it up in class and you're a know-it-all on top of it. Now where are those—here they are—oop, goddamn it!"

"What about you?" I said. "You'd never get an A in deportment, I'm sure of it. Not in any school in the country."

It was clear she wasn't listening, but really she was terrible. Always so impatient and ready to holler. No faults when she was my age, right.

We almost whammed a pickup truck.

My hand grabbed the dashboard but there was nothing to grab onto. I said, "Why aren't you looking? Step on the brake!" I imagined the worst. Slam, splat, ambulance, funeral. I didn't want to die.

Her fingers found a cigarette. "Ah." She stuck it in her mouth and jabbed at the lighter. "I mean, I wasn't a perfect angel. I once read Shakespeare with a 'lithp.' In front of the whole thophomore clath." Oh boy. Here it came. She'd told me this story a hundred million times already. *"Friendth, Romanth, countrymen. Lend me your eerth."* She laughed too long. "Ha-ha-ha-ha!" It wasn't that funny.

What if she crashed for real one day when I wasn't around? What if it was *her own stupid head* that went flying through the windshield? Just think of the attention I'd get. All the grownups concerned for my future and happiness. Poor orphan. What a darling. Let's adopt him. Yes, let's.

But she wasn't that bad, come on now, was she? She could crack you up singing silly songs like "Mairzy Doats" and "Your Feet's Too Big." She loved the messy paintings at the modern museum and the black-and-white photos of greasy-haired teens in Washington Square who looked like they could rob you. She liked those record-your-own-voice booths and artichokes with ketchup-and-mayonnaise and "Doctor Zhivago" (the movie) and "Another Country" (the book) by that Negro writer with the bulging eyes, and the smell when you walked into Ohrbach's department store. Plus everyone got along with her. At temple and in the neighborhood. Well, just about everyone. And how would we survive if she died in an accident anyway?

Vroom.

Screech.

Whizz.

Woosh.

I was more upset about the route she was taking than her cuckoo swerving all over the place. She should've turned left on Monticello Street a couple blocks back but instead she went straight.

The lighter popped.

"I come to bury Thaethar, not to praithe him," she said.

She yanked it out of the socket, lit up her cigarette and ha-ha-ha'd again.

I mean, there were groceries in the car that we couldn't afford to go rotten. Minute steaks and Fudgsicles and a bag of frozen succotash and all of it was melting. Plus the breads were squishing and the milk was spoiling and the bananas were getting those ugly black bruises, the kind that force you to throw them out. All because of this hair-raising long cut.

As the motor overheated and clanged and grouched.

Rrrrrrr. Whizzzzz. Rrrrrrr. Kzt.

But more than the food and the money it cost, *I'd been counting on being home by now.* My best friend Georgie Garr was in his downstairs apartment, next building over, waiting for me to come over and play.

She blew some more smoke, ran through a stop sign and flew across Oak Street.

I grabbed again where there was nothing to grab onto. "It's like you're trying to kill us!" I said.

She said, "Boy, can you exaggerate," and returned to the Shakespeare. *"Yet Brututh was ambithiouth. And Brututh wath an honorable man.* You wouldn't believe what a riot I was. My teacher was so impressed. Mr. Aristotle Fabian. Can you believe that name? And incidentally. He was gorgeous."

At least she'd dropped the report card business. I'd just brought it home to her. The only surprise was **Deportment: F**, final entry in the list. I loved my sixth-grade teacher, Miss Dewess, but now she'd double-crossed me, stabbed me in the heart, repaying my devotion to her (I'd figured I was her favorite student) with a wormy potato. So what, I talked in class. So what, I called out the answers.

As The Bomb continued to kidnap us.

My mother nicknamed her car The Bomb, a beat-up Plymouth shaped like a bee that she bought for fifty bucks and which rattled and buzzed as it sped us across Route 80, barreled down Peru Street where the people with money (well, more money than us) lived, with their rainbow sprinklers and porches and carports, as it zipped past the three-little-pigs of a firehouse (a hundred percent brick) and the milk machine and the Church of Christ, Scientist (pillars in front) and our paper-maché synagogue, Temple Shir Shalom, under two tremendous yellow-leaf trees, at the corner of Peru and Salem, with a screee of a left onto Salem Street.

This was the third time in a week that The Bomb had made this roundabout backwards rush to get home.

"Ma. Please. What is wrong with you? Stop!"

Grr.

Kumph.

The car slowed down—just like that—just like the last time—a dizzy drop to maybe two miles an hour—like somebody walking—like the day was being filmed through a slow-motion camera—as her head turned left—ever so slowly—so that her cheek was facing Salem Street—eyes off the road—*completely off the road!*—and The Bomb crept creepily past the rabbi's house, around the corner from the temple.

Ohhh...

sooo...

slowwwwly.

There's...

that...

house.

Who...

is

in

there?

Her head darted around like a woodpecker head, checking every window, peck-peck-peck, quick-quick-quick, because a car couldn't stop in the middle of the street when you had to keep driving.

"Come on," I said. "We shoulda been home already."

A shade went down in the front—the living room, most likely—as if a ghost were shutting the daylight out.

My mother jumped on the brake.

My stomach lurched. "Hey!"

A screech and a jolt.

Another shade went down in the window next to it. Someone was in there. You could just see the fingers.

My mother stretched her neck and scouted around dementedly, trying to see inside. It was like I wasn't there.

I was worried she'd circle the block again and re-travel this crackpot detour. She'd done it before. Just circled around and repeated the search, every window in the rabbi's house.

Now we'd *never* get home. When all I wanted was to run upstairs to finish my homework and run downstairs, as I said before, to play with Georgie Garr.

A car beeped behind us.

It joggled my mother out of her stupor and she drove like a normal person. But her mood was different. She honked at a squirrel. She said, "Jesus Christ, squirrel!" She turned on the radio but a commercial was blaring *("This is the Pepsi generation!")* so she snapped it off. She sucked on her cigarette and returned to being mad at me. "Really. I don't get you. What is the matter with you? Why can't you behave like a good little boy and get a decent fucking report card?"

"I got a *great* fucking report card."

"Don't get fresh."

"And I'm not a little boy. I'm eleven."

"That's still a little boy."

"It's not."

"Don't argue with me."

"Why not?"

"Shut up!"

"I won't."

"You'd better."

"I will not shut up."

She reached across to hit me but I ducked it.

I said, "Leave me alone!"

She gunned the car faster.

My life was a catastrophe. An F in deportment. A teacher you couldn't trust anymore. A mother who whacked you. And to make matters worse, a yellowjacket flew in the car and dived around my eyes.

◆ ◆ ◆

The Bomb wobbled and scraped as it took us home in silence.

Soon we were back in the poor part of Montevideo (we called it Monta Video) with its measly trees and kids playing punchball and a garbage picker farther up pulling a pineapple out of a trash can.

We turned onto East Monadnock Road at the bottom of the hill and skidded around the corner bar as the door swung open—"You Can't Hurry Love" came booming outside—with a man stumbling out of it.

As we passed the row of connected brick apartments (like a giant carton of Pall Mall Reds that a cyclops had dropped on a hill), Mrs. Garr strutted out of her street-level living room on spiky high heels. She was on the way to her night job at Kitty Korners in Hackensack where she served cocktails to drunks till three in the morning. Her hair was piled up like a cinnamon bun and her blouse had two torpedo points. She was my best friend Georgie's mother.

"Get a load of Miss Universe," my mother said.

All the sudden I felt better. She was talking to me again. Joking even.

Mrs. Garr stared into our windshield and put her cigarette up to stop us. "Hey." Her voice always sounded like she had a bad cold. "Wait a minute!" She had a swollen chin like a boxer's.

The Bomb pulled up and my mother leaned across me to talk through the open window. "I'll be down in a minute to get him, Mayda. Just need to bring these groceries up."

"I don't want you leaving your mischief here whenever you feel like." She meant my brother Toby. He was four and a half and rascally and my mother would drop him off at the Garrs' because there was always someone there to watch him. The Garrs had seven kids and were a nonstop shock to the neighbors with their missing teeth and filthy hair and shaking naked bodies in the window in the back. My mother had left my brother there today because he'd been pulling things off the shelves at the Shop-Rite and my mother would wind up paying for them without noticing it.

Mrs. Garr hollered backwards, into her apartment, "HEY, ATHENA! Bring out the mischief!"

"Please don't call him that," my mother said.

Mrs. Garr turned back. She had frosty blue coyote eyes. "You want a babysitter then pay me." A perfume smell gushed out of her, like dish liquid mixed with Christmas tree. "He jumps off dressers. He bothers the cats. I was snappin' curlers into Sherry-Marie's hair just now, minding my own business, when I look up and there's your mischief, just standing there, gawping."

"His name is Toby."

"And I says to him, 'Can't you see I'm on the goddamn toilet!'"

Their bathroom had no door.

Mrs. Garr liked to waltz around naked, especially when Mr. Garr wasn't home. If I showed up early to pick up Athena to walk her to school (she was also in Miss Dewess's class), Mrs. Garr might be spread out dead asleep and stripped on the Castro like an uncooked turkey. None of her kids would cover her up or even act like she was lying there in the front room with her legs open. So I knew that whatever Toby had gawped at, it wasn't his fault.

"I got circus enough in this place as it is," Mrs. Garr said. She grabbed my mother's wrist. "Time is it? Cockshit!" She dropped the arm, chucked her cigarette and hopped into her Cadillac, racing it out of her parking spot on squealing tires. (I never understood where they got the dough for a car like that.)

My mother said, "Well!"

Toby stepped out of the Garrs' apartment—he looked spit out like a gumball—and my mother turned the motor off.

"Why do I have to go?" Toby said.

"Because..." My mother and I got out of the car. "♪♪...the party's over ♪♪..."

"It was not a party," Toby said. "I was playing ting-a-ling phone call with Georgie Garr."

I could smell the Garrs' apartment odor puffing out of their screens, a pukey mix of dirty diapers, roach spray and 99 slinking Siamese cats which they entered in contests.

"You can play with Georgie again tomorrow," my mother said. "Outside. I don't want you over there anymore."

She was unloading grocery bags and handing them to me.

"Why not?" Toby said.

"Because."

"But I like to play in Georgie's room."

"He's too old for you."

"His mother never says that."

"She's an alcoholic, sweetie. She doesn't have any judgment."

"I'm gonna go back tomorrow."

My mother put her hand up, a prelude to a smack. "Don't argue with me. I'm warning you."

Toby sulked.

We all ended up with grocery bags, Toby included—she handed him one of the smallest ones—and started up the hill, trudging past the red-brick apartments (like Paul Bunyan's staircase, two units per step) with ours at the sunny top of the climb.

The neighborhood boys liked playing with Georgie Garr. He was older than us, almost fourteen, with F's in every subject and always kind of sleepy-eyed, but a whiz kid with electrical gadgets. The ting-a-ling game that Toby liked playing included a real working phone that Georgie had hooked up from the front of his smelly apartment to the back of his smelly apartment. It rang. You answered. You talked. No dialing. We couldn't believe it.

"Georgie wants to put a phone in my bedroom," Toby told me, swinging a grocery bag like he was ready to pitch it.

I said, "It's my bedroom too."

"I hope he could do it," Toby said. "He could call me up. I could hear it ring. I could answer and talk to him all day long."

My mother said, "Stop swinging that."

Toby stopped walking. "I. Am. Not. Swinging!"

"And no telephone either." She nudged him forward with her pocketbook.

"Why??"

I heard the rumble and crash of the bowling lanes across the street, like thunder in another town.

"Because," my mother said. "Now shah!"

My brother half-swung the grocery bag, just to aggravate her.

My mother said, "I already warned you!"

My brother said, "I am a good little boy."

And I said, "Why are you yelling at him?"

"Oh, I don't know." My mother shrugged. "I'm feeling a little aggressive today."

There was no one on the street but us and there wasn't a single tree.

Naomi's TV was blasting behind her bedroom door as we entered the apartment at the top of the stairs, a skinny row of tiny rooms over Gagliano's candy store. (Even though we had very little furniture, the rooms were so small they looked crammed with tables and seats and beds like that cheapskate store for the Salvation Army.)

"I thought you were sleeping over Debbie's tonight," my mother called through the bedroom door.

Naomi called back, so loud she sounded insane, "I CHANGED MY MIND!!"

"Well if you changed your mind, why didn't you pick up your brother at Mrs. Garr's?"

"I AM NOT THAT CHILD'S MOTHER!!"

"It's the least you could do when you know I'm at work all day and have all this other crap to take care of."

"YOU WORK HALF A DAY!! I'M IN SCHOOL A LOT LONGER!!"

My mother answered phones in a church from 10 to 3, four days a week. She'd been forced to get the job after my father ran off with a mystery lady two years prior.

She said, "Don't smart-mouth me, young lady."

"WOULD YOU PLEASE?? I AM WATCHING A PROGRAM!!"

"Don't you *would-you-please* me. You want me to smack you?"

"JUST LEAVE ME THE FUCK ALONE!!"

My mother sighed. Normally she'd keep the fight going until she wound up cracking my sister in the head but not today. "I don't have the strength," she muttered.

My sister Naomi was three years older than me. Lately she'd been smushing on eyeshadow, French-kissing seniors, writing in a diary, stamping into her bedroom and slamming the door. She was the only one of us in touch with my father. Postcards sometimes, and sometimes a letter. I was jealous that he loved her best but I'd never admit it. (Oh and by the way, it's pretty apparent that my sister would never get an A in deportment either.)

My mother said, "Help me put the groceries away," and I said, "No. Later. I gotta find Georgie," so she hit me in the face and I just stood there a while.

Our kitchen was as tiny as a bathroom.

Toby was playing with plastic soldiers on the floor and singing "Oh beautiful for basic skies" to his little green men, but his singing stopped when my mother hit me.

My mother made us slam chops for dinner: turn on broiler, throw in chops, slam broiler shut.

2

A week or so later my mother and I were in the car again, headed home from the Shop-Rite (she had asked me to help carry bags again—"I need your brains," she joked) and The Bomb took the same exact Indy 500 of a detour past the rabbi's house.

Vroom.

Screech.

Whizz.

Woosh.

Then the slowdown—kumph.

And the looks in his windows.

Peck-peck-peck.

It was just since *Rush Hashunnah* that we'd met Rabbi Landy of Hollywood, Pennsylvania. (It was news to me that there was more than one Hollywood.) We'd gone through a slew of rabbis because we were a tiny congregation and the salary must've been crappy. (There was the free house to live in, however.) Rabbi Landy was new and exciting and different, and we were hoping he would stay for good. He was tall as well and handsome. His suits looked expensive. That first day of *Rush Hashunnah* he paraded into the temple, taking extra-long steps toward the *beema* up front while smoothing his hair-tonicked hair back into his yarmulke. He reminded me of a ringmaster, full of confidence and pizzazzy strides with his chin ducked down as he glided into the tent.

He smelled good to boot. Cigarettes and cut lime and the inside of a cedar chest. A big improvement over hamster-faced Rabbi Edelman who smelled like stew and retired to Florida.

Right away I got the feeling that everyone wanted to know the new rabbi, be his pal, call him Rick. It was obvious he was goodhearted. It was there in the splintery lines of his smile and in his quiet tone of talking. On that first day, when everyone was crowded around him and looking at him and laughing just to laugh, he went over to people one by one and talked to them, introduced himself, and even came over to me, just a kid, and put out his hand and asked me my name from his deep dark throat and shook my hand and touched my shoulder. It was a pleasure just to look at him and enjoy his manly pride.

So we were racing toward his house again as my mother smoked and jabbered like a carefree flirt in a chewing gum commercial, but I wasn't really listening because she was saying something boring (about what nice clean people the Italians were) and she was probably in one of those lousy moods that'd only get lousier as the car ride continued.

"Haven't you ever heard of a speed limit?" I said. But I didn't exist. Not at the moment. Normally she'd argue with me about what qualified as freshtalk, but her mind was blowing elsewhere, hurrying toward Salem Street.

So I returned to my private worries, such as my teacher Miss Dewess's infuriating double-cross.

Who cared if she thought that passing notes in class or debating during recess about Jews vs. Christians was some kind of proof of my failing deportment? If she was so worried, why didn't she stop me? I'll drop out of school and run away with Georgie, I thought, who looked different to me now, after the stuff we'd done in my bedroom.

"Phyllis won't put up with this forever," my mother was saying, having switched to the subject of Toby. (She'd left my brother with her best friend Phyllis today instead of Mrs. Garr.) (With every word my mother spoke, a smoke signal tumbled out of her.) "You know your brother's a handful. And that Sheldon of hers is such a goody two-shoes. But I can't afford to pay her. You know that too. And it's not like I need her to do this every day. Or like I'll leave him there for hours on end. And your sister for cripe's sake. Why can't she just watch him now and then? I can't believe I'm raising such a shrew. It's Mayda Garr's fault. I mean, I never even asked her to make him a lousy sandwich. And how can she stand the smell of that flea-trap anyway? But I know. You're right. Let's see how Phyllis made out with him. Let's see if she's still breathing."

Georgie Garr and I had crawled around under the sheets in my bedroom and wiggled out of our underpants. It was my first time doing such stuff with a kid and I wanted to repeat it. Georgie had lots of hair down there and smelled like ham cold cuts. After a couple of minutes he coughed through his nose and said, "I come off," as the sticky goo I'd heard about came squirting out of him without any notice. (Giant shock!) And though my thoughts about him were bad for the most part—about his stinky apartment, his disgusting green teeth and the fact that he never smiled—it was great to fool around with him and join in his grownup ways. Naomi walked in on us at one point and said, "I'm gonna tell!" but I knew she wouldn't. The last thing she'd ever do was team up with our mother.

But then there we were, as I started to say, driving by the rabbi's house, finally slowing down, and my mother's head was turning till her eyes were off Salem Street—completely off Salem Street—as she looked into every window of the house (color of peanut taffy) including the teeny attic window. She saw that there were no cars in the driveway. She said "shit" under her breath.

What was her problem? How could this possibly matter to her? She wasn't a religious person. She only went to temple out of habit Friday nights and lit Hanukkah candles out of habit as well and didn't serve bread or noodles on Passover. That was the limit of her Jewishness. Besides, she cursed too much for God to accept her. Maybe all she wanted was for the rabbi to spot her from one of his living room windows and run out to meet her, tell her shalom and reward her with a complimentary challah.

But the only thing that happened was a nearby kaboom, most likely the backfire of a truck or a jalopy.

My mother jumped but her eyes stayed focused. "What's with the thunder all the sudden?"

"You can't have thunder when it's sunny out," I said.

She turned to me and stared, like she was surprised she had company.

I said, "A jalopy must've backfired."

I was ready for one of her outbursts—some kind of crabby wisecrack—but instead she parked and shifted the shift, unaware of anything else but the house, and watched for another ten or so seconds.

Then, "Ope!" she said. "Almost forgot. Gotta get cigs," and maybe three minutes later we were pulling up to Joseph's Drugs on Main Street with a screeching halt.

"Stay here," she said.

"No."

"Two minutes."

"We'll be late to get Toby."

She coughed a couple times, then flew into a choking fit. "Ahook, ahack, aheck, aheck, ahok! Ahok! Ahok!!" It went on for too long.

"You okay?" I said.

She was wheezing, "I'm fine!" like she was mad at me for asking.

I worried I'd have to squeeze around and drive her to the hospital.

She left the car gasping.

Her choking fits were horrible.

The car was still running, filling with fumes.

I snapped on the radio. There it was again. *"You can't hurry love. You just have to wait."* So heartsick and creamy. But what did they mean by *"it's a game of give and take"*? When my parents were together, it hadn't felt like a game at all. Unless it was one of those deadly games like Russian roulette.

My mother: "You're drunk."

My father: "Go to hell."

My mother: "Too late. I'm already there."

My father: "Like that matters to me."

Long minute of silence.

Then my mother: "You're disgusting! Oh my God! Oh my God!"

I imagined my father had peed on the wall—something like that—what else could it be?—in a whiskey-sour dizzy spell.

I watched as various adults left the drugstore. They all had nicer clothes than my mother's and they all looked a lot more relaxed. A bouncy-haired lady in hot-pink culottes. A man in plaid pants with a crewcut and freckles—I pictured him in a golf course locker room, a big naked man with a big friendly voice saying, "You sank quite a putt on the ninth there, Jimbo."

I should ask Georgie Garr to come strip with me again. I should ask him to hook up that homemade phone in mine and Toby's bedroom. One of his ting-a-ling hotline devices would be great for scheming our plans together. (He wasn't just my closest friend—he was basically my only friend.) But my mother wouldn't let him interconnect our apartments—she'd made that clear to my brother already—and her nos were usually final. I could fight her about it, slam around and bang and holler like Naomi did—it's not like I never threw a tantrum before—but then I remembered Miss Dewess's blot on my report card and sighed upon the glove compartment.

Deportment: F

Miss Dewess was right. I talked in class and told dirty jokes and called out the answers. I made fun of Jesus's magical powers at lineup one morning, right to Linda Lally's face. I pretended Ronnie Moro tripped me. I could feel there was something obnoxious in me, on the line between brat and delinquent, but it hurt my head to think beyond that. It was better just to forget those thoughts, hide them away, because once they were out, you couldn't prevent yourself from reaching the end of your deportment rope and screaming or hitting.

Used to be my father was the one to sign my report card.

I didn't miss him.

Not at all.

The Supremes were singing with hope in their hearts.

"You can't hurry love. You just have to wait."

I could no longer breathe because of the fumes in The Bomb. I was worried I'd collapse into a coughing fit myself. And annoyed that we'd get home too late for *Sex and the Single Girl* which was showing on the 4:30 Movie and which I was dying to watch with Naomi on her TV. I imagined my mother talking at 78 revolutions per minute with pharmacist Joe at the pharmacy counter. He was totally bald and totally patient. She was excellent at boring people.

Eventually she reappeared at the entryway, smoking a cigarette, with a tall man holding the door for her. The pharmacist? Nope. The rabbi!

Whoa. Just standing there. Holding the door for her. Rabbi Landy. Holy camoly.

The sun was out and shining on him, so his forehead hid his eyes, and the shadow of his nose hung an awning over his mouth, making him spookier (and handsomer) than he looked when he prayed on the *beema* at temple.

It was like seeing someone famous.

He was nodding while she talked. He was smoking too and smiling like he enjoyed what she was saying. Something dopey about the Jews, I bet. Showbizzy Jews like Joey Bishop and Alan King. She loved those types and was constantly yakking about what she loved about them. Their chutzpah, their smarts, how they came from New York. She was nuts about Tony Curtis too because he was *absolutely gorgeous* and came from the Bronx and was Bernie Schwartz in his actual life, believe it or not, about as Jewish as it gets.

So they were smoking in front of the drugstore, all palsy-walsy and close to each other. And it was then that I realized his head was bare. You could see it when he tilted. Nothing on top. I'd always figured rabbis wore their yarmulkes every minute, like priests with their cardboard collars. That's what the rabbis before him had done. But Rabbi Landy didn't care about mere rules or traditions. He was practically a gangster when you thought about it, with his slicked-backed hair and fancy suits and prominent cufflinks. He was the coolest person I knew at the time.

My mother meanwhile talked and talked—synagogue gossip? *Valley of the Dolls*? her rotten children? Nobody cared. Though she could easily have won an Oscar for best performance by a supporting bigmouth. And the rabbi kept nodding though you could see he was losing interest.

Then he broke off the meeting and my mother waved bye but he didn't wave back as he walked away.

"He was buying cigs too," she said as she got back into the car. "We smoke the same brand. I could tell he was impressed."

I said, "This car is making me nauseous."

"Let's pick up your brother. Gotta be quick. Wait'll I tell P'hill." My mother thought it was funny to pronounce the silent P. (I did too.)

She turned the key and jiggled the shift, eager to get to Phyllis's, but I kept my eye in the sideview mirror.

The rabbi was walking toward a car a bit behind us, walking his pizzazzy ringmaster steps. He got in on the passenger side. His wife was at the wheel. His wife whom I was scared of. I'd seen her a lot at temple over the past few weeks because of the ho-hum High Holidays. She had a sharp tan face, hard as an anvil, and was as beautiful as an evil queen in a fairy tale, but she was always so tough and harsh and frowning that no one really talked about how beautiful she was.

As my mother pulled away, unaware of the rabbi's wife, it looked like Mrs. Landy was yelling at the rabbi in the shrinking rearview mirror. He didn't react. He just looked through the windshield.

My mother pressed a radio button and "How Much Is That Doggie in the Window?" came sugaring out of the speaker, a hit from her heyday, and she sang along in her tuneless croak.

"The one with the waggly tail!"

Meanwhile, it confused me to see a husband (the rabbi) being driven away in a car by his wife.

3

Phyllis lived in Beechwood, just above Montevideo, with its pretty painted houses under oversized trees. We pulled into Phyllis's driveway and my mother said, "I'll be right back," as she left the car, walked up the path and rang the doorbell. Phyllis came out. I was close enough to hear.

Phyllis said, "Hey, darlin'." (Phyllis was from the South.) "Toby's on the commode." She waved at me. "Hah there, Andy!"

I waved back. "Hi."

My mother tried to whisper. "I ran into Rabbi Landy on Main Street."

Phyllis screamed, "YOU DID?!"

"Shush! Just now. At Joseph's."

"Did you talk?"

"Oh Phyllis, you've met him."

"Not in the drugstore for gosh sake."

"He smokes Winstons."

"He does?"

"In the soft pack."

"Zowie! Just lahk you."

"I was coming back from work. He was surprised I had a job. I said a woman in my sitch had to find herself employment."

"Course. Your sitch."

"Something wild about that guy."

My brother squeezed out from behind Phyllis's legs and ran into the car.

"Say excuse me," my mother said. But my brother was already sliding in beside me.

"Well, well," my mother said.

"Pell-mell," Phyllis said.

"Gotta run."

"Y'all be careful."

"Ah am always careful, honey child," my mother said.

"Call you later."

"Don't forget."

Which ended her jolly jabber with Phyllis.

Driving away, my mother said, "That woman is just so classy," and turned around to Toby.

"Why don't you look at the road!?" I said.

My mother ignored me. "You better not've given P'hill any trouble today, small fry."

Toby squinched his face up. "I am a good little boy."

"That's what you think. And there's nobody else to leave you with if P'hill backs out."

A van screeched ahead of us and honked a long honk.

"Oh quiet!" my mother said, returning to the road.

She liked to say about Phyllis that she'd never met a Dixie Jewgirl before. Phyllis was president of the Temple Shir Shalom Sisterhood, which meant she sprinkled her funny Southern expressions into her announcements after services: "Tonaht's raisin cake jamboree is brought to you by Francine Rabinowitz in honor of her daughter Rona's *bozz* mitzvah. Ah wish yall a rootin'-tootin' mazel tov, y'hear?"

◆ ◆ ◆

I went to bed remembering how giddy Phyllis had been about Rabbi Landy. *"YOU DID?! Did you talk?"* What a Carolina kook she was. Okay, he was interesting. But not *that* interesting.

My brother was bothering me from his bed across the room. "Wrestle me," he said.

"Go to sleep."

He jumped on me anyway and we were at it with the lights out. He grunted and puffed as he struggled to pin me down with his Dipsy Doodle breath on me. I didn't fight back until I flipped it around and sat on his stomach and he yelled for me to stop. It was fun to have power over him, like a wildcat on a puppy.

Pretty soon, he conked out.

I forgot about Phyllis and the rabbi and the temple and was up even later imagining Georgie Garr with his clothes off and wiggly. I considered leaving my family forever, to live in a treehouse naked with Georgie.

◆ ◆ ◆

In the morning I heard my mother on the phone—she and Phyllis started their mornings with hour-long phone calls—saying something about a friend of theirs, Irma Somethingorother, who had pronounced the movie title *Grand Prix* as *Grand Pricks*, and they were laughing their heads off. (I heard Phyllis's laugh through the telephone wire.) Then there was something about a tiger being a *stripped* animal (ha ha ha) as opposed to a striped, and a male lobster being a *cock*. They enjoyed sharing screams about sexy topics, like giggly teenagers.

And again I remembered that scream from the day before, when my mother told Phyllis about her run-in with Rabbi at the pharmacy on Main Street.

"YOU DID?! Did you talk?"

Why had Phyllis screamed like a nut when it came to Rabbi Landy? Maybe it had something to do with Phyllis's husband Ef. Maybe he was too potbellied to please her. My mother was correct, Phyllis was classy. She always wore a dress and heels and never bad-mouthed anyone. And there was something you might say sad about Phyllis which I connected to the hunchback that made her look broken.

Her husband Ef was sweet and friendly but he was wet-lipped and sweaty and his shirts were always untucking themselves. So maybe Rabbi Landy was more of what Phyllis liked in a husband. Neat and good-looking, with an excellent way of speaking. Maybe that was what tickled her. She got me to look more closely.

4

I started looking Friday.

> *"It is good to give thanks unto the Lord*
> *And to sing praises in his name o most high."*

The rabbi was leading us in Friday night *Shobbis* services.

My brother and I sat on either side of my mother in the fifth pew back. (Our sister Naomi never went with us anymore.) Toby was swinging his legs.

> *"To declare thy lovingkindness in the morning*
> *And they faithfulness every night."*

My mother grabbed Toby's legs and mouthed *Stop it*.

"Though the wicked spring up like the grass..." the rabbi said, as square-haired and solid as the father on *Flipper*, "...and all the workers of iniquity do flourish..." the rabbi continued.

(I wondered if Georgie Garr and I were workers of iniquity.)

The congregation mumbled back, "...it is they that shall be destroyed forever."

The words jumped out at me: *destroyed forever*.

I looked around at the lake of faces, the sparkly glasses and mushy mouths and hairsprayed ringlets, overflowing because of Rabbi, because everyone wanted to see him and say hello to him and shake his big hand. Were there workers of iniquity among this congregation of Israelites? Did they steal from their neighbors? Whip their kids? Would God Almighty *destroy them forever?*

I scouted around for Phyllis as the air seemed to sizzle around me—Phyllis among the sinners. I wanted to see if I could recognize, just by looking at her, what she felt about the rabbi, after the giddy screaming she'd screamed at my mother—all that tittering and gushing when she was already married. Did her feelings make her as wicked as grass?

It is they that shall be destroyed forever.

My mother's life had already been destroyed forever by a vicious home-wrecking bar-stool lady whose name was Adele (Dell for short), as far as I could figure, and who my father fell in love with and escaped with to Orlando Florida where the cops couldn't trap him and throw him in jail for refusing to pay child support because New Jersey had no power there. They'd met at the place where he bartended, based on a fight I'd snooped through a wall. Twilight Tavern on Route 17. I didn't know any more than that and I didn't want to know, although my sister Naomi always acted like she was dying to tell me.

But then Rabbi Landy was up on the *beema*, and any gloom about my father did a boomerang out the swinging doors.

And the funny thing was, without the rabbi as our leader—the handsome six-foot movie-star rabbi—this service would've been nothing more than the same old words in a mumbly singsong. "Workers of iniquity *mumble mumble* destroyed forever *mumble mumble* the wicked spring up like the *mumble mumble.*"

I caught Mrs. Rodetsky, the widow with the thinning hair, smiling with excitement, excited about the rabbi, pronouncing with happy pushed-out lips.

I caught Kenny Blumstein, formerly an Eagle Scout, now a big doctor, his cheeks as sharp as a Cherokee Indian's, blaring his prayers for the sake of the rabbi.

And his father right next to him, saying *Gawd* extra loud whenever the word showed up in a prayer, staring straight ahead with his push-broom mustache, like the only thing that mattered was a nod from the rabbi.

Rabbi lovers. Rabbi fanatics. Rabbi watchers. Rabbi believers.

So where the heck was Phyllis? Her latenesses seemed pathetic for the president of the Sisterhood.

"The righteous shall give generously," the congregation said.

And the rabbi declared, "But the wicked shall borrow and not repay."

Congregation again: "Thou o Lord art forever on high."

And Rabbi again: "Thine enemies shall perish. You have exalted my horn."

These flouncy, strangely angry prayers meant nothing to me. God sounded worse than Georgie Garr's father (all beer gut and redface) eager to wallop you. It seemed like God'd murder you with a pestilence or a thunderbolt if you sneezed at even a single commandment. I was beginning to think that God was made up.

Then Phyllis finally pushed through the swinging doors at the back, her giant husband Ef behind her with his shirt tucked out. They sat near the door, the only seats open.

My mother turned around when she heard the doors wobble and sent her friend Phyllis a goofy hello by popping her eyeballs.

Phyllis responded with a kitty-cat smile and a shrug of the shoulders.

The rabbi and the rest of us continued back and forth:

"I shall be anointed with fragrant oils."
"And the righteous shall flourish like the palm."

My eyes wandered off to the rabbi's sons, also at the back, handsome and tough, with a pair of matching scowls. They had been to a kibbutz, someone had said, and were fluent in Hebrew.

And back to Phyllis—there, to the right—pulling her gloves off, feeling for a prayerbook, unfocused on the rabbi, wondering if she'd defrosted the veal, something like that, so I doubted how deeply in love she could be if he didn't soak up all her attention.

"The Lord is upright."
"There's no unrighteousness unto him."

My mother, meanwhile, sitting right next to me, recited like the prayers were the prettiest description of her loveliest hopes and her girliest daydreams. She even knew the words by heart—"Mine eyes have seen the defeat of my foes!"—exclaiming with inappropriate pride. (How embarrassing, what a showoff.)

So I acted like the others and focused on the rabbi, as dramatic as Charlton Heston with the clouds lit up behind him. And though the prayers we recited were basically nonsense, they added to the shivers of fascination.

I remembered back to *Yum Kipper* and the crying. Not very long ago. It was the worst of all the holidays. The only good thing about it was you got to wear sneakers to temple. Otherwise, you couldn't eat, you prayed all day and most of that time you prayed standing up.

But *Yum Kipper* the rabbi was new to us. We'd only known him since *Rush Hashunnah* and his razzmatazzy intro on the *beema*. All we knew was that the last temple he'd worked at was in Hollywood, Pennsylvania, that he got your attention and had a scary wife and two stuck-up sons who had gone to a kibbutz.

On *Rush Hashunnah* we learned this too: When he spoke, it was exciting. Everyone listened carefully. No one even ahemed. I didn't know rabbis could interest you like that.

> "God created heaven and earth and everything in it in just six days. Light! Dark! Mosquitoes! Pistachio nuts! And us! In his image. Kit and caboodle. Six days flat."

Pause.

> "Hey God."

Longer pause.

> "What took you so long?"

The congregation laughed like a TV studio audience.

> "You're God, for God's sake. God the all-powerful. God the Father. You could've gotten it all done with a snap of your fingers. Would've added to your mystique. Would've added to your power. Why take six days? What did you have to prove? Tell us, o God the father."

He looked around with a bashful smile. Then switched to a look of confident wisdom.

> "I think the answer is simple. A father who competes with his children isn't much of a father. A father who has to outdo his kids has a screw loose.
>
> "Think about it.
>
> "God doesn't create us in order to dominate us. He creates us so he can be equal to us. By spending a week on creation—eight hours a day—God lets us know that our work is as important as his. He labors over creation and, like us, he rests. Because God doesn't merely create us in his image."

Pause.

> "He creates himself in *our* image too. He encourages us to be more like him, to be more godly, by being more like us. Creation is his tribute to our humanness."

Mr. Rothstein was sitting next to me during the *Rush Hashunnah* sermon and he whispered, "What *narishkeit!*" (My mother liked to call him the Backseat Rabbi because he'd never finished rabbi school and was now just a sourball with Brillo hair and a shiny suit and retirement money from an embroidery factory. I was the only one in the temple, I think, who liked him.)

But everyone else was in awe of the rabbi with his Moses shoulders and his nonconformist creation story. All the other rabbis we'd ever hired told storybook stories about blind Isaac (we should open our eyes) and vicious Haman (we should stamp out viciousness) and faithful Abraham (in God we trust). But Rabbi Landy's sermons were meant for grownups and intended to help them think for themselves.

Small correction. His wife Tehila was the one other hold-out. She'd sit there alone while the rabbi gave speeches with her beachy brown legs crossed and pick at her hair.

But everyone else was in a hypnotized trance. Even his two stuck-up sons (they sat in a separate pew from their mother) leaned forward during the sermon, like their father was their hero.

When the sermon was over the cantor tooted a pitch pipe and the choir stood with a clunk and a shuffle and boomed out in Hebrew about how your fate for the year is written on *Rush Hashunnah* and finalized ten days later on the fast of *Yum Kipper*.

> *"How many shall pass away and how many shall be born?*
> *Who shall have rest and who shall wander?*
> *Who shall be at peace and who shall be pursued?*
> *Who shall be at rest and who shall be tormented?"*

I read it in the side-by-side English translation. Pretty hair-raising list. Who would drop dead between now and next summer? Someone wrinkled? Someone young? Someone poisoned? Bayonetted? Pistol-whipped? Strangled?

The choir shout-sang the prayer in a harmony that had cracks in it but was actually kind of nice.

And then the crying on *Yum Kipper*, ten days later, after hours and hours of boring temple torture, during an afternoon prayer when the rabbi made a display of himself by sobbing in public.

"*Avinuuuuu!*" he cried.
"*Malkeinuuuuuu!*" he sobbed.

The only song the cantor didn't sing for us that day. (I looked at the English on the opposite page: Our father, our king, we have sinned before thee.)

He sobbed out the words with humongous gasps of sadness. I stretched my neck to search for his tears. Everyone was stretching. It thrilled the congregation. No rabbi had ever performed like this.

Avinu!

(Sob!)

Malkeinu!
    (Sah-hob!)

Our father, our king.
We have sinned.
Have compassion.
Inscribe us in the book of life.

I glimpsed the tears, like rain on his face. I wondered about his secret unhappiness.

When I looked at my mother, she was crying as well.

Her mother had died when she was six years old but I'd never seen her cry about it. Maybe the sadness had been stuck in her throat for 28 years and was loosened by the rabbi's crying, by the Hebrew words *kol tsar umastin*, bring an end to our oppression.

Or maybe my father was the why of her crying.

Whatever it was, I thought that she and the rabbi shared a tragedy together that I could never be a part of.

5

Then my mother signed me up for special classes on Saturdays out in Watterridge where the countryside started. I could pick from chemistry, astronomy or Welsh. I chose astronomy. She didn't explain why, but I figured it had something to do with my teacher Miss Dewess and my F in deportment. Maybe these difficult classes would challenge me out of my wiseguy behavior.

My mother drove me over in The Bomb, taking the familiar roundabout detour past the rabbi's house, but my sister and brother were with us this time (she would drive them to their friends after she dropped me off in Watterridge) so Naomi piped up: "Why are you turning here?"

My mother said, "Because."

Naomi said, "But this isn't the way." She was in front and turned to look at me. "Is she taking you to temple?"

"Weren't you listening?" I said. "I have astronomy starting today. Special class for the smart kids."

Naomi said, "How can you be smart when you're an idiot?"

Toby said, "Mommy always drives in front of the rabbi's house."

"You are not taking me back for more of that junior congregation crap," Naomi said. "That boss mitzvah was enough."

Toby said, "She cursed."

Naomi said, "Crap is not a curse."

I said, "Every single day. Directly past the rabbi's house."

Toby said, "Rabbi, scab eye, tab eye, shab eye."

My mother said, "Would you all just—please! Shut up already, damn it."

But my mother never scared Naomi. "You couldn't *pay* me to return to that tedious pointless junior congregation. I sleep late on weekends and nothing's going to change that. Not even with that dreamy new rabbi on the pulpit, no way, not even with him could you get me to—oh!" My sister stopped. "Wups."

I was glad for the quiet.

My mother peeked sideways at her darling daughter. Must've had something to do with a feminine situation. Why else would Naomi say "wups" and stop talking? (I'd studied the diagram in the 32-count Tampax box any number of times and still couldn't figure out where they stuck in those applicators.)

◆ ◆ ◆

I couldn't figure out what the stars were made of either. Light, gas, water, chalk? None of it made sense to me. And the astronomy teacher didn't explain. The students laughed when I asked if an astronaut could get sucked up into a big black hole. Which made me embarrassed. There was one boy I liked, Thornton Vanoosten, who was taller than the rest, with extra-long eyelashes, but he didn't even look at me. All I got from the special Saturday class was the promise of a telescope (the church my mother worked at offered to buy me one) and the sense that I was wasting my time with the gifted kids because how gifted could I be if I couldn't grasp a word of it?

Oh, and I had Thornton Vanoosten to daydream about. With his extra-long eyelashes.

Back at school, Miss Dewess asked me about astronomy class and I lied to her that I liked it because I no longer trusted her. How could I after that F?

The only people I felt comfortable with were my brother and Georgie Garr.

Georgie and I took our clothes off again when Naomi and Toby were out somewhere and my mother was working. I loved to crawl around with him and look at his big-boy body.

Later he said, "When can I put dat phone in here?" He looked at me and looked away. He always looked away after he said anything.

"My mother said no. She said I couldn't have one."

"She don't live with you in your bedroom. I can do it by secret."

"What do you mean?"

"I can do it tomorrow."

"Great idea. Let's do it when she's at work."

"Do your mother beat you up? If I put in a phone?"

I thought about his father. He was famous on the block for losing his temper and hitting his kids in flipped-out rages. He'd even whack the kids of other families if they got in his way. He painted people's houses for a living (with a terrifying sci-fi spray gun) and had a watermelon belly and was horribly ugly.

"Don't worry," I said. "My mother hits *us*, but she won't hit *you*."

Georgie snuffed. His snuffs were tough to translate. Did he trust what I was saying? Was he worried I'd call him a scaredy-cat? Regardless, I was guessing that the phone would make it easier for us to meet like this and wiggle our clothes off.

He wired it up that same day in fact, sooner than I expected, before my mother got home from work—I guess he was impatient—but he had problems with the wires so it was dead in the beginning.

6

We were driving again to Phyllis's. It had nothing to do with babysitting. Toby just wanted to play with her Sheldon, and my mother just wanted to jabber with Phyllis. I joined them because I had nothing else to do, and Phyllis and Ef had a color TV.

Toby and Sheldon hurried outside to their big backyard, and I boogalooed into the sunken den to sample the Zenith color console, but I couldn't pay my complete attention because my mother and Phyllis were talking too loud in the nearby kitchen though it seemed they were trying not to.

Phyllis said, "Yeah, but she's a beauty. A first-class stunner."

My mother said, "Frankly my dear. She's a first-class bitch."

"Oh come on now," Phyllis said. "I think she looks like Mizz Tennessee. Remember from the pageant?"

"It's a hard beauty, Phyllis. Nothing sensuous about her. I'm sure she doesn't make him happy."

"Nona says he's gettin' his Ph. D.," Phyllis said. (Nona Tower, boss lady know-it-all at temple.)

"In what?"

"In Freudian psychoanalysis."

"A clergyman *and* a doctor. Well well! Paging Dr. Martin Luther King. How does he find the time?"

"Beats me. Sounds dangerous."

"Oh Phyllis. He's a pussycat."

"I got the scoop on Señor Rabbi, sugah," Phyllis said.

"Warmed-over hearsay."

"From Ruthie Zimmer." My mother always said that Ruthie Zimmer had the biggest yap in all of Montevideo.

My mother stopped, then started again. "Aaa, Ruth's untruths. What does she know? If it came from Nona Tower maybe I'd listen." I remembered that Mrs. Tower's sister Dina Klotz had belonged to the rabbi's temple in Pennsylvania before he moved here.

"Ruthie is friends with Nona's sister."

My mother stopped again. "And?"

"Seems Ricky-doo and company are headed for splitsville."

"No!"

"There's a history to this." I couldn't hear what she said after that because of a TV siren. Something to do with a thief on the loose in Dick Tracy's precinct. (It was a show for littler kids, that's true, but it was the only thing on, besides a soap opera and *The Match Game*.) Then Phyllis said: "...but they reconciled and patched it up."

"Oh I don't know. Ruthie? From the desk of a lonely housewife. Maybe Nona's sister Tina—"

"Dina."

"—made the whole thing up."

"The whole what up?"

"The splitsville stuff."

"Nona's sister is the president of that Sisterhood," Phyllis said.

"And you are the president of this Sisterhood. Big deal."

"What's that supposed to mean?" Phyllis said.

"Shit. I'm sorry. What's the matter with me?"

"Ah want you to be careful, missus."

"Ah am always careful, honey child."

Splitsville, dangerous, hearsay, reconciled, Freudian psychoanalysis. I wasn't quite old enough to add it all up. And I wouldn't ask my mother about it anyway. Her talks with Phyllis were not my concern.

Yet the rabbi was a student. Which made no sense. How could you be a student at *his* age?

Meanwhile, Dick Tracy radioed Go-Go Gomez to say that Sketch Paree was wearing a Dick Tracy mask and robbing the terrified big-city citizens.

◆ ◆ ◆

Oh and about Nona Tower. Before I forget.

Phyllis might've been president of the Sisterhood, but Mrs. Tower had been president for many terms before her and still behaved like president, boss, and hostess of Temple Shir Shalom no matter what was on schedule or who led the Sisterhood or even the more significant men's division (our dentist Hy Rosenzweig). When Rabbi Landy first showed up, it was Nona Tower who introduced him to us and set up the reception to toast his new beginning the night before *Rush Hashunnah*. She always decided what to do for these events and no one said no. (We were used to it.) But with Rabbi Landy she was extra annoying, using pushy expressions like "This way, Rick" and "Come close everybody to welcome Rabbi" like he was her very own life-size rabbi robot. (Somebody whispered that she'd known him in Pennsylvania and their families had gone to Bermuda together.) The strange thing was, she refused to introduce him to my mother. She made a point of it as she glided right past her while ushering him around on the tiles of the social hall. Nona Tower had those streaky green bangs and those flashy white teeth and that big swinging rear and on top of it she was rich, rich, rich— so she didn't have to worry that my mother might outshine her.

My mother looked nice but not that nice. Nona Tower was the one with the beauty and the say-so. But then women were always fighting. I'd learned it from stories like Rapunzel and Sleeping Beauty and I'd seen it in the snarling pusses of Lucy and Ethel after they had a big fight which was practically every episode of *I Love Lucy* despite their unbreakable friendship. And like everyone at temple, I was afraid of Nona Tower. So smart, so breathy, so fancy, so fake. Her annoying smell of flowers and cantaloupe (and some kind of medicine) could smother the temple whenever she was in it. And she was always blabbing and smiling through her big flashing choppers about "our adorable Beechwood cul-de-sac" (I had to look up *cul-de-sac*) and her good-looking husband and her three spectacular Coppertone kids and all of them so welcoming and likeable.

But Mrs. Tower wasn't.

Mrs. Tower was awful.

7

A warm day came and took my mind off temple. It was like summer again on East Monadnock Road with the mothers out on the sidewalk in their beach chairs smoking while their kids ran screaming in the street. There was a game of tag going which my brother Toby joined because he loved to run and hit although the other kids rarely tagged him as he was the puniest and the youngest. I was too old for tag and feeling a little lonely, lonelier than usual, so I sat on the curb and peeled a twig between the mothers and the taggers.

I heard the taggers tramp and gasp.

I heard a freight train coming, down by the tracks.

I heard the mothers going on about the price of meat ("69 cents a pound." "You're kidding." "At Acme. Here's the receipt.") and a mother who drank.

"Some days, she doesn't even get out of bed."

"How do you know?"

"I saw her. I visited her. She answered the door in a nightgown. She was guzzling beer at ten in the morning. Gives those sorry-ass kids of hers Sugar Pops and Cocoa Puffs for dinner every night."

"No wonder that bozo is cheating on her."

"If he's a bozo, then she's a booze-o."

"I thought she was a wino."

"Hey Dumbo!"

"No, beer-o. Miss Pabst Blue Ribbon of '66."

"Hey Big-ears..."

"Let him be."

"...is that what they call you?"

I realized one of the women (Jackie-Gleason-size Mrs. Kohlmeier, who had a toilet paper turban wrapped around her hair) was talking to me.

I turned to her and turned away. "I'm not bothering anyone," I said.

"You're bothering *me*. Stop snooping like that."

"It's a free sidewalk. I can sit where I want."

The ladies snickered.

My mother said, "Watch your mouth, yon wise-ass."

The ladies guffawed.

I continued to peel the twig.

"You should hear the mouth on that daughter of hers," Mrs. Pepp said, meaning my sister Naomi. "Every other word. F this, F that."

"Oh who are you to talk?" my mother said. Mrs. Pepp was as scraggly as Mammy Yokum from the comics (though only around thirty) and as much of a curser as Mrs. Garr.

They switched from the topic of bratty kids to bratty Paul Newman with his sparkly blue eyes and the hunky fellow who played Ben Casey and the endless legs on Cyd Charisse, who'd done a fancy dance on Ed Sullivan last night.

"She's so elegant," my mother said. "Can you believe she's forty-four?"

"I didn't care for her," Mrs. Zellman said. "I preferred the trained poodles." Mrs. Zellman had red lips and thick black eyebrows and was always out her second-floor window yelling for her kids. "Margaret! Holly! Carlton! Doreen!" (She pronounced the last one Daw-veen.) Like most of the mothers on the street that day, she wore a housedress that looked like pajamas.

My mother dressed nicer, no curlers twisted up in her hair like grenades. Her hair was up with bobby pins. She wore clean white jeans and a white summer top with a bra strap showing, conspicuously black.

I heard the tag players switching to hide-and-go-seek. "One one-thousand, two one-thousand..."

I heard a radio playing, *"You keep lyin' when you oughta be truthin'."*

I heard a screen door slam as Mrs. Garr stepped out, dragging a beach chair and clutching a cigarette case. I wondered why she wasn't at Kitty Korners serving drinks to the drunks but then I remembered she had

Mondays off. She was wearing a housedress too, but with a pointy bra underneath, smelling like a head full of hairspray.

I heard a loud girl holler, "Ready or not, here I come!"

I heard Mrs. Kohlmeier whisper, "Oh no. Mayda Garr."

I heard Mrs. Garr blat like a grouchy trombone, "Who blew a fart?" as she opened the beach chair.

Then she called back into her putrid apartment. "DON'T YOU BURN THOSE FUCKIN' FISH STICKS, ATHENA!"

With her giantess height and pointing-out breasts, Mrs. Garr reminded me of the 50-Foot Woman, which I'd seen on TV a couple weeks back. She wasn't very different from that snarly-mouthed monster in peekaboo duds, squashing restaurants and people and dismantling electrical towers.

She positioned her beach chair next to my mother's.

They didn't look at each other.

The train had arrived at the end of the street, bottom of the hill, hooting a spooky hoot. It went on and on as it passed through Montevideo, boxcar after boxcar—hamburger brown, basketball orange, washed-out green. It moved so slow it made you wonder how it got to wherever it was going. Pittsburgh? Kansas City?

I looked again, and my Winston-smoking mother and Mrs. Garr of the Tareyton filters had their heads together, talking. They seemed serious and friendly (hard to believe) but the freight car racket drowned out their voices.

I was worried they were talking about how Georgie and I were getting naked together and wagging our penises. Maybe Naomi had ended up tattling after all—of course, why not?—that no-good double-crosser. *Wait'll I tell George Senior,* Mrs. Garr might be saying. *He'll wallop the turd-manure out of those punks.*

I was scared that she would notice me so I slid away slinkily, with my backside on the curb.

But then Naomi of all people was coming at me across the street in—surprise!—a skirt and waving c'mere.

I hurried around the corner with her where the train noise wasn't as clanky. "Why are you dressed like that?" I said.

She put her face up to mine. "Daddy's picking me up in ten minutes."

"What??"

"He wants me to meet him on Hobart Street. Not that I care. "

"I thought he was in Florida!"

"I lied to Mommy. I told her I was sleeping over Debbie's tonight. I need you to cover for me. Don't you tell her what I'm up to. I'm warning you." She was walking away.

"WAIT A MINUTE DAMN IT!"

She hurried back and clamped my mouth shut.

I was huffing into her hand. My nose exploded with crying.

"Are you with me or against me?" she said.

I yanked her off my lips as hard as I could. (I realized I was stronger than her.) "Are you crazy?" I said. "Why didn't you tell me?" I forced myself to stop crying.

She wiped her hand on the belly of my T-shirt. "Because I knew you'd tell *her*."

"No I wouldn't! And if you thought I would, why do you trust me all the sudden?"

"He's taking me to dinner."

"You are seriously insane," I said. "What is he here for? Where's the money he owes us? Why are you doing this behind our backs?"

"Behind *her* back."

"You're not answering me *anything*."

"Look." She put her hand on my shoulder. "The point is I do trust you. You just have to face certain realities. I'm a daddy's girl and you're a mama's boy."

I shook her off me. "You say that again and I'll slaughter you!"

"I'm merely stating the obvious."

"I got an F in deportment for your information. Plus I'm stronger than you muscle-wise so you better watch what you say to me."

"Hey, no need to throw a shit fit. Man, what a temper. He's here to make a record at some kind of studio in New York, okay?"

"A wrecker?"

"A record! The kind they play on the radio."

"Like a 45?"

"For RCA Victor. They call it a demo. He said he can make a ton of money if some talent scout or, I don't know, some agent signs him a contract. Then he can pay us all the money he owes us. If you remember correctly, he has a voice like Wayne Newton."

More like Simon of Alvin and the Chipmunks, I thought. "And what? He's bringing you along with him to the studio?" I imagined headphones in a soundproof booth and the label with the gramophone and dog in the center, spinning in a control room. I imagined it was *me* tagging along instead of my sister, after meeting him on Hobart Street.

"He's taking me to dinner. I already told you. Who cares? I just need you to cover for me."

"Why didn't he contact *me*?"

She sighed. "He said he wanted to."

I felt the crying starting up again. "Well tell him to go to hell. You can both go to hell for all I care."

She put her arms around me and hugged me tight. "Just cover for me, all right?"

"No."

"I know you don't mean that."

I pushed away hard but kept looking at her. You could hear the bowling pins crashing across the street. "Did you tell on me? About that thing with Georgie Garr? You know, when you saw us under the sheets together?"

"Silly boy. Of course not. What do you think?"

"I don't know what to think."

"So you see? We're even."

"Even how?"

"I've got my secret and you've got yours."

"You're lousy."

"*You're* lousy."

8

Indian summer lasted a day and we were at temple again for Friday night services, in zippered jackets and plastic coats, waiting for things to happen. My brother Toby was running in the lobby like an escaped pet monkey, and I was talking to the cantor's son Bobby (hair all shiny, parted down the side), and my mother and Phyllis were off in a corner, talking.

All the voices were coming at me like baseballs out of a pitching machine.

"I am seriously disappointed in them," Bobby was saying, regarding the Yankees.

"Ah just wanted you to say a word about Max downstairs," Phyllis was saying to my mother. "At the reception after services."

"Last place," Bobby said. "That's eighty-nine losses for the season."

"Little ol' me?" my mother said. "Toby! Stop that!"

"Max requested it," Phyllis said.

"I am dying for a smoke," Mrs. Cohen said from elsewhere in the lobby.

A kiddush reception was scheduled for after services to honor Max Gertner, the ladieswear salesman with the muttonchop sideburns—honey cake and challah and percolator coffee set up in the social hall by the Shir Shalom Sisterhood—because Mr. Gertner had donated jillions to refurbish the social hall and establish a Judaica library at the back of the temple basement.

The cantor's son Bobby said, "Are you listening to me?" He was upset about the Yankees' worst whatever in history.

"Sorry," I said. "What?"

I was thinking about Naomi. How she hadn't come home last night. How she'd stayed overnight in New York with my father while pretending to be at Debbie's. She was obviously his favorite and it burned me up.

My mother whispered too loud to Phyllis, "What can I possibly say about Him of the Fabric Samples? That he made a pass at me last week?"

A pass? Max Gertner? At my mother? Really?

"I've got it all written up," Phyllis said, handing my mother an index card. "Come."

"Does Nona know?" (Nona Tower.)

"We're going to surprise her."

And what was a pass exactly? Did it mean that Mr. Gertner had passed his meaty hands all over my mother's body?

I heard a mannish-voiced woman say, "Terrific personality. Good-looking. Relaxed. Excellent sort of rabbi for this kind of—"

What?? Someone had erupted into a sneezing fit and drowned her out.

Then:

"—Freudian psychoanalysis."

There it was again. With its mischievous syllables. But what exactly was it?

Bobby said, "That stadium's cursed."

And my mother said, "Where are you taking me?"

And Phyllis said, "The rabbi's office," grabbing my mother's bracelet and pulling her toward the rabbi's office. Then they looked at each other and smirked.

"Now?" my mother said.

"Joe Pepitone," Bobby said.

"Studying psychiatry," Mrs. Cohen whispered. "Some schmancy institution on the Upper West Side. I wonder if he gets them to lie on the couch."

Another voice clucked, "That couch of his'll never get cold, that's for sure," which made me guess it wasn't leather.

"Rabbi's office," Phyllis said. "Come on. Let's go. You can read him your speech. Your ode to Max Gertner."

"My ode to a Grecian horndog," my mother said.

Eight o'clock rolled around and we all shuffled into the temple, all except my mother and Rabbi. She was still with him in his office, discussing her speech for the Gertner reception.

I sat in a pew with Toby, who was swinging a leg.

After a couple uncomfortable minutes, my mother tiptoed in and squeezed between me and my brother. She put a hand on Toby's swinging leg and mouthed the words *Stop it.*

The rabbi strode in a couple minutes later, more like a swami than a rabbi, with his flowing black robes and his thrown-back shoulders, smelling like a spice rack.

I looked at the rabbi's wife across the way. She was studying her nails.

I looked at Mr. Rothstein, the Backseat Rabbi, next to me as usual. His face was a pickled tomato.

I looked at everyone else in the room and they were one big tooth-twinkle, pink-lipped smile.

Then the prayers started up.

"It is good to give thanks unto the Lord," the rabbi said, "and to sing praises to his name o most high."

◆ ◆ ◆

Naomi dragged me into her bedroom when we got back from temple.

"Oh Andy. Oh God." She busted up crying. "He never showed up. I waited two hours. Like an idiot. What a dope. I went to sleep at Debbie's last night. I couldn't come home. I just couldn't face it."

"Face what?" I said.

She put her head on my shoulder and kept on crying.

There were many things I wanted to say, like Why do you bother? And I could've told you. And What did you expect? And Next time tell him to send us money. But I stopped myself.

9

Next morning the phone woke me—the phone Georgie Garr had put in our room!—and I answered it. "Hello?"

"Come play wid me."

"Georgie! It works! I can't believe it!"

"Come over and play."

"It's six o'clock in the morning, Georgie. And on top of that, it's Saturday."

"Come. Come now."

"I can't come now. I've got my special class this morning."

Georgie hung up.

My brother slept through it.

I fell back to sleep.

I woke up later to my mother yakkety-yakking on her grownup phone across the apartment. It had to be Phyllis. I was sure they'd never think twice about calling each other before it was even light out.

I heard my mother say, "Okay, call me back," and hang up the phone.

When I entered the dining room, she was smoking in a nightgown, dialing someone else.

I said, "I'm not going back to that ridiculous astronomy class," though we were supposed to head out shortly.

My mother put the phone down.

"I thought about it," I said, "and that's that." Yes, I'd miss my peeks at Thornton Vanoosten with his beautiful eyelashes from the other side of the room—I'd dreamt about wrestling him in a boxcar the night before—but I couldn't take any more of the teacher's astronomy gobbledygook and the students' talking down to me.

"I'm just not going," I told my mother. "And you can't make me."

"Gee Andy," my mother said. "And the church just bought you a telescope."

"Give it back."

"What's a church going to do with a telescope?"

"I don't care. I didn't ask for it."

"Well you're not sitting around all day doing nothing, mister."

"I've got homework."

"That'll take you ten minutes. You're going to temple."

"I went last night."

"Junior congregation."

"Why do I have to sit in that torture chamber for two days straight? Last night was enough." I knew why I had to do it but I wasn't as bold as Naomi, not enough to scold my mother for jumping at every chance she got to run to the temple.

"No arguments," she said. "Go on. Take a bath."

"What about Toby?"

"He's going too."

"What about Naomi?"

"She had her bas mitzvah already. You know that."

"In other words, you can't control her."

She put her cigarette out with a jab. "What's wrong with you, honey? You feeling all right? Let me feel your keppie. Come over here. You're not sleeping enough. Where's your brother? Go get Toby."

"You go get him. I am not your slave."

She raised her hand to hit me but I ducked it.

"I'm gonna run away," I said. "I'm gonna run away and never come back."

"Really? Where to?"

"I'm serious."

"Sure you are, dollface."

"Why do you have to hit like that?"

"I did not hit. Now go. Get ready."

"I won't."

"You'd better."

I left the room.

I ended up going. Only after she followed me into the kitchen and said, "If you refuse to go, you can forget about those comic books you asked for."

She drove us over and came in with us.

The lobby was a lot like the lobby the night before. The cantor's son Bobby (hair all shiny, parted down the side) yammered about the Yankees, Toby ran in circles like an escaped pet monkey and my mother slipped into the rabbi's office.

I could see the rabbi's roughneck sons conferring with each other—they were handsome boys, one tall, one short, both as fuzzy as werewolves—and it seemed like their topic was the Yankees again. (Jeez Louise, enough with the Yankees.) (Not to mention the season was over already!) They stood separate from the rest of us.

I wasn't a regular but the other kids were, so at exactly 10:30, all seventeen of us shuffled into the temple and peopled the pews. Unlike last night, there weren't any grownups present. And unlike last night, the rabbi didn't stroll in a few minutes later.

It was a whole half hour later!

Eleven o'goddamn clock!

Thirty minutes of us flat-left kids all irritated and fidgeting, kicking the pews and groaning, including the rabbi's snotty boys all snooty to each other with their whispery Hebrew Yankee-fan chins up, and my brother tugging my sleeve and saying, "I'm bored. Let's go."

Rabbi Landy declared, "All right, juniors," as he giant-stepped into the temple, adjusting his silver tallis collar. (No apologies, no nothing!)

I could hear the front door of the building swing shut, just outside the temple.

(My mother escaping.)

"Give praise to the Lord. Proclaim his name," the rabbi said.

(I could hear her gun the motor as The Bomb pulled away.)

"Make known among the nations what he has done."

◆ ◆ ◆

What an embarrassment. It was all her fault. I could have thrown her out a window.

All her fault.
All her fault.
All her fault.
All her fault.

She had cornered him in his office. She had talked and talked and smoked and talked, directly into his face. She'd cornered him and trapped him and caused him to walk in late.

Later than late.

I refused to say a word to her when she picked us up to drive us home and asked me how the service went.

"Okay," she said, "be that way." No yelling, no hitting.

She turned around and looked at Toby. "And what about you, Kimosabe? What's the inside scoop on junior congregation?"

"Actually? I hate it."

◆ ◆ ◆

Back at home later, Naomi was eating a tomato sandwich with a glass of grape soda and I was eating Beefaroni with a mug of banana milk.

She said, "He called me at Debbie's. He never left Florida. I hate his guts. I'll never speak to him again."

"Good decision," I said.

She harrumphed.

"What about his singing career?" I said.

"Who knows. He never mentioned it. You ever meet his new wife Dell?" She took a braggy sip of soda.

"You know I didn't. Why do you ask me like that? Look, I'm sorry you're upset, but if he thinks you're so special, why don't you tell him to send us money?"

"You never gave him the chance to explain himself."

"Oh God. I'm going to throw up on your tomato sandwich! I swear to you, I really am."

Patiently she tilted her head. "Temper-temper."

I hated letting her get to me like this. I buttoned my mouth and breathed through my nose. I put my hands in my lap.

She said, "I met Dell maybe a year ago. He took me and her for Italian food. She drank a lot of cocktails. Did you know they met in a bar?"

"I don't want to hear about it."

She looked out the window. "Fine by me."

We went back to eating. There was sun on the table, and the smack and jangle of a delivery to the candy store was ringing from the street downstairs. I thought about the Chunky bars and Pez dispensers and pies for a quarter being rolled into the store on hand trucks.

She said, "What do you think of the rabbi's boys?"

"Why are you asking?"

"That Avi is cute." She finger-combed her slept-on hair. (She really did sleep until noon on weekends.) "I mean the older one. Whatever his name is."

"Those boys are stuck up."

"How can you say that?"

"You only saw them *Rush Hashunnah*. I see them every week. They never talk to anyone, they just whisper to each other. In Hebrew! And they're always sniffing, like the rest of us smell bad."

"Well that's probably because they go to yeshiva. And that Avi's adorable. And if anyone's a stuck-up snot, it's that Mrs. of his."

"Mrs. Landy. Tehila."

"The name alone. Ew. It's like she's sick with something. 'I came down with a case of double tehila. Help me. Please.' But the rabbi. Mm. Now *him* I love."

"He's an excellent speaker."

"He is dreamboat numero uno in Dullsville USA. I bet Mommy gets all trashy around him, you know? Basically throwing herself at him when he'd never be interested in...ukhh...not possible."

"I don't know what you're talking about."

"So what. I don't care."

The phone rang, a different ring from the usual ring, like a bike bell going haywire. I remembered my phone link to Georgie Garr and ran to my room and picked it up quick before my mother figured out there was a phone in there. (She was reading a racy paperback in the living room.)

Georgie asked if he could come upstairs and show me his peter. I said let's go out for a mystery walk because no one had left our apartment yet so it wasn't safe to have him visit. I got the idea of a mystery walk from a pal I'd had a couple years back named Arthur Vilsac who had moved away. He used to lead me out of our neighborhood down scary blocks where the trees were dead. (Afterwards, he'd pick a fight and punch me.) I missed Arthur Vilsac.

Georgie said okay.

I heard his mother, Mrs. Garr, in the background yelling something about *this Christ-forsaken fucking shit pit!*

I remembered to take my telescope before I went out, perfect for our mystery walk. Luckily my mother's church hadn't asked her to give the telescope back. Though I no longer needed it since dumping astronomy, it was still in my possession. It was mine—all mine. It was shaped like a rocket and swooshed when you twisted it. I wasn't interested in pointing it at the sky. I only wanted it for snooping on people in their houses during a mystery walk. Hopefully naked people.

I told that to Georgie, and he said, "Me too. Let's look in the windows. Let's look at someones nakit."

We walked up the hill past the bowling alley and turned down a spooky side street. I'd never gone anywhere with Georgie before so I was surprised to see that he didn't walk straight, his body kept aiming for the curb, like his steering was broken. I wondered if he was born that way. I wondered how someone as crooked and seemingly stupid as him could hook up a phone. We passed a bunch of dirty houses, no gardens in front, not even grass, and a crumbling apartment house with shadowy shapes in the second-floor windows. There was no one on the street but us.

Georgie took my hand. "This scary," he said.

I enjoyed the cool of his palm in mine though it was swollen like a sponge and sticky.

When we turned onto busy King Street at the top of the hill, we hurried across and his hand let go.

A speeding cement mixer almost killed us.

"Phew," I said.

"I'm glad we left them frighty streets," Georgie said.

I got him to look through the telescope with me at a no-parking sign a couple blocks down, then up into a tree to peek at a bird's nest.

"I like it," he said.

There weren't any windows with open curtains and naked people which I found frustrating. "We've been rooked," I said.

Georgie said, "Yeah."

I had a dime in my pocket so I took him into a soda fountain to buy us some candy. The store owner wore a soda-jerk jacket and slid his eyes at Georgie like *Who's this trash* but Georgie didn't notice.

I bought a Three Musketeers bar and split it with him and we walked along the busy stretch of King Street in the sun, past a fat man walking a dachshund and an old lady humming "It's a Grand Old Flag" and the chop suey restaurant and the Melody House where you could buy hit singles for 59 cents, enjoying ourselves, smell of hot dogs in the air, and—abracadabra!—there he was—Rabbi Landy—walking out of the post office—chomping gum and wearing sunglasses which made him look blind.

He noticed me and shot me a smile, then a bigger one when he saw I had a friend with me.

"Good afternoon, Andy," he said. "How delightful to run into you."

I was excited that he remembered my name and spoke to me warmly, like we were friends since I was born. "Hello, Rabbi Landy."

I'd never seen him this close before. (And again, without a yarmulke.) His face was still handsome but this time I noticed tiny pinhole marks across his cheeks like termite bites.

"And who is this young fellow?" He put his hand under Georgie's chin. (He really looked blind in those sunglasses.)

"This is my friend Georgie Garr," I said.

Georgie looked at the sidewalk and said, "Hello, rib-eye."

"Georgie lives downstairs from us."

"Ah!" The rabbi let go of Georgie's face. "What are you rascals up to?" he said.

Georgie squinted and took my hand. "Mystery walk."

"Ah, mystery walk. How wonderful." The rabbi put his hands on our backs and kind of pushed us a little. "You misters enjoy your mystery walk." He was smiling hard. "Sensational," he said.

We moseyed toward home.

"He a nice man," Georgie said.

"He's a rabbi," I said.

"What's that?"

"Like a priest but for the Jews."

"My dad *hate* the Jews."

"Except rabbis are allowed to get married."

"My dad said Hitler shoulda killed all the Jews."

I dropped Georgie's hand.

The words felt like bowling balls thrown at my neck. I turned around and walked backwards—to protect myself from Georgie and physically change the subject—but it was hard not to think of how awful my friend was (although I'm sure he was too thick to understand what he'd said).

He copied me and walked backwards too.

The hurt went scrabbling down my throat, like a poison spider. I remembered the telescope and put it up to my eye and used it to explore, up and down King Street, to take my mind off Georgie.

A faraway license plate. A twisted-up windbreaker stuck in a tree. A kite in a sewer. The rabbi in front of the post office, talking to...

Oh.

Nona Tower. Wearing sunglasses too, like a second blind person.

"What you lookin' at?" Georgie said.

She was bending toward him and waving her arms in the circle of the telescope.

"The rabbi," I said, still detesting Georgie's guts. "He's still in front of the post office."

Her Highness Mrs. Tower, vulture lady of temple, the one who'd shown him off like a rabbi robot on the night we first met him, was out there in front of the post office with him and gritting her teeth like she wanted something—give it!—and was mad enough to slap him. Then I saw the letter F on her lips.

It was crazy how much I could see from this far: her teeth, her wrinkles, the green in her bangs. She usually seemed so phony with her breathy breathing and satisfied smiling, her voice like a stream over chilly pebbles, but she didn't seem phony now. She was mad at him and showing it. She looked wickeder than ever.

I brought the telescope down from my eye.

Georgie said, "Let's go back and play in your bedroom."

"Not today," I said.

10

A couple days later I came home from school and my mother was on the phone with "The Secret Storm" on in the background. One of the women on the TV show was smoking on a phone call while my mother in real life was smoking on a phone call.

The actress was saying into the mouthpiece, "I'm sorry to hear your father is dead," though she was smiling while she said it.

My mother looked at me but didn't see me. She tapped her nails on the coffee-stained placemat. She couldn't wait to butt into the conversation, you could tell from the tapping and the jut of her elbow. It had to be Phyllis on the other end of the line, the only person she talked to like this, with a soap opera blasting and a cigarette smoking and two unfinished bowls of Maypo, crusted over from breakfast, never cleared away from the table.

I left to do homework but lingered outside the dining room. I'd been learning so much out of the corner of my ear that I found myself getting interested.

"So don't tell anybody," I heard my mother say. "We had coffee together. At Brinkerhoff's. On Sunnyside."

Pause for Phyllis to speak.

"Rick. Who do you think?"

Pause.

"Rabbi. That's right."

Pause.

"I don't even know why I tell you any of this. You get so hysterical."

Pause.

"Remind me in the future not to tell you any of this."

I heard the TV actress say, "How fair was it to trap him into marrying you?"

And a second actress said, "It wasn't my fault that he found me irresistible."

Then back to the first: "What's your mother going to think when she learns you committed adultery?"

I wasn't completely sure about adultery. I knew it involved adults and sex but beyond that I was hazy.

I must have blanked out because when I focused on her again, my mother was saying, "I'm ready to sell her. Want a kid?" with a jokey tone, when the last thing I'd heard was her lecturing Phyllis for getting hysterical. Somehow they'd switched subjects (and moods). Now the subject was my sister.

"Oh Andy'll never give me trouble," my mother said. "He puts up a fuss but he's clearly not rebellious." (Just wait, I thought.) "But Naomi. Oy. She's always had that mouth on her. You know the name of *that* tune."

All safe-talk now, after they'd dropped the topic of Rabbi. I wished I could've heard what Phyllis had said to annoy my mother. Something disgusting about the rabbi, I bet. Something gross about her wish to commit adultery with him.

I heard trumpety commercial music. It was the one where a white knight goes galloping through some Phyllisy neighborhood and zaps people clean with a blast of his lance.

My mother cooked up a couple more speeches and hung up on Phyl and I hurried away.

◆ ◆ ◆

Later—after a dinner of not-completely-defrosted chicken cutlets and a comic book in which the Green Hornet's sexy girlfriend peels off her face to reveal that she's a hideous monster—I wondered if maybe my mother's boast to Phyllis about coffee with the rabbi was a hideous lie. Maybe my mother had gone to lunch at Brinkerhoff's with one of her priests and saw Rabbi Landy in a booth with his family and that was the extent of it. Maybe she wanted Phyllis to think of her as the rabbi's pet in a way that she wasn't. Maybe nothing she said was true.

I remembered Naomi saying our mother must be getting all trashy around the rabbi, and of course he couldn't bear it. What else could she be doing in his temple office or at Joseph's Drugs or wherever else they ran into each other but hoodwinking him with her endless chatter, her boring opinions, her messy drooling—begging for his kisses—and him too polite to say *Leave me alone*.

And all that cigarette smoke gushing out of the two of them! How could they even breathe?

But I had a spelling test to study for.

◆ ◆ ◆

Later I got a phone-call phone call, not a Georgie Garr phone call.

My mother shouted for me, "Andy!" and then dangled the receiver. "*Pour vous*."

"Hello?"

"Andrew? Thornton Vanoosten here. From astronomy class."

"Thornton. How did you get my number?"

"You're the only Montevidean Baers in the phone book," he said. "I just want to say you were missed at class last Saturday. Is everything copacetic?"

"Oh sure. Yes. Fine. Goodbye." He made me so nervous (just the thought of those eyelashes) that I could only think of hanging up.

"Wait! Don't go. The class isn't remotely as enjoyable without your hilarious questions."

"I thought my questions were stupid."

"You were the only one courageous enough to ask them."

"Well it's nice of you to call me, Thornton."

"Courageous enough and silly enough."

"Turns out I won't be returning to the class. For religious reasons. I'm Jewish. And the class is on our sabbath." What a flimsy transparent exposeable excuse. If I was that concerned about sabbath observance, I never would've signed up for astronomy in the first place. But I certainly wasn't courageous enough to admit that a class for gifted children made me feel like a dope.

"I see. Well."

"Sorry about that."

"Sure thing. I get it. *Pob loook*, young lad."

"Sorry?"

"That's Welsh for good luck."

Jeez, he was enrolled in the gifted Welsh class too. What a boy this was. So dashing and strong and courageously brilliant. You'd be wasting your time getting jealous of him.

"*Ciao*, Andrew," he said.

◆ ◆ ◆

Meanwhile, Friday, back at temple:

"Guard my tongue from evil," the rabbi said, "And my lips from speaking guile. May my soul be humble and forgiving unto all."

And the rest of us responded, "Open thou my heart O Lord unto thy sacred law."

My mother didn't read, she recited by heart, with her eyes on the rabbi, her prayer book closed on her dress-and-stocking lap.

I glanced at Mrs. Landy, the rabbi's wife Tehila. She was also reciting the prayers by heart but she was looking at her ankle, turning her shoe, no looks at her husband. Her nostrils flared, her cheeks were tight, her eyes seemed as sharp as carving knives. What a mismatch, I thought, the rabbi and her. He was welcoming and smiling and peaceful and kind, and she had the jaws of a screaming hyena.

Then Phyllis pushed in through the doors at the back, using her lips to split a bobby pin and poke it into her veil. (Ef lumbered in behind her, hiding a yawn by keeping his mouth small.)

And for the first time ever, my mother and Phyllis didn't look at each other and grimace like goofballs.

The cantor sang, *"Ba-roooch ata oddonoy..."* (blessed art thou O Lord...) with what sounded like an Irish accent.

My mother stared ahead. My mother looked joyful. Her shoulders were back and her chest was out, a total mom embarrassment. *Look at me! I'm reciting by heart. I'm exultant unto the Lord.* She might as well've been nine months pregnant, she was showing that much.

Then the rabbi called Mrs. Flawless, Nona Tower, up to the *beema*. She wore a green paisley dress and her underthings were swishing, sending that roses-and-cantaloupe medicine smell all over the temple.

She popped into the circle of the reading light and read with her usual gasping romantics:

> *"It is good to give thanks unto the Lord,*
> *And to sing praises unto his name, o most high."*

Her frosted bouffant looked green in this light, and her eyes smiled coldness.

I looked to my right at old Mr. Rothstein, to distract myself from the excruciating fakeness of Mrs. Tower's reading style. "Windbag," he muttered. I liked that he didn't pretend to like her.

I wondered if Mrs. Tower always acted like this. How could she call her kids in for dinner when she whispered like Jackie Kennedy? And why had she been with the rabbi on King Street when I caught her through the telescope?

My mother, meanwhile, just to my left, was watching Mrs. Tower. My mother's smile was a melting cough drop, a medicated brown one, as she continued with her reciting:

> *"To show thy lovingkindness in the morning,*
> *And thy faithfulness every night."*

And Rabbi Landy just sat there in his seat on the *beema*, like a U.N. ambassador, prayer book in his mitts, in the background of the service, overseeing the situation from his high-level distance...

...as Mrs. Tower continued reading aloud with her spine-chilling breathiness:

*"Though the wicked spring up like the grass,
And all the workers of iniquity do flourish..."*

She read smoother than the velvet on the curtain of the ark.

"...it is they," my mother called back with the congregation, "that will be destroyed forever."

11

Next morning, junior congregation.

My mother drove Toby and me and hurried into the rabbi's office. And all of us kids filed into the temple—only, yet again, to have the rabbi keep us waiting (the rabbi and my mother), cracking our knuckles, punching our thighs, turned into idiots. What kind of rabbi would abandon you like this, leave you to fidget, minute by minute, squirm by squirm?

10:45.

11 o'clock.

No sign of Rabbi.

All her fault!

Trapping him in his office, corralling him with her talking.

I've had it, I thought. I've got to do something. I couldn't just sit there like a goody-goody moron, not doing anything, with my F in deportment wasting away.

But what in actuality could I do? Run around back and peek in the window? Barge in on the two of them as she reached to adjust his tallis or tie and he twisted to escape her clutches? Unless she was talking so goddamn much—annoyingly, absentmindedly—talking and talking—that she hadn't observed that he'd fallen asleep.

"Where you going?" Toby said.

"To the bathroom," I whispered and scooted off the pew.

"Wait!" Toby said.

He followed me through the swinging doors and out into the lobby.

"Stop following," I said.

"I gotta go too."

I pointed past the tallis rack toward the rabbi's office. "Mommy's in there with the rabbi."

"She is?"

"I'm gonna go get her."

"Don't. She will hit you."

I was standing in front of his office already, on the right side of the lobby. I put my ear on the door. I could hear her inside, middle of a sentence, saying "your work with adolescents" or "you work without a license" or "you look like David Janssen."

I jiggled the handle. "Ma?"

Quick quiet.

"Mom?"

No answer.

"It's locked," Toby whispered, moving in closer. His whispers weren't quiet.

I jiggled again. "Hey Mom? Are you in there?"

Again. Nothing.

It was locked.

But I'd heard her.

(A rustle, then quiet.)

"Maybe she went back home," Toby whispered. "Maybe the rabbi is downstairs in the boys' room making a doody." He sniffed.

"I don't think so."

I'd heard her.

No question.

"Come on," my brother said. He pulled me downstairs to the men's room where he opened every stall, one after the other, like a janitor checking the toilet paper.

"The rabbi isn't down here," I said.

"He prolly went to his home. He's prolly smoking a cigarette and watching Dudley Do-Right."

"The rabbi wouldn't smoke and watch cartoons on *Shobbis*, Toby, believe me."

We both took a leak.

We returned upstairs. I sat in the pew again, alongside my brother, upset with our mother's trickery and the rabbi's audacity and the ticking of the morning's clocks on mantels around the planet.

I touched my brother's knee. "Stop fidgeting."

"I am. Not. Fidgeting." He pushed me away.

When the rabbi finally pranced through the doors at a quarter after eleven, he acted like it was normal for him to be 45 minutes late—after whatever he and my mother were up to—to parade up front, not looking at anyone, focused on the future and fiddling with his tallis.

The only other person I knew with power like that was the principal at my grammar school, Miss Flora Buchanan, who was 92 years old. (She was ancient, yes, but her hair looked as young as Annette Funicello's and was equally poofy.)

I raised my hand illogically (no one raised their hand at temple) but the rabbi ignored me.

"Starting next week," he said from the *beema*, "we will try something different. You will begin the service without me. I'll appoint someone new each week—one week a boy, next week a girl—to act as the rabbi, and that kid'll stand at the *beema*, like me, and call out the pages. You'll read out loud and back and forth and sing in Hebrew, like your parents do, but with a junior rabbi here in my place. It's a way to work on your leadership skills," he said. All of which was arranged so he could continue to stroll in shockingly late, halfway through the service, avoiding any eye contact, after whiling away his time with my mother, clearing his throat and pushing his hair-tonicked hair back into his yarmulke. "You'll all enjoy it, I guarantee it."

After services we poured into the lobby to grab our coats and run outside and locate our parents waiting in their cars and there was my mother, in the middle of the lobby, sitting with her legs crossed under the portrait of an old-time rabbi, in a beard and tefillin, hugging a Torah.

Man, did she annoy me, sitting there where the rabbi had left her, sitting there with her legs crossed for as long as it took a junior congregation to run its full schedule—my underhanded mother, who wouldn't even acknowledge me when I jiggled the rabbi's door, looking like she'd just had a bath or an ice cream.

I couldn't wonder further because a hand was on my shoulder and the rabbi was pulling me into his office.

"Andy...

...come."

Prickles of itch-rash assaulted my face.

I'd never been in his office before. I'd imagined it was grand and green, like Principal Buchanan's, but it was dark and small, like a stall in a men's room, and so narrow that the rabbi's desk could only fit sideways. I smelled my mother's spray-on deodorant.

"Have a seat," he said, putting his hand out.

I sat near his desk.

He smiled. "How are you?"

I was too confused to talk.

"Andy!" Then quieter. "Andy."

I had nothing to say to him.

"Don't be nervous," he said. His smile fizzled out. He touched my arm for a kind-hearted second. "I wanted to spend some time with you, Andy. Get to talk to you a bit. What a coincidence running into you on King Street the other day."

Why was he bringing up King Street? Was he suspicious that I'd seen him with Mrs. Tower through the telescope, waving her arms around and hollering at him in front of the post office?

I looked away. I looked at his desk. Sunglasses, Dixie cup, Parker pen, matchbook.

Matchbook. From Brinkerhoff's. With a picture of a steaming cup of coffee on the front. Where the rabbi and my mother had had lunch together—the two of them—or so my mother had insisted to Phyllis. Didn't the reality of the matchbook prove it?

I took a deep breath. I caught a whiff of his tobacco-and-lime smell.

"Tell me about your friend," the rabbi said.

"What friend?"

"The one I saw you with on King Street the other day."

"Oh Georgie Garr. I introduced you."

"Tell me more about him. What's he like?"

"He isn't a moron if that's what you're thinking."

"I wasn't thinking anything."

"I know people think he's feeble. But he's a super intelligent person."

"May I offer some advice?"

I shrugged.

"Why don't you take a deep breath first?" he said.

"I already took one."

His eyebrows tensed up. "You're all bottled up."

"What's that supposed to mean?"

"You're like a hose with a cork in it. The hose fills with water—fills and fills—until the water has nowhere to go. And it explodes."

Psychology. He was studying it. Or so the adults at temple were saying. Studying in some college. Learning about the thoughts in your head. The thoughts and the feelings.

Like backed-up water.

About to explode.

Lies and secrets.

Liar. Faker.

Stop bothering me.

"That doesn't sound like advice," I said.

He took a breath himself. "Listen." He lifted his yarmulke and smoothed down his hair and pushed it back under the yarmulke. "I don't think it's wise for you to be friends with Georgie Garr."

"Why not?"

"Because he's—not of your caliber."

"What's that supposed to mean?"

"He's dirty for one."

"No he isn't. Just his teeth."

"Does he clean his nails? Does he brush his hair?"

"My mother told you to talk to me, didn't she?"

"Of course not!" He looked so hurt that I almost believed him. "Andy. This is between us men."

All I could think of was my mother and him when I'd jiggled the doorknob.

Between us men. Don't make me laugh.

Between a man and a woman.

Then I pictured my mother complaining to the rabbi about their sons getting naked.

"Georgie Garr is my friend, Rabbi Landy," I said.

"So you say."

"I should know when a friend's a friend," I said.

He smiled nicely, all patience and goodness, like I'd hurt him profoundly when he was only trying to help.

I remembered Georgie's comment. *Hitler shoulda killed all the Jews.* What if Rabbi Landy was right? Maybe I shouldn't have let that go. Maybe Georgie Garr really *wasn't* of my caliber and I should've hollered at him for siding with Hitler.

But wait.

No.

Back it up, I thought. It was Rabbi who'd hurt *me* profoundly, pretending he wasn't in his office with my mother.

"Don't you have other friends?" the rabbi asked. "Andy?"

I was reluctant to respond. "Not since Arthur Vilsac," I said. "He moved away. To Suffern, New York."

"Or any other boys to get friendlier with?"

Thornton Vanoosten. He'd called. He was friendly. With his Elvis Presley eyelashes and his smarty-pants personality. Maybe he could become my friend. Maybe I could call Information, ask for his number and return his call.

"I'm sure you know plenty of boys," the rabbi said.

I couldn't hold back. The words shot out of me: "Why didn't you answer when I knocked on the door?"

"Door? What door?"

Because I didn't trust him, not after that, and not with my mother still out there in the lobby, crossing her legs, uncrossing her legs, waiting for me while the other kids' mothers had already driven them home and made them lunch.

"I knocked on your door," I said. "This door right here. I heard you inside. I heard you with my mother."

"That's impossible," the rabbi said.

"But I heard you."

"I forgot my tallis. I went home to get it. I wasn't on the premises."

"I'm positive I heard you."

"You couldn't have. I'm sorry. But that simply isn't possible."

"Well I know I heard *her*."

"Who?"

"My mother. She was in here."

"Oh, she might've been in here making a call. She said she had to use my office to make an important phone call, yes. But hey. Andy. Let's forget about your mother. What are you feeling? Right this second?"

"Feeling?"

Betrayed.

But I didn't want to say. It already seemed like I'd said too much. And the foolish thing was that, even though the rabbi was full of phony smiles and a phony tone of comfort, his attention made it seem like I had a big man's arm around my shoulder, the best kind of comfort for a kid without a father.

I stretched my legs and my knee bones popped. I grunted. I yawned. "I'm tired," I said.

"Just think about what I told you. You're an excellent young fellow and you should surround yourself with other excellent young fellows."

◆ ◆ ◆

"What Did He Say To You Come On Now Tell Me!"

My mother was so frantic to worm it out of me that I guessed that the rabbi was telling the truth and our talk had nothing to do with her. If she didn't know about the topics of discussion, then maybe they hadn't conferred together beforehand. Maybe they hadn't cooked up a plan to knife me in the back by ridiculing Georgie and insulting my psychology. And maybe it was really only her in his office, like the rabbi had said, making a phone call.

"None of your business," I said.

My mother sighed and drove off.

"None of your business," Toby parroted in the back.

"Would you please drive slower?" I said.

"You have to tell me *something*, Andy."

"No I don't."

"Oh yes you do. I can make you. Watch."

"How? You gonna pull out my fucking hair like you do to Naomi?"

"He cursed," Toby said.

My mother drove another block and parked at a curb. She was a pro at hasty parallel parking. She turned off the motor, put her elbows on the wheel and dug her hands in her hair. "All right," she said. "You're right. All right?" She didn't drive away.

She never mentioned my father but he was here now, I could feel him, like a shadow on our backs. She didn't want me to see her as the hitter and screamer that he was. She wished he was around to share her parental duties. She might've even missed him. She was alone as a parent in any case and had no one to decide things with. It was enough to make you pity her and for the moment, at least, I did.

◆ ◆ ◆

I wondered if the rabbi ever talked to my mother like he'd just talked to me, like some kind of mind reader. I hated what he'd said about Georgie Garr's hygiene but it was hard to forget his concern. No wonder my mother liked sitting with him all comfortable in his office. Did he talk to his wife with the same consideration? I doubted she would go for such nonsense. She'd probably reach for an emery board and start filing her nails if he asked her what she was feeling, right now Tehila, don't hold back.

And besides, Phyllis had said they were headed for splitsville. If a couple thinks about splitsville, how can they ever forget it?

But Georgie Garr. The rabbi had advised me to dump my best friend. How strange that Thornton Vanoosten should call and say hi at the very same moment. I thought about it some more and concluded that Rabbi Landy sure had chutzpah, trying to decide things for me when the last thing I wanted was another powerful adult with say-so over me. Especially someone who had say-so over my mother. In the end, I didn't know what to think so I took Georgie's phone off the hook so he couldn't reach me until I decided.

12

Then things got worse.

Some mornings my mother left the apartment super early, before we were up, before it was light out, without an explanation. Where could she be going at five in the morning? To spread frosting on cupcakes in the bakery up on King Street? To wash corpses at the funeral parlor? Were we that hard up for dough?

Many nights, after we'd all gone to bed, she'd be typing in the living room, way past midnight—I'd get up to pee and hear the tap-a-tap tapping—but there was never any evidence the following morning of what she'd been typing. Story of her life? College paper? If so, for what school? On one particular two in the morning, I could've sworn I heard someone else in the living room, typing alongside her.

A couple days a week I'd come home from school and she'd be locked in the bathroom, crying—big dramatic wails like her world was at an end. Maybe her boss, Father Quinn, had bawled her out for screwing things up (though she always liked to tell you how perfect she was, how everybody said so), and she just couldn't stand it.

My sister was never up early enough so I'm sure she never witnessed any of the mystery departures. And if she overheard the crying, she didn't make fun. She was tough all right, but she wasn't mean. Besides, she might've felt bad for our mother. Naomi had tried again and again to get our father to rescue her, to whisk her away to never-never daddyland, and she'd cry herself to sleep as sadly as our mother did when he shattered her chances.

◆ ◆ ◆

Thornton Vanoosten called me again before I remembered to look up his number. His manly voice excited me so much I accidentally licked the receiver. He asked if I wanted to play with him Sunday. He said his father could pick me up and bring me to their house. This was like something out of a fairy tale, with a prince and a pumpkin.

When I covered the mouthpiece to ask if I could go, my mother said she'd drive me over, "Don't make them schlep," if only, I figured, so she could tootle past the rabbi's house on the ride over.

(I didn't know the story but I started to wonder if her escapes before dawn and her crying in the bathroom had to do with Rabbi Landy. Something he'd yelled at her about in one of their private moments that had hurt her so deep that she was driving around with no destination, at foolish hours.)

Thornton's town was grander than Phyllis's. It was forest mostly with far-apart houses on streets without sidewalks between splashing brooks and stables for horses. And Thornton's place, as we drove up to it, had columns in front.

My mother crushed a cigarette. "Goodness gracious, Mizz Scarlett!"

My mother dropped me off.

Thornton's mother served us dinner for lunch (fish, corn, potatoes) and added my name to the end of every sentence. "Take a seat here, Andy." "Can I get you a glass of chocolate milk, Andy?" She wore a baby blue dress and had wonderful posture. My throat tightened up because of some mind-boggling dryness so I ended up not saying much. Thornton ate with his mouth open, gabbing about dissecting worms.

He and I played Scrabble in the cork-paneled den which had a fireplace and hard plaid couches. I beat him by 38 points. Afterwards he said he wanted to take a walk. I said let's make it a mystery walk and he liked the idea. I imagined him taking my hand, like Georgie.

(I didn't feel any guilt about ignoring Georgie Garr by the way, not one bit, because of the Hitler situation.)

"If I turn left here," Thornton said, "it's a mystery walk already because I never turn left here." The block had only three or four buildings on it and every one was a mansion. "On the other hand," Thornton added, "no mysteries here."

"Are you kidding?" I said. "Where did all this moolah come from?"

Thornton laughed. "You really do say the funniest things, Andrew. Hey, what's that?"

It was a red dirt foundation.

"Another bazillion-dollar mansion in the works," I said.

"Let's play in the hole," he said.

We ran and shouted like we were a few years younger. Thornton slid down a mountain of dirt that scraped away the seat of his corduroys and underpants. His tush showed in the back like honeydews. He tried hiding it with his hands but couldn't completely.

Sexy feelings split my body, like I was Wile E. Coyote in the middle of nowhere struck by lightning.

He said we should sneak into his house by way of the mudroom because his mother would be angry about the rip. (It was hard to imagine her angry.) (And what was a mudroom?? Gee, this family was rich!)

I couldn't bend my knees out of inner commotion as we hurried off the construction site.

"What's the matter with you?" he said.

"I'm paralyzed."

"Ha ha!"

We got to his bedroom without being noticed. He sat me on the edge of the bed and put his honeydews in my face.

"How bad is it?" He bent way forward.

"Does your mother have a sewing machine?"

"Try pulling the ends together. I'll sew it myself."

"This is a big job, Thornton."

"Do the ends come together?"

"No." I could feel the cool of his goosey flesh as I tried to pull the rip together.

"Can you see anything?"

"What do you mean? I can see both buttocks." I pronounced them *byoo-tox*.

"Can you see my balls?" He bent over farther.

"Yes. Both."

We wound up doing what I'd done with Georgie Garr (naked under the sheets, pulling each other's penises) but this boy was moanier as he shot out the sperm. There wasn't enough time for me to shoot out because his father called upstairs and said he was ready to take me home.

I wondered where he'd been all day. Swimming in the built-in pool in their finished basement? He was over six feet and amazingly peppy. It was nice to have two people—two men—both of whom needed their hair cut, incidentally—so happy to be my footmen. (I would've lived with them forever in their palace if they'd asked me.) They drove me home in a Ford Country Squire, older than The Bomb, with wood along the sides. Thornton talked nonstop about the "phonology of Welsh" and honked out some vowels that sounded like elf talk. The car had the smell of a pigeon coop.

No one was home when I got there which surprised me but not entirely because of my mother's recent unexplained absences.

I went to my room to masturbate while the coast was clear—my Thornton time had been so thrilling that I figured I'd be rubbing about it until I was in high school, maybe college—and there was Georgie's phone off the hook, lying on the toy chest at the foot of Toby's bed like a clobbered otter.

I thought about hanging it up and fixing the link between Georgie and me, but I wasn't sure I should. Rabbi Landy had told me not to. Georgie hated Jews.

Or was he copycatting his father?

No.

Wait.

Yes.

No.

I still didn't know what to think.

I was too obsessed about the rip in Thornton's pants and his tush hanging out to keep my mind on Georgie Garr. I yanked down my pants and flopped into bed and rubbed with the fingertips on both my hands until the goo gushed out.

I used a sock to clean it up and heard a radio in the street. Not music but talk, like it was floating up from the candy store. Then it sounded like the news. Maybe the weather. Maybe the football scores. Where was it coming from?

I put my ear on different walls and searched in the corners. Then I traced the sound to the phone.

The phone!

Of course, the phone. It didn't have a dial tone. It was always connected to Georgie's phone. I should've expected this. I put my hand around the mouthpiece and listened.

The voices were metallic.

"You can do this, baby." (Mrs. Garr.)

"He'll have a conniption. How can I tell him?" (My mother.) (My mother?! Talking with Mrs. Garr! Unbelievable. Crazy.) (But was it really any crazier than me and her Georgie stripping together?)

My mother started crying.

Mrs. Garr said, "Fuck him. Who gives a shit? You should fuckin' forget him. Are you listening to me?"

"I gotta go."

"I ain't talking out of my craphole, missy."

"I know." Sigh. "I know. I know." My mother muttered something I couldn't make out, then said, "This is Phyllis's fault. If it hadn't'a been for Phyllis. She was the one who—" Her sentence melted away.

"Do not ignore what I'm saying to you. F - U - C - K - H - I - M."

"Okay. I got it."

"And that wife of his? Don't make me spit. That wife of his? She's all dried up."

"Oh Mayda. You think?"

"She ain't nothing but a high-class bitch-tit."

"Yes, that's it, what else could she be? But I really gotta go now. Time to make dinner."

"Fuck dinner too. Get that lazy-ass thunder-cunt daughter of yours to cook it."

"I may be depressed but I'm not suicidal."

They laughed themselves into a double smoker's coughing fit.

Afterwards I thought: Phyllis's fault? All dried up? What had the rabbi done to my mother? And how on earth could Mrs. Garr—nasty Mrs. Garr!—be a comfort to her?

13

I couldn't ask questions because she'd figure out I snooped. Yet she wouldn't've explained it anyway because, really, why would she? Whatever it was, it made her ashamed. And since there weren't any dead people or fingerprints to dust for, I had to get my clues at temple.

Friday night.

The rabbi said, "These words, which I command thee this day shall stay in thy heart."

And the rest of us responded, "Thou shalt teach them diligently unto thy children when thou sittest in thy house and when thou walkest by the way."

First thing I noticed was Mrs. Landy wasn't around. I looked across the way for her, fourth pew back, and Mrs. Rodetsky was in her place—retired teacher, thinning red hair—tilting her head as she gawked at the rabbi. Where was Mrs. Landy? I'd never gone to a Friday night service that she hadn't been in her regular place, checking her watch, smoothing her skirt, proving to us brainwashed pinheads that her husband wasn't worth much. I wondered what could've happened to her.

Meanwhile, the rabbi said, "True and Certain. Page 26," twinkling at his congregants—twinkle, twinkle—and my mother twinkled back—twinkle for twinkle—looking stronger than she'd looked in weeks, erasing any traces of the sobbing and the midnight typing, as she answered back with the rest of us:

"True and certain it is that there is one God.
His wonders are without number."

True and Certain. Page 26. I couldn't imagine anything more comforting. The prayer might as well have said:

*"True and certain it is that there is one rabbi,
And he oxygenateth only me."*

◆ ◆ ◆

After services, I overheard comments as I headed to the men's room and peed at the urinal and bee-lined from the men's room to the checkerboard floor of the social hall where I moved between the cookies and the challah and the punch bowl.

"Trouble in Tahiti."

"I can only imagine."

"Major blowout."

"Bonnie Teplitsky."

"You heard it from Bonnie?"

"One-way ticket. Boca Raton."

"I know. I heard. She's down there with the mother-in-law."

"He has a very long résumé of extracurricular you-know-what."

"Non-stop to splitsville."

"Who says?"

"My sources."

"Your yentas."

"Ask Nona."

"Ask who?"

"Nona Tower."

"It all comes back to the mother-in-law."

"My lips are sealed. With a paperclip. And a staple gun."

"You say that now, Harriet, but why don't I trust you?"

In Florida with her mother-in-law. That seemed to be the gist of it. Where the Mrs. had disappeared to.

Chatterboxes.

Busybodies.

None of my business.

What did I care?

Then I found myself next to the two sons by accident, loitering at the kiddish table, as I reached for a kichel.

"Excuse me," I said.

The older one, Avi, was reaching for a kichel too, in his pinstripe suit, with a pinstripe sleeve, so I let him go first, and he grabbed about a dozen cookies and shoveled them onto a coffee saucer, not looking at me, like I didn't exist, which pissed me off big time. Then his elbow went into my face and that pissed me off even more.

"Hey," I said.

He turned to me. "Hey what?"

"You elbowed me."

His eyes narrowed. "You were in my way."

He started to walk, but in a rumble of a snit I said, "What happened to your mother?"

Avi turned back. His eyes were even slittier. He had the solidness of a Budweiser draft horse. He said, "What happened to your *father*?"

I didn't have a comeback.

My mother came over. She ignored me too. "*Shobbis*, Avi. *Shobbis*, Yussie."

And while the younger son Yussie tottled away, Avi puffed his chest out and talked to my mother. "Hello, Mrs. B."

"You've certainly got an appetite."

"Heh heh. Always hungry."

"I bet you are."

"Come on already, Ma," I said. "We gotta get going."

"Fi more mits," my mother said, not looking at me.

◆ ◆ ◆

I heard her on the phone that night as I stumbled into the bathroom, after waking up from a nightmare. "What good is she? I'm serious. Lotta highfalutin haughty, with a cherry on top...No, Boca. That's right. Good riddance, bad rubbish...I never, nope...The mother-in-law. You got that right...I had my suspicions...She's the one with the money, you know. She's the one with the power. All you have to do is fill in the blanks."

14

Later that week, on the way to spend my allowance on a 45 of "96 Tears" for 59 cents at Melody House, I saw the rabbi and his sons a half a block ahead of me, exiting Dubin's Dresses on King Street, across from the Micmac movie theater.

They were loaded up with shopping bags, the three of them, and Avi and Yussie were swinging them at each other—a blur of Dubin's shopping bags. The rabbi ignored them. He put his own bags down and dug into his pocket for a cigarette and lit it. The boys kept swinging, harder and harder, like rock'em sock'em shoppers. Their father just searched in the sky and smoked.

❖ ❖ ❖

Mrs. Landy was still away from her pew when the rabbi gave his sermon the following evening. (Had he shipped her the dress-bribes from Dubin's already, care of his mother-in-law in Boca Raton? Would he ever win his Tehila back?)

His sermon dealt with the patriarch Joseph.

> "Imagine their faces carved in stone—60 feet high!—the Mount Rushmore of Judaism: Abraham, Isaac, Jacob, Joseph. Otherwise known as The Righteous, The Obedient, The Crafty and…" Long pause. "…The Crybaby.
>
> "You might not remember this, but Joseph is a crier. There are seven accounts in Genesis of his crying his eyes out. Not a couple, or five. Seven! This is a very emotional man, our

Joseph. And why not? Makes sense. He lived a rollercoaster existence. Sold into slavery by his very own brothers! Promoted to enormous power in the world of Egyptian politics! Doomed to perpetual bad nights' sleeps because of those psychedelic nightmares of his!"

He paused like he was pausing for an explosion of laughter, but nobody laughed.

"And indeed, he is a crier.

"A weeper.

"A waterworks. And I venture to suggest that the crying is a form of self-administered psychotherapy. When Joseph's unhappy and words escape him, he breaks down and cries. His emotional dam bursts. And don't be fooled. There ain't nothin' especially pretty about a grown man crying. A grown man crying is like a little baby crying. His tears are the tears of the stymied communicator, of the human who doesn't verbalize. When a grown man cries, it's like the world has fallen apart. Think James Dean in *East of Eden*. Think Marlon Brando in a tattered T-shirt wailing for Stella."

Even *I* understood the psychology here. The wailer was the rabbi, and this Stella woman was Mrs. Landy.

Mr. Rothstein huffed. "One *shegetz* after another."

◆ ◆ ◆

Then Thornton Vanoosten called me again. I was overjoyed. He wanted to come to my place this time, just to be fair. How about Saturday?

"Sure," I said.

So what if he saw how poor we were? He'd already seen my meager street—all cement, no trees—when his father dropped me off that time. He must've had some inkling.

I couldn't stop thinking about his tallness, his handsomeness, his funniness, his boyness. The days dragged on.

◆ ◆ ◆

My mother and I were driving home from Shop-Rite. The Bomb slowed down. I smelled something burning. The days were getting darker. And there in the middle of Salem Street were the Landy boys throwing a football.

My mother parked the car and got out. It was a cold afternoon. She leaned against the hood, lit a cigarette and watched. A faraway dog barked.

I got out too. I said, "What are you doing??"

The older son did zigzags as the younger son counted, "One Mississippi. Two Mississippi." You could see their breath. There were church bells somewhere. The ball went flying.

My mother said nothing.

I was angry all over, forehead to sweat socks. "Would you please get back in the car already??"

A seaplane buzzed. The air was wet. Something was burning—fireplace? leaves? a house on Peru Street?

The bells kept going.

Gong bagong.

The Landy boys shouted. The ball was out of bounds. They were too involved in their game to see us. Or too plain arrogant.

Despite my mother's outrageousness and my history of detesting them, the rabbi's sons had my sympathy that day. Their mother had abandoned them. Their mother was gone.

Gong bagong.

Then a Buick drove up Salem Street, blowing fallen leaves around. I couldn't believe it. Their mother was in it. At just this moment. Could my mother have planned it? I didn't see how.

The boys stopped playing. The boys were frozen. The boys were smiling. (First time I'd ever seen the Landy boys smile.) Their mother steered the Buick into the two-car driveway. She switched off the motor, exited the car, saluted like a general and unlocked the trunk. Avi trotted over and hefted out the suitcase. Yussie slammed the trunk shut. Avi put the suitcase down and hugged his mom possessively. Yussie joined in for a three-way embrace. Mrs. Landy peered out from the top of the hug and noticed my mother leaning on a car, smoking and watching, and shot her an eye-beam, full of contempt, straight to the head, like an alien determined to blow up the brains of an inconvenient earthling.

As the church bells rang.

Gong bagong.

15

My mother served us tuna on toast with potato chips and a glass of milk. You could tell she enjoyed how handsome Thornton was from all the smirking she did.

As soon as we entered my bedroom after lunch he noticed the Georgie Garr telephone.

"Hey neat. What's this?"

I told him it was busted.

"But what is it?"

I explained.

"I'd like to meet this Georgie Automobile," he joked.

I said, "It's Garr, not Carr."

"Aha! Well I'd still like to meet him."

"Sure. Sometime." Truth is, I wanted Thornton all to myself.

"I'd love to try it." He picked up the phone without any warning.

I grabbed it out of his hand and put it up to my ear. "Huh," I said. "Funny. Maybe he fixed it." I waited for it to ring. "How about that," I said. "It's ringing."

Mrs. Garr answered, "Why you busybody pissflap! Stop calling here damn it!" and slammed down the phone.

I shrugged at Thornton. "Gee. No answer. He must be out playing." I waited a bit and hung up the phone.

I'd never wanted a playmate all to myself like this. The feeling was only partially positive. Because I felt like my friend might be taken away.

We played parcheesi, crazy eights and half a Stratego. After an hour or two, my mother opened my bedroom door and batted her eyes at

Thornton. "I'm taking your brother to the movies. Wanna come? We're seeing *The Fortune Cookie*."

"Didn't you ever hear of knocking?" I said.

My mother said, "All four of us can go. What do you say? Master Vanoosten?"

"I already saw it," Thornton said. "Excellent choice though. Thanks anyway."

My mother pouted like a hammy comedian. I could tell she was hurt because she wasn't that good of an actress.

As soon as she and Toby left, Thornton reminded me of the pants-ripping incident—wasn't that hilarious?—and we stripped and had more penis fun. After we wiped up the goo, he suggested we take a mystery walk *in my own apartment!* "Parents and sibs are always leaving the nuttiest things just lying around and you gotta wonder if they secretly want you to find them." (Sibs. What a word.)

I tried to discourage him but he wouldn't stop talking about it. He raised an eyebrow. He enjoyed being teasey. "Come on. It'll be fascinating. I stumbled on some playing cards once in my father's sock drawer. Nudie jacks with giant dicks. And queens with big tits." He was trying to persuade me, and in the end I couldn't resist because of his self-assured sweet-talk and swaggering spontaneousness.

So we barged into my sister's room and right away I discovered her diary. Page after page about missing Daddy, that cheater, that prick, his girlfriend's a slob, Dell this, Dell that. Then some insecure thoughts about her kissing a senior. What should her tongue do? Would he dump her for a better kisser? I felt suffocatedly guilty.

Meanwhile, Thornton was attacking an underwear drawer, sifting through bras. "This is terrific, isn't it?"

I didn't agree but I said, "Yeah."

He even put a bra on over his polo shirt and minced around in my sister's mirror saying, "I want your baby, Andy," in a ridiculous high-pitched Aunt Bee voice, "plus a box of cherry chocolates," which was somewhat arousing and somewhat depressing.

When we got to the living room where my mother slept, Thornton picked through her drawers like a robber and through her closet like a bargain hunter. He didn't find much (a girdle and a garter) before the phone rang—I jumped—it was Mr. Vanoosten, ready to pick his son up—but I did glimpse a looseleaf that I'd never noticed before, hidden behind an endtable. I decided I'd look at it later, alone, after Thornton went home. (Maybe it was the book my mother was writing!)

I felt terrible after Thornton left. I imagined shouting, "Thornton! Why did you leave me!" like someone in a movie after the hero goes on a bus, but as soon as he disappeared I forgot about my misery and tiptoed into the living room and pulled out the looseleaf from behind the endtable, thinking it was safe to snoop because my mother and Toby were at *The Fortune Cookie* and Naomi was at Debbie's.

The looseleaf was full of speeches typed out like a play.

> DR. LANDY: So talk. Don't think. Whatever comes to mind.
>
> PATIENT: What? No foreplay?
>
> DR. LANDY: Not sure what you mean.
>
> PATIENT: What the patient can expect. The ground rules. You know.
>
> DR. LANDY: Just talk. Don't censor. Those are the only ground rules. This is a critical piece of my training. To practice with actual patients and tape-record the sessions.
>
> PATIENT: So I'm a guinea pig.
>
> DR. LANDY: No, no. I've had years of training.
>
> PATIENT: I'm a guinea pig and you think I'm crazy.
>
> DR. LANDY: I would never say that.
>
> PATIENT: Yes, but you'd think it.
>
> DR. LANDY: Not at all. People have problems. Everybody does.
>
> PATIENT: And you're confident you can cure me.

DR. LANDY: You've got nothing that needs curing.

PATIENT: In other words, I'm perfect.

DR. LANDY: There are elements of your personal history that affect your life as you live it now, and it would be helpful for you to explore them with me, to get to the bottom of them. If you're willing. You're an inquisitive woman. Why not use that inquisitiveness to gain insight into the influence of your parental upbringing, the secret demands of your inner life, the shifting course of your emotional development? Don't you imagine that that would help you?

PATIENT: Can you reach me a cig? This isn't exactly conventional, you know.

DR. LANDY: These techniques have been used by medical professionals all over the world for almost a century.

PATIENT: No, I mean this isn't conventional because you and I are, you know...doing it.

DR. LANDY: All right, Bea. Listen. You're going to have to edit that out when you type this, okay? In fact, start typing from this point forward. Oh, but leave in what I said about your personal history. That whole bit.

PATIENT: You wanna light me?

DR. LANDY: Did you hear what I said?

PATIENT: Yes, dear.

DR. LANDY: Don't call me that.

PATIENT: Sorry. Let's start over.

DR. LANDY: Just talk.

PATIENT: Talk.

DR. LANDY: Whatever comes to mind.

PATIENT: Don't censor. Got it. I read you. Over.

Doing it?? Like boyfriend and girlfriend?? The rabbi and my mother?? The psychiatrist and his *patient*?? *A devoted member of his **smiling congregation**????* And what about his wife? What about his boys? Did they realize what was going on? His wife must know everything. Why else would she run to Florida? And here he was, all set up in some office somewhere (maybe his tiny temple office!) (of course! that office!) to discuss my mother's most personal private intimate problems. And she typed it at night. She typed him as DR. LANDY. Not doctor of medicine but doctor of psychos. It was just like Naomi told me. My wackadoo mother was forcing herself on the rabbi and he was just too nice to stop her. I had it in writing. She was urging him in disgusting directions. I flipped to the middle.

> PATIENT: For one, I didn't love him. I didn't even pretend to love him. I was desperate to get married. Thought no one else would want me. We were all of nineteen.
>
> DR. LANDY: Lots of people marry people they're not in love with.
>
> PATIENT: Such as thou?
>
> DR. LANDY: This isn't about me.
>
> PATIENT: She clearly can't stand you. That'll never change. But did you ever love her?
>
> DR. LANDY: I'm serious.
>
> PATIENT: At any point in your marriage?
>
> DR. LANDY: This is not about me!
>
> PATIENT: Okay. All right. You don't have to yell.
>
> DR. LANDY: That wasn't a yell.
>
> PATIENT: Forget it.
>
> DR. LANDY: Back to Johnny.
>
> PATIENT: Whatever.

DR. LANDY: Was he Jewish? You never mentioned.

PATIENT: Ng.

DR. LANDY: One of those rare Jewish Johnnys. Go on. Please.

PATIENT: Listen. You're starting to get on my nerves. Why don't you leave me the fuck alone?

DR. LANDY: Ah. That's perfect. Speak as freely as you'd like.

PATIENT: You're exasperating, you know that?

DR. LANDY: How so?

PATIENT: He was unfaithful to me on our honeymoon, all right?

DR. LANDY: And how did that make you feel?

PATIENT: Like a goddamn treasure.

DR. LANDY: What difference did it make if you didn't love him?

PATIENT: Just because I said I didn't, doesn't mean it's true.

Yes it helped that my mother might've actually loved my father, but he didn't love her back. And he'd cheated on her from the *start of their marriage—ON THEIR ACTUAL HONEYMOON!*—so what difference did it make? And the rabbi, I was beginning to realize, must be SOME KIND OF CRIMINAL! I flipped ahead.

PATIENT: I thought I told you. Twenty-nine.

DR. LANDY: I'd've remembered that. What a shocker. How tragic.

PATIENT: I was in kindergarten. I was six. Worst thing that ever happened to me. Well, that and meeting you. Ha!

DR. LANDY: Were you close to her?

PATIENT: She was my mother. What do you think? But my parents were divorced already by the time she died. Divorce was only for movie stars back then, not for the parents where we grew up.

DR. LANDY: This is all very important for us to discuss here certainly but I'm afraid you're leaving the feelings out.

PATIENT: What do you mean?

DR. LANDY: There isn't any prize for being the smartest girl in the class.

PATIENT: There you go again.

DR. LANDY: What?

PATIENT: Making me feel like a piece of shit.

DR. LANDY: That wasn't my intention.

PATIENT: I wanted her dead, okay? How's that for a feeling? I wanted her dead for divorcing my father. Then she died. Tada! So I thought it was me. That my anger had killed her.

DR. LANDY: Of course. It's only logical. What else could you think? But guilt like that can be tremendously paralyzing. It's a struggle to recover from the guilt of a parent's death, especially when it occurs that early.

I flipped a chunk forward.

PATIENT: Oh, Toby was a mistake. Is it okay for me to say that? I'd never tell Toby. But think about it. Seven years after the last one. Just as Johnny and I were getting ready to call it quits. We thought it might help if we fucked. So we fucked. But it didn't help. And look at what happened. No wonder I resent the little pisher.

Yeesh. Poor Toby. My poor little pisher mistake of a brother. I flipped more forward still.

PATIENT: I keep hoping Nona Tower drives by and sees my car out in front. She might've even seen it already. Now isn't that childish?

DR. LANDY: All of our behavior has a logic—an understandable psychological explanation—in other words, a reason.

PATIENT: Oh come off it, Rick. Don't you think it's a trifle, I don't know, perverted of me? That it gives me a thrill? To imagine getting Nona's goat?

DR. LANDY: Now, now. This is important. Especially as it points up your neurotic competitiveness. And the pleasure you get from your exhibitionism, your delight in being looked at, in showing your body.

PATIENT: That's quite a leap, mister, from Nona Tower seeing my car to my showing her my goddamn body.

DR. LANDY: I detect hostility.

PATIENT: Do you?

DR. LANDY: What are your feelings about me?

PATIENT: Don't toy with me, Rabbi.

DR. LANDY: What do you mean?

PATIENT: You know what I mean.

DR. LANDY: I don't think I do.

PATIENT: Then think a little harder. Darling rabbi. Dearest Rick.

DR. LANDY: I'm afraid our time is up.

I had that fantasy again of throwing her out a window. Her and her copy of *Warped Desires* which she was leaving out in the dining room lately, with the back of a naked lady on the cover, kneeling before a man, like she was begging for sex.

I flipped to this blocky paragraph:

> PATIENT: Never told you I went to nursing school, did I? Not exactly my finest hour. One tumultuous fall and winter. Had to leave when I learned I was pregnant with Naomi. But so at the hospital—it was a teaching hospital—in Atlantic City—there was this doctor, Dr. Hertzberg, up and down the halls. He had a Jewfro and a rooster strut. It was love at first sight. But he never loved me back. He never even looked at me. I'd spy on him as he walked down the hall. I'd follow him out to the parking lot. I'd time my appearances so I'd accidentally on purpose run into him in the elevator. I'd say hello but that was it. I was paralyzed. I was tongue-tied. I was a lowly first-year nursing student. Oh, he might say hi so as not to seem rude but he'd look away as soon as he said it. We never so much as shared a sentence together. I remember looking his number up once and calling him at home. Soon as he answered I hung up. And then one day—can you throw me a cig?—I was up in my dorm. I was wondering how to get him to notice me. Thanks. I was scouting around, scrounging for ideas, and I noticed my hairbrush, this big brown hairbrush, and I grabbed it without thinking and sat on the bed and crossed my legs. I drew back the brush and slammed it against my ankle and. It broke. My ankle. I broke my own ankle. Dr. Hertzberg saw me at once.

As horrible as it was (horrible, horrible, horrible, horrible) that wasn't the worst of it. I flipped even farther forward.

> DR. LANDY: Sounds like a certain amount of healthy separation going on.
>
> PATIENT: Oh yes. Very healthy. He's developed quite a mouth on him.
>
> DR. LANDY: Nobody says you should give him up.
>
> PATIENT: Johnny used to say that. <u>He's your son, not your girlfriend, and you have to give him up.</u> That it's part of growing up.
>
> DR. LANDY: Well he does have a point. You don't want him growing up to be, well, you know.

What Miss Dewess had suggested. A permanent troublemaker with a permanent F in deportment. My mother must've told him about the blot on my report card.

>PATIENT: I hate it when people talk like that.
>
>DR. LANDY: That's why I'm spending time with him.
>
>PATIENT: And I appreciate it.
>
>DR. LANDY: Just try and understand what Andy's feeling.
>
>PATIENT: I know what Andy's feeling. I lost a parent too.
>
>DR. LANDY: Of course. Right.
>
>PATIENT: You begin to feel like you caused it. Like it's all your fault. But in this case it was Johnny's fault.
>
>DR. LANDY: What?
>
>PATIENT: The, you know, the divorce. It was all his fucking fault. God. If I only hadn't had those kids.

I closed the looseleaf and put it back.

16

Four or Five Months Later

She made the dreaded turn onto Salem Street and I think by now, all three of us, even Toby, knew what she was thinking as she checked the rabbi's windows and the cars in his driveway.

"Oh!" my mother said. "He's back, kids. Look!" There were two cars in the driveway, a Buick and an Olds. "He's finally back from Israel." She parked The Bomb with a quick couple turns. "Can you believe it? He's back. He's home already. Come, kids, quick!"

She hurried out of the car with Naomi and Toby behind her.

I scowled and said, "I'm staying," but my mother didn't hear.

They crossed the street, my mother in front, forgetting to check for traffic. She clomped up the steps of the rabbi's house like she lived there with him, and my sister clomped too, Toby trailing.

My mother knocked and Mrs. Landy came to the door with an oven fork clutched in her oven mitt. She had lady-style sideburns like poison-tipped darts that sharpened her jaguar jawbone, adding to her scariness.

I stayed inside The Bomb, pissed at my mother for race-walking in to see Rabbi. I refused to join her puppy litter. I was proud of myself for not yapping up the steps behind her. Naomi wasn't the only one who could stand up to our mother. What a bunch of suckers.

But it was hot in the car. Already my neck and eyelids were sweating.

Meanwhile, my mother slid into the house, right past Mrs. Landy, leading the way for my lobotomized sibs. I imagined her barreling straight for the rabbi, who'd be sitting under a reading lamp, running a finger down the verses in a jewel-encrusted bible. Even caught off guard by a cuckoo from temple (his intimate sex lover!!), he'd be gracious enough to say *Happy to see you* with his big hands out.

"I brought the kids," she'd say. "All three of them. Hey—where the fuck is Andy?" I imagined her looking all over for me, even under her shoes. She'd been counting on a hundred percent attendance from the family and here I'd ruined it for her. She would kill me for this. I knew how she was.

So I blew out a gust of frustrated bravery, exited the car, walked across the street and stomped up the steps. I looked at the mailbox, blacksmith black. I looked at the doorbell with a starburst around it. I twisted my feet into the bristles of the welcome mat and let myself in. The door was unlocked.

Rabbi Landy was talking his head off as I entered. He was waving around a cigarette, saying something excited about the discotheques in Tel Aviv. There were a couple of unpacked, partially exploded suitcases open on the coffee table and on one of the sofas. The group was sitting in a sort of a circle, the rabbi, my mother, my sister, my brother and the rabbi's wife, standing at the back, brandishing the oven fork.

The rabbi was saying, "I'm not kidding. Take your pick. Tel Aviv, Jaffa, even Jerusalem."

I couldn't hold it in. I said, "It's a hundred degrees in that stupid car."

Everyone looked.

My brother said, "You are *opposed* to say excuse me."

My mother said, "Andy. Come. We were waiting for you," like she wasn't annoyed. "Right over here." She patted an empty spot on the sofa.

I stayed where I was.

The rabbi said, "Nice to see you, Andy," with an extra-strength smile. Then he slanted his eyes for a peek at Mrs. Landy, standing sentry at the back.

Her hair was high and perfect, like a stack of honey dessert balls. "Of course you're overheated," she said. "It's awful out there." She was trying to smile, but it looked like a gas pain. "And here I am attempting to cook in this heat. When we're only back a minute. Speaking of which. I've got a pot roast on the range and it's your fault if I burn it." She turned around sharply and marched into the kitchen, swing door swishing after her like an unpronounced curse word. I thought she meant me, that it was my fault if she burned the roast, but then I realized she meant my mother. Or possibly her husband. She might've even been joking. But she had to be fuming, in any event, at the sight of her husband's sexual girlfriend making googoo eyes at her criminal spouse. I imagined her jabbing the roast with the fork. Jab jab jab.

Rabbi Landy said, "Thank goodness at least it's cool inside. And so nice to have the four of you here, all at once, to welcome me back." He stood from his chair and walked in my direction and put a hand on my head, half rabbi, half dad. His cigarette smoke went straight for my eyes.

My mother lounged on the sofa, meanwhile, gazing up at her living god. Nothing else mattered but her idol back from Israel, standing there before her. She said, "So what were you saying?"

I heard a song I wasn't crazy about—"I'm Your Puppet" by the Purifies—floating down from the second floor where the rabbi's sons must've been catching up on American radio.

Naomi cleared her throat. "He, uh." She was gazing up at the rabbi too. "He was talking about his trip."

Toby said, "To Isrul."

My mother said, "I'd love to go to the holy land. Just once before I die."

Rabbi Landy said, "Yes. Well. We've still got a bit of unpacking to do. As you can see. We're not back an hour."

My mother ignored the hint, she just kept talking, about her dream to dance in Israel, her love of nightclubs, her jitterbugs with senior boys at Atlantic City High School, and her horas at weddings and cha-chas in the Catskills before my father flew the coop.

Naomi said, "Please. Those are old-lady dances. I can do the Watusi, Rabbi. And the shing-a-ling." She shimmied around with her dodo-bird shoulders like a frantic ignoramus, without even leaving her seat. She's as bad as my mother, I thought, trying to jiggle her dinky breasts at the rabbi.

My mother said, "Those aren't dances. Those are allergic reactions."

Meantime, the smell of Mrs. Landy's roast came seeping through the cracks and jumped up the noses of her low-class intruders, turning the house into *her*, even more than if she'd stayed out here and shot lasers at us.

Rabbi Landy just smiled.

A short time later the storm door banged and my mother, brother, sister and I went tottering down the front wood steps. My mother looked like she'd been fixed somehow. And Naomi and Toby were grinning like nitwits.

I got into the car first, the seat behind my mother. The driver's door opened and my mother's bag flew in. Naomi and Toby walked to the other side and got in as well. My mother sat down and slammed the door shut and turned around and hit me hard, right in the face. Wham!

"How dare you not come in with us and humiliate me like that!"

My face was burning and messed with tears, but I looked right back, straight into her pupils, and in a threatening voice I'd learned from my sister said, "You do that again and I'll break your arm."

◆ ◆ ◆

A boy can take all kinds of shocks: a crack in the face, a nosy rabbi, a worthless father, a friend's green teeth, a shameless mother like a temptress out of the Torah, with her confessions typed out in an unprotected looseleaf.

And even as he takes what he takes, week after week, shock after shock, after observing from the pews and overhearing phone calls and stumbling on a transcript, things start to change.

His mother stops talking to him. Georgie Garr stops calling him. Shoulders turn away from him in the lobby at the temple. A grumpier gruffness gruffs out of Mr. Rothstein, the Backseat Rabbi. And nothing at all, not even a glance, is glanced his way from Mrs. Tower or Phyllis or her husband Ef or the rabbi's sons or his wicked wife Tehila. They pretend he doesn't exist. Because he reminds them of her.

◆ ◆ ◆

Then my mother was drinking coffee and I was eating a Pop-Tart when she blurted it out: "We want you to go to yeshiva."

I swallowed funny. "Who's we?"

I knew.

Her and Rabbi.

"Miss Dewess and I," my mother lied, "who else?" The room smelled of cigarette smoke and sour milk and her meshy nightgown. "To help solve the problem of, you know, your deportment."

"You're lying," I said.

She made like I hadn't said anything. "We think it's a good idea."

"Well I don't."

"Oh come on. You're just saying that."

"Miss Dewess would never say to go to yeshiva."

"Just take some time to think it through."

"It's an hour away and I don't know anyone. I refuse."

"You know Avi and Yussie."

"I despise those jerks."

"Look. It just makes sense. You'll have more of a challenge than you've had at Van Buren. We thought about skipping you but that would only complicate things in terms of your maturity. So how about you finish up this year at Van Buren and start at the yeshiva in September?"

I'd never seen the school but I knew about it. It was down in Hudson County, in a tough Cuban neighborhood not far from the Lincoln Tunnel. I imagined there were gangs in the street with switchblades in their socks like in *West Side Story*. I said, "Everybody says it's like a mental institution."

"I'm sure it's a lovely modern place."

"How can you say that? You've never even been there. And how on earth could you afford the tuition anyway?"

"Rabbi Rick says you're eligible for a hundred-percent scholarship."

Rabbi Rick. I knew it. Just another sneaky way for her to feel closer to her boyfriend.

"I won't go. Never."

"I don't think you know what you're saying, honey."

I bulldozered out of the dining room.

◆ ◆ ◆

She brought it up again a few days later but I didn't want to hear it.

"You don't just walk away like that..." She followed me out of the room. "...in the middle of my talking to you."

"You can't force me to do something I don't want to do."

"I'm not forcing."

"Then why are you bringing it up again?"

"I'm being subliminal."

"Get out of my room."

Toby was in there. "Too much yelling," he said. "I do not enjoy the yelling."

My mother told him that no one was yelling and ordered me to do the damn dishes.

"No."

"Do them or I'll call Mr. Garr and he'll come upstairs and *make* you do them."

Toby said, "Do them, Andy. If he comes up here, he'll beat me too."

So I did the dishes but I didn't use soap and I made sure the water was icicle cold.

17

I didn't talk much to my mother that summer but I did agree to yeshiva in July ("Okay, all right, I'll go") because even though I resented giving in to her (especially when she was using me as the dog piece in her Monopoly love game), I liked the yeshiva before I even saw it. I mean, they took you in a school bus, you ate in a cafeteria, you had all new classmates, you really learned Hebrew and your time away from home was longer than normal. Not to mention half the teachers were men. It sounded like an adventure I'd be a doofus to say no to.

But the summer sucked. Nothing happened. Thornton never called me. I never called Thornton. (Because if Thornton wasn't calling me, there had to be a reason and I knew the reason would hurt me.) Georgie Garr tried calling on his single-purpose hookup but I was too upset about Thornton to answer. I was longing for Thornton. It hurt me to remember him. Our friendship had slipped away somehow.

Meanwhile, the rabbi and his family were away all summer at a Jewish camp on Seneca Lake where he was director and his wife was head counselor so my mother suffered her own kind of longing.

Toby played outside all day with the hollering neighbors.

My sister and I sat in front of the air conditioner (we had just the one) and watched game shows like *The Dating Game* and reruns like *The Beverly Hillbillies* which she and I just loved.

I thought I should tell my sister about the shocks in the looseleaf and the riddles it solved but I didn't after all because it was just too embarrassing. And besides, I wanted to keep some secrets of my own after her secrets about our father. But wow. So much scandal down on paper, indisputable proof that my mother was filthy and the rabbi even filthier.

I went to the dentist, Dr. Hy Rosenzweig. He found three cavities. As he drilled in my mouth, I listed my favorite sweets in my head to counteract the pain, counting on my fingers: Jujyfruits, jelly beans, jelly rings, Swedish fish, candy corn, cotton candy, circus peanuts, cherry chocolates, chocolate frosting, nonpareils, Nestlé's Crunch, Milk Duds, Sugar Babies, sugar cookies, Pixy Stix, Peeps, Lick-m-aid, lemon ice, frozen custard, dipped cones, Ring Dings, Fudge Stripe cookies, Kisses, Dots. I got to twenty-four.

◆ ◆ ◆

Toward the end of the summer my mother said, "You need a haircut before you start yeshiva. How about a nice one?"

"No thanks."

"I talked to Tehila."

"Why do you call her that?"

"They just got back from summer camp."

"Why don't you call her Mrs. Landy for heaven's sake? Why are you even mentioning her?"

"I don't—I just—can't I finish a fucking thought?"

"Who's stopping you?"

"I can't wait until they throw you into that yeshiva dungeon already. I'm sick and tired of your lip."

"I can't wait either."

She took an extensive breath. She refused to let me get to her beyond where I'd already gotten her. "Seems Tehila has a barber come to the house every month to cut Rabbi's hair along with the boys' and she offered to let you use her."

"Mrs. Landy just offered?"

"Though you clearly don't deserve it."

"Just like that?"

"She knows you're starting yeshiva next week."

"And what do you mean by use *her*? The barber's a lady?"

"The barber's a lady."

Figures the rabbi would have a lady cut his hair. They probably have intercourse in his office at the temple—right around the block—after she cuts the whole family. I scoffed. "No thanks."

"She'll do it for free."

"Who told you that?"

"Tehila."

"Stop calling her that."

"She'll cut your hair like Illya Kuryakin."

"Really?"

I went.

There was no one cooler on TV than Illya.

My mother dropped me off without coming in. I was ready to tell her, "Don't come in, I'm warning you," so I was disappointed when I didn't get the chance.

The older son Avi (his hair was freshly cut—though he still resembled a werewolf) answered the door without a hello and led me back through the spotless house. (At least I wasn't expected to talk to him.) He led me past the modern sofas and Red Sea and Dead Sea travel posters and the swirling silver mezuzahs and menorahs.

I could smell something frying.

In the kitchen, the younger son Yussie was under a barber's tent getting his neckline perfected with a bumblebee of a buzzer so I guessed I was next. The perfector was the haircutter (all in black) and she had an Illya Kuryakin haircut herself. It looked like she had no bra on underneath.

Mrs. Landy said, "Tonya." It rhymed with phone ya. "This is Andrew Baer."

Again no hellos from the stuck-up Landy brothers.

And no sign of Rabbi. His absence didn't surprise me. He was probably with my mother in his cramped temple office right around the corner, right this minute, patting her vagina.

Tonya however was nice. She had cheerful cheeks and shadows of beautician exhaustion pouching under her eyes. She smiled and said, "Pleased to meet you, Andy. I'm just about ready for you."

"Thank you," I said.

Mrs. Landy gave her a look like she resented this hospitality. Mrs. Landy was wearing an apron and a sleeveless top and her hair was up and perfect as usual, like a *Rush Hashunnah* challah. She leaned against a cabinet and watched the application of her younger son's talcum with zero expression on her lips. Her lips were clamped tight. As onions and burger meat sizzled in a skillet behind her.

Tonya took the tent off Yussie, and he waggled his head to get any hair off. Then Tonya swept the floor while Yussie and his brother grabbed some macaroons out of a cookie jar shaped like a dreidel and split—no thank-yous to Tonya, no ta-tas to Mom, just some arrogant Hebrew back and forth, which was meant to leave me out, I'm sure (and Tonya too).

She patted the stool and I sat.

"An Illya Kuryakin cut," she said. "Brave man."

I loved that she called me brave and a man, but it didn't prevent my kneecaps from ricketing. I perched on the stool. She flourished the cape and snapped it around my neck.

"He's my favorite on *The Man from U.N.C.L.E.*," she said.

"Mine too," I said.

Mrs. Landy kept watching, out of her high beams of annoyance. I was privy to the secrets of her rat-fink husband. I was the offspring of the woman who was wrecking her marriage. I was a literal son of a bitch, I thought.

Did she know that I knew?

Snip, snip.

Perhaps she knew nothing.

Snip, snip, snip.

I was sure I stood out, whatever she knew, because I couldn't have possibly felt more awkward—half anteater, half ant—about to be zapped by Tehila Landy's seven-foot tongue.

"So you're going to yeshiva," she said without any pleasantness as Tonya kept snipping.

"Next Tuesday," I said.

Mrs. Landy snapped, "I know when it starts!" and returned to the stove. "It'll be horrid for you. Just the Hebrew alone. You'll be extremely far behind." I hadn't thought about that. I remembered she was a Hebrew teacher. I panicked.

Mrs. Landy stirred the skillet and sprinkled in salt and banged in the cabinets and turned back around to continue watching the haircut.

"Here comes the hard part," Tonya said, her breasts up against me. "I have to apply my razor knife. I'm afraid this is going to hurt."

Like a rusted machete! It hurt so bad my eyes started tearing.

"Youch," I said.

And in a low hard voice, with the sizzle of onions and meat behind her, Mrs. Landy said, "Youch is not enough." She was disgusted with me. "Scream if it hurts." Disgusted and impatient. "If it hurts—for God's sake—scream."

18

"Ma? Hey Ma. It's 6:15. Time to get up."

"Fi more mits."

Normally I'd do as she asked and return in five minutes but today I said, "No! Get up! This is my first day of school, at a school you forced me to go to, and I refuse to let you lie there like her royal highness and make me late."

Long pause.

Then a sound like she was laughing. "You're funny, you know that. You really are, Andy." She laughed a little more, and though it sounded insincere, it was real enough to turn into a coughing fit. "Ahook, ahack, aheck, aheck, ahok! Ahok! Ahok!!" She coughed and coughed, like her brains'd pop out.

Finally, in a wheezy voice, she said, "First day. Course, honey. Go in the other room. I'm awake. Just a sec."

In less than a minute she was tramping into the dining room with a look like an earthquake had thrown her out of bed—eyes sprung open and hair shocked up. She sat at the table and felt around with her feet. She'd left her heels underneath last night. She slid them on. Then she hurried out of the room, threw on a raincoat over her nightgown and led me downstairs and out into the street.

She smoked in The Bomb and talked about how clever I was and how super the yeshiva would be and yawned and coughed and said something dumb about how I may've gotten my legs from my father but my brains I got from her.

I said, "I got my brains from me. Just drive."

We were on our way to the rabbi's house because our apartment was "simply too far off the route"—or so she claimed—meaning I'd catch the school bus every morning from the rabbi's curb with the rabbi's sons. (Ichh.) I imagined the driver throwing a tantrum earlier when he was asked to take the detour through our shoddier streets just to pick up the one Montevideo student enrolled in the yeshiva. "I won't. I refuse."

But when I thought about it later, I guessed that my mother had schemed it more sneakily. It was too completely perfect for her. Every morning. Five days a week. A visit with the rabbi. *Ooh la la.* "Don't go out of your way, Mr. Driver. I'll gladly take him to the Landys' every morning—hardship that it is." I imagined her rolling slowly up Salem Street, eyes on the rabbi as he picked up the *Times* from his front-yard grass, parking at the curb, bounding out of The Bomb, cigarette burning, with a nauseating "good morning, Rick," in her raincoat over a nightgown with a psychological hope in her heart that the wind'd blow the raincoat open and the nightgown up. ("Your delight in being looked at, in showing your body.")

The rabbi's sons were on the sidewalk when we got there, with accordion briefcases, like commuters to Manhattan—no rabbi in sight.

A yellow school bus turned the corner.

It felt like a shish was kebobbing my stomach.

As I stepped out of the car, my mother said, "Have fun, darling."

She lingered behind the wheel that day (no reason to scramble out because, as I said, there wasn't a rabbi in sight). She just drove away slowly, staring at the windows of the rabbi's house, her head way up in the windshield, her breasts squashed flat against the steering wheel, her eyes passing over his windows like searchlights.

Nude Taking a Shower
1969

19

I cooked up a plan. I'd write him a letter. I'd write it on the bus, using paper torn from my spiral notebook. I figured if I wrote it all in caps over the bumps on Kennedy Boulevard he wouldn't know it was me. And no "dear anyone." No barriers between my feelings for him and my uninhibited expression of them.

> I KNOW YOU DON'T KNOW WHO THIS IS BUT I HAVE TO LET YOU KNOW THAT I THINK YOU'RE A PEERLESS TEACHER. I'M EXHILARATED TO BE IN YOUR CLASS BECAUSE YOU REALLY ARE A STIMULATING PERSON. MY PARENTS SPLIT FOUR YEARS AGO. MY MOTHER'S NO HELP. SHE MAKES THINGS WORSE. IT'S NOT THAT I'M LONELY OR UNHAPPY ~~OR~~. JUST TO LET YOU KNOW WHAT AN INCOMPARABLE PERSON I THINK YOU ARE AND HOW EXCITING YOUR METHOD OF TEACHING IS.

I didn't read it over. I just folded it in quarters and slid it into my bookbag. I knew exactly when to deliver it.

◆ ◆ ◆

Three mornings earlier, a hot September Tuesday, he'd introduced himself to us freshmen boys. (The girls had separate religious classes.)

"My name is Rabbi Aaron Loobling, I'm thirty-two years old, born in Garden City, Long Island, and I'll be schooling you in the consciousness-bending intricacies of the Talmud every Monday through Friday, except holidays both sacred and secular, from 8:45 to 11:15 ante meridiem, until the temperatures register as sultry again."

No teacher had ever spoken to us so fancily before or told us his age or announced his first name.

"But how in fact can a dusty old Talmud bend a young man's consciousness?" His eyebrows snaked around like the curlicues on the tops of the Hebrew letters. He had thick black glasses and a red plaid jacket and his shoulders were almost as wide as the door. He was the only beardless rabbi in the yeshiva, as handsome as one of the Lacosta boys in the Italian part of Montevideo, with a powerful build and a scary stare, his yarmulke pushed forward on his big square head like a fedora on a flamenco dancer.

"An irrelevant storybook," he continued, "spinning tales of liability law in the eighth and ninth centuries, with its intrigues of divorce and baking and the do's and don'ts of festival days and the consequences of human error and divine coincidence, testing law and logic and ordinary horse sense, with a fair amount of wiggle room. Why should we care?" He looked at every kid in the class. His pause made me think of those exaggerated pauses in a Rabbi Landy sermon. But this guy wasn't slick. "It's the discipline itself," he said. "The argument per se, the burrowing deeper, the scrupulous analysis, the collaborative pursuit of the single thread in accordance with your school of thought, and the equal pursuit of the logic of the other school of thought. It's the willingness to ask the question that no one dares to ask. And then to ask the next question. To never give up on the hunt for the truth while considering every possible means for arriving at that truth."

He picked up a leatherette book from his desk—humongous as an atlas, the kind that goes in a slot behind a row of encyclopedias (we all of us boys had the same maroon slab in front of us on our desks)—and he slapped its mighty binding.

"Third order *Nashim*, seventh tractate *Kidushin*, Mishnah number two," he said. Then he opened to the page and quoted from the text:

> "'A Hebrew slave is acquired by money and by contract and regains his freedom after six years of service or in the jubilee year or by deduction from the purchase price.'"

I already knew about the Talmud. It's made up of scores of these books, full of thousands of similar sentences, and was written by rabbis, not by God. As my teacher explained, the Talmud is laws—and arguments about the application of those laws—under every possible circumstance, perfect for sharpening youthful noggins. A more adult form of study than the Torah, I thought, with its tales of Samson's magical hairdo and Sarah's nonagenarian pregnancy and Jonah's vacation in a fish. There wasn't any magic in the Talmud.

Rabbi Loobling cleared his throat and it rumbled like a hotrod. (Everything he did made noise.) He read the snippet again, the whole thing over, but he accented different words this time. He wanted us to listen:

> "'A Hebrew slave is acquired by money
> *and*
> by contract
> *and*
> regains his freedom after six years of service
> *or*
> in the jubilee year
> *or*
> by deduction from the purchase price.'

"Typical Talmudic pronouncement," he said, booming like a Broadway actor. "So condensed, Carnation could've canned it. But what was the going rate for a slave in the Persian Empire? What about slaves who refused to leave their masters? Or slaves who were women? Women could be slaves, you know. And how about sex between a slave and a master?" Someone snickered behind me, but Rabbi Loobling glowered so arrogantly that the snickerer started sneezing. (Irwin Werblowsky.) "The answers to these questions—and there are more of them, you'll see—will concern us till roughly Chanu KAH [he pronounced it like an Israeli, with the accent on the KAH], the first and longest leg of our sedentary journey. We will ponder nothing but the fate of a slave for the next two months." He clapped his happy hands together, as noisy as a cherry bomb exploding in an underpass.

I was totally afraid of him. He was totally too tall and strong and overconfident.

"And what about this?" he said. "A slave steals a hundred shekels, *BUT* in fact he's worth only fifty shekels, *AND* when the time comes to sell him, you must sell him once...*and then sell him again!*" His eyes swept a double-dare-you beam around the room, as if all of us were suspects in the theft of the hundred shekels.

I had no idea what he was talking about. I was lost and excited and excited that I was lost. Because there was definitely something fun about him. Something devilish in the eyebrows, in the too many muscles doing pushups along his forehead, and his over-expressive rabbi face, like he could force you to appreciate the Talmud in a stare-down.

"Imagine the emotional consequences of being a thief and a slave, sold in the *form of your own human body*, not once but *twice* in a filthy cacophonous Babylonian slave market. For the price of a two-pant suit!"

I really didn't get it. It was just too hard to follow.

"This isn't a light read, gentlemen," he said. (At least he admitted it.) "This isn't the Bobbsey Twins in Babylonia. The point is to. Well. What is the point? Somebody?" The screw of his face was so tight, he looked hurt.

I glanced around the room at my classmates back from summer. Giant-size Jerry. Allergic Irwin. Lenny of the key chains. Horowitz the limper. No one looked remotely interested in taking up the question.

I raised my hand.

"Ar-yay?" My Hebrew name. How did he know it already?

"To keep asking questions. Isn't that the uh point?"

"Questions. Ah. What sorts of questions?"

"Well." I had to think fast. I wanted to please him. "What about the benefits of a slave's enslavement?"

"Benefits?" The rabbi turned his lip corners down. "Like what?"

"Like job security. And, and room and board."

He smacked his desk—bam! "We'll get to those. Hold on!"

Irwin Werblowsky would call me a *tukhis licker* later but I didn't care. It was my first few minutes of high school (after three long years in yeshiva elementary, after fourteen years alone in the desert) and I was alone no longer.

◆ ◆ ◆

I came early to school a few days later to watch Rabbi Loobling's sky-blue car take a turn into the parking lot at the back of the yeshiva. It was a foreign car, an *Italian* car, with a tough little face and a body like a toaster. I imagined the cool of the seats inside and the scrape of his stubble. I imagined the Fiat squealing to a stop and him, out of nowhere, yanking me into the front, spiriting me away, in a muscle-bound kidnapping.

I waited in a shadow.

He parked, but he didn't see me.

I hadn't delivered the letter yet. I was planning to do it that morning. I promised myself I would. I didn't imagine what would happen after that, but I knew I had to do it.

◆ ◆ ◆

Later, after an hour of Rabbi Loobling on the subject of a Hebrew slave ("in this morning's lesson," he told us, "our manservant claims he's got to be released from the drudge of his servitude because of the disgrace to his family"), he announced it was time for break.

My trigger word.

Break.

Most of my classmates either shuffled to their lockers or raced to the gym where the school nurse put out chocolate donuts on a folding table or hightailed it out to the parking lot for a quick game of handball against the cinderblock of the building. Rabbi Loobling spent his break in the teachers' lounge next to the principal's office, talking to other teachers and marking his attendance. Two boys stayed back in the classroom with me. Irwin Werblowsky had his head on his desk, and Herman Ziggleman was doing the Jumble in the *Daily News*. (Herman's hair was cut in Moe Howard bangs—Moe of the Three Stooges—and he swung his hips like a girl when he walked.) I was fingering the note in the pocket of my shirt (watermelon red with a tie the same color—you bought them together). I'd rehearsed it in my head. I'd stroll to the front, cool as a pickpocket, draw a gallows on the board like I was starting a game of hangman (solitaire hangman??), reconsider—cough—and slide the note in Loobling's open-top briefcase.

Later, at home, under a reading lamp, about to grade papers, he'd discover my gift. And how joyous he would be!

So I sauntered up front, drew a gallows on the board, coughed in my fist and...fumbled the note!...so that it fell on the teacher's open Talmud. And since I'd better not draw attention to myself by fixing the mistake, I rushed to sit down again, flustered and trembling but proud of my daring. He was going to read my letter. He didn't have a choice.

I could feel the thud of blood in my temples, like handballs whacking on cinderblock.

The boys were returning from break. Rabbi Loobling wasn't back yet.

Jerry Leshinsky plunked down in the desk beside me and his closeness felt terrific. He was the tallest, friendliest, best-looking boy in class, although he always made me conscious of the sorrow of his father, who had a blurry concentration camp number branded on his arm.

Jerry liked to grab you by the back of the neck and shake you. "Andy old boy." Which was what he did now. "How's freshman life treating you?"

"Just great," I said. "Summer was boring."

"You missed the gang."

I smiled like it was true, although I'd never been part of the gang he referred to (Horowitz, Irwin, Lenny, himself).

I glanced up front toward the teacher's Talmud, open on his desk, with my letter tented on top of it. It looked like it had a spotlight on it.

Jerry leered. "How's Myra?"

"How?"

"How was your reunion?"

"Ah. I guess it was okay."

"What do you mean *okay*? I want details, morning glory."

Myra Schwartzberg and I had talked on the phone only once that summer, even though we'd been one of June's notorious kissing couples (including Jerry Leshinksy and bosomy Andrée Koplowitz) during a bunch of eighth-grade graduation parties in darkened finished basements from Woodbridge to Bridgewood. My reunion with Myra had been dead on arrival.

I said, "Not much to tell you. I saw her though, yeah."

Jerry sounded titillated. "What did she say?"

"Oh you know. I don't know."

"You mean she said it with her strawberry lip gloss?"

"Yeah."

Jerry leered. "She's ready, And." He liked to call me And.

"For what?"

He grinned. "Little Jack Horner. Stuck in his thumb. Pulled out a plum."

My face hurt from smiling. "Oh I don't know, Jerry."

All the students were back from break now.

Everyone was murmuring.

Then ta-da! Curtain up. The door swung open and Rabbi Loobling strode in.

Act two, scene one.

He swerved around the desks and made a hammy crash-landing in his chair up front. He tilted his thick black glasses forward, dementedly askew, and slouched way down, his oversize shoes poking out from under the front of his desk.

Then he saw the letter, folded in quarters, like one of those fortune-teller things you poke your fingertips into to predict a friend's future.

He tilted his head like a myna bird and opened the letter.

I was trembling.

I thought, *I've wrecked my life*.

The murmur picked up again (rumba, samba, ha, ha, ha), as Jerry was saying, "Eating his Christmas pie—no, his Chanukah latke," and I smiled lamely, like Little Jack Horner, while noticing everything else in the room—that the teacher was reading with his lips pushed out—that the murmur of the students included Horowitz howling and Irwin boasting and had nothing to do with suspicion about the letter our teacher was reading or any impatience to get the Talmud lesson going—that none of my classmates gave a hoot about the letter—that the room went hot and I went cold—that the teacher got intensely intent as he read to the end of the unsigned letter.

Under the cover of the murmur, he looked at me (I was looking at him) and he said in a normal voice, that no one but I paid attention to, "Did you write this?"

"Yes."

He began part two of the lesson.

◆ ◆ ◆

There weren't any trees or beaches near the school but I heard tree leaves tossing and the ocean slapping all through the rest of the lesson.

As the class wound down ("A slave belongs bodily to his master," the teacher taught us), I only felt worse, as if Rabbi Loobling had banished me to a reject planet where all it did was sleet and thunder.

First there'd been the jolt of his knowing right away who'd written the letter. Then the complete humiliation of his saying nothing else about it, staying on schedule, proceeding with the lesson. Then he hadn't even accidentally glanced at me the rest of the hour.

It was all so excruciating.

Who cares, I thought.

But it wormed around inside me. The complete excruciation.

Meanwhile, echoes and fragments swirled in the classroom, in the form of his voice, on the breath of his manliness: "...how far does that kind of promise go?..." "...he is nothing more than real estate..." "...which means bastard by the way..." "...because a heathen slave is the property of his master..." "...do you gentlemen know what a heathen is?..." "...as a result of his romance with a gentile slave..."

I didn't hear the bell ring.

Everyone was leaving.

Then most of us were gone. The room seemed to slant and decant the stragglers. I got my stuff together and joined the shuffle out toward the hallway. Someone was excited about the outlines of Dorothy Janoff's nipples ("she's got on *thee* tightest sweater") and someone said something about a New York Met sitting naked on a birthday cake—a story that would normally get me to pump the kid for details—but I could barely hide my grief.

Jerry asked me to save him a seat in Rabbi Minkowitz's class which was coming up next and ran to say hello to Andrée Koplowitz at her locker.

I said, "Sure thing, Jerry," depressed that I no longer had Myra Schwartzberg to meet in front of *her* locker.

Then a fifty-pound slam came down on my shoulder and I jumped with fright.

Couldn't be Jerry. Jerry was gone. "Hey!" I said and turned around.

Rabbi Loobling was glaring down at me.

The sky could've sent down a lightning bolt, the moment was that dramatic. His hot eyes and crazy hair made it look as if a blood balloon had burst in his head and might splatter all over me. He yanked me out of the classroom by the arm and into the hallway.

"You're hurting me," I said. But I wouldn't have cared if he ripped my arm off and everyone witnessed or nobody noticed. Rabbi Loobling had slammed his hand on my shoulder and the floodlights fired (clunk!) (woosh!) and the test cars crashed and all the ancient and modern bridges collapsed across the rivers of the Middle East and Asia Minor.

He was pulling me up stairs I didn't know about, tugging me along like he'd captured a runaway Hebrew slave and was about to slap the shackles on. But I didn't feel hurt. I didn't feel anything but the thrill of his attention and his physical ka-blam.

Before I could picture it, we were out on the roof, all summery sun and blazing gravel, a rooftop studded with colossal metallic ventilation mushrooms like pinball bumpers. My pinball heart was plungered into position.

"What do you want from me?" Rabbi Loobling asked.

We were face-to-face. He was still holding onto me. He wasn't much taller than me but his face seemed high in the sky like an angel's, one of those angels you have to wrestle.

Grim-faced.

Lunatic.

Sensational slab of a he-man curiosity.

He let my arm go. "Sounds like you want a lot from me," he said.

I rubbed my bicep. I thought he might've pulled something. I was proud of myself. I think I already had what I wanted.

He didn't wait for an answer. "And this stuff about your mother only making things worse. How could I possibly help you with that?"

"I didn't say you could."

"I'm sorry she's disturbed but it's not my problem."

I didn't respond.

"You know," Rabbi Loobling said, as a look of gloom came storming down into him, "this isn't the first time I received a letter like this."

I had a hard time keeping the sentence together. I rubbed again where he'd grabbed my arm.

Other.

Admirers.

How many?

A hundred?

I wanted to be the only one.

My worship felt worthless.

The moment was ruined.

I wished I'd never met him.

I'd heard he was a teacher once at Birnbaum Yeshiva, the same yeshiva Rabbi Landy's wife Tehila taught at. (Tehila the horrible.) Herman Ziggleman had mentioned it the first day after summer vacation. (Herman of the Moe Howard bangs and feminine hipsway.) Herman had been at Birnbaum, he'd said, for all of elementary. (Our high school corralled from yeshivas like Birnbaum plus a nearby lousy public school.) How many batty Birnbaum boys had written anonymous notes to Loobling? How many batty Birnbaum girls? Did they line up at his desk? Did he have them take numbers?

"So what do you want?" the rabbi repeated. "What should I do?"

Wrestle me, I thought.

"Do you want me to be your friend?" he said.

I waited to hear more options. I loved how he stood there staring at me. I loved how he let me stare right back. We didn't look alike, except for our glasses and extra-long legs, but those two things meant a lot to me.

He tilted his head. He squinted in the sun.

I tilted my head. I squinted in the sun.

"Well?" the rabbi said.

There were no more options. Either he became my friend or he ignored me completely, like he'd ignored me in class after reading my letter.

"Yes," I said, still struggling to keep the sentences together.

"Yes what?"

"Yes, Rabbi."

He shook his head disapprovingly. "Do you know what this means?"

"No. Not entirely. What is your intention?" I knew I sounded stilted but I couldn't control how I sounded.

"It'll take a lot out of you. To be my friend. Half of it will come from me—I'm fair that way—but that's a mighty portion for you, Andrew Baer. I expect quite a bit from my friends." He clasped his hands together.

"Of course." I clasped mine too. I noticed his wedding ring. I'd never noticed anybody's wedding ring before. It dented his hairy finger. It glittered self-importantly.

"You look worried," he said.

"I'm scared, that's all."

"Don't worry."

"I won't. I'm scared, not worried."

Rabbi Loobling shook his head again. I remembered my father's negative headshakes when I was nine or ten and he caught me reading my sister's copy of *Nancy Drew and the Haunted Showboat*, basking in front of the air conditioner. His headshakes communicated better than anything how much I'd let him down.

But the headshakes on the roof felt different. They made Rabbi Loobling seem tolerant and nice, although the look on his face was anything but.

"I can't promise anything," he said.

"I know."

"You know?"

"I could tell that about you."

"What else could you tell?"

"That you're prone to melancholia."

Rabbi Loobling smiled in spite of himself, inaugural crack in the wall of his hardness.

"And you know what *I* know?" the teacher said.

"No."

The rabbi grimaced. "That you're a delightfully brilliant sad young person."

He swatted me on the side of my head, catching my ear and temple.

Which was the second crack in the hardness.

◆ ◆ ◆

Wide awake that night, at one in the morning, way past my bedtime, while my brother was snoring, I decided that if Rabbi Loobling had received any other letters like mine, from a lonely loser or a long-haired rebel or the spoiled son of another rabbi, no way could he compete with my sad delightful brilliance.

I decided I wouldn't tell anyone. Particularly not my mother. I didn't want her turning what I told her about myself into something she was an expert in. Like when I told her how much I enjoyed learning French and she sang the *Marseillaise* and went on and on about the Frenchies she had crushes on like Charles Boyer and Yves Montand.

My legs, my feet, my eyesight, my appetite, they all belonged to me, and I didn't want her messing up the realities of my life. I could picture her falling instantly in love with Rabbi Loobling at some PTA meeting and saying something crass to me later like "Wow, what a man!" as if she were Betty Grable and Loobling were Victor Mature. I didn't want her batting her eyes and talking his ear off and claiming him as her latest accomplishment. (That wouldn't happen in any case because the school was in a different county and they never had parent-teacher nights anyway, but why take the risk?) I'd never tell her a thing about him. Never ever.

I figured, though, awake in bed, that she wouldn't like him anyhow. He wasn't nearly splashy enough. He wasn't a smooth-talking lectern-grabbing fire-spitting sermon giver like her precious Rabbi You-know-who. He was scholarly and honest, principled and true. He could never stand up at the front of a fancy synagogue and cry hot tears in a flowing white robe at the climax of *Yum Kipper*. He wasn't that kind of rabbi.

Rabbi Loobling looked right at you. He told you what was what.

Morning prayers at the yeshiva, I watched as he put on tefillin. First he rolled up his sleeve, a cuff at a time, revealing his arm which was covered in hair. He shook out a strap, long as a whip, attached to a box, and strapped it around his bicep. Then he wound the whip seven times around his arm, murmuring a prayer, rocking as he murmured. Next he squeezed another strap, attached to another box, around his hatline like a headband. I'd wound my tefillin around my own head and arm, but on the rabbi they seemed more effective. I imagined Rabbi Loobling unwrapping his tefillin and rewrapping me in his. Show me how to do it. I was never sure I was doing it right.

Then I noticed the principal, Rabbi Nass, staring at Rabbi Loobling. Rabbi Nass was among us in the davening room and focused on my teacher with his eyes like incisions from a spot near the door. He was Canadian and fat and secretly rolled up his beard with a rubber band that you could see from a certain angle. He was new to me and already pretty friendly when he passed me in the hall ("Good morning, Herr Baer") but at morning prayers his eyes were shifty. You could tell by the way he stroked his beard that there was something about my idolized teacher he didn't approve of.

Rabbi Loobling didn't notice or pretended not to notice. He just closed his eyes and rocked and prayed, bound up in his tefillin.

20

I tuned out the school and the students.

I focused down hallways, looking for Rabbi Loobling, for his off-kilter yarmulke, slipping glasses, tortured eyebrows, giant strides. In biology class I stared at the door, wishing he'd pass. In the second-floor boys' room I fumbled over my fly, taking my time, hoping he'd appear and wizz alongside me. By my locker, during break, at assembly or in another class, I dawdled and mooned, without comprehending: "Define the value of x." "Every Hebrew verb is regular." "What does the poet mean by 'the fog comes in on little cat feet'?" Was that him teaching? Were those his vowels and consonants bellowing out of a classroom? How long until donuts when I'd pass through the gym and race to the parking lot to see where his car was and notice its direction (left? right?), thinking it might clue me in to the scenes of his life I'd never be part of. There he stood, over Mrs. Paris, the principal's secretary, initialing his timesheet. There he sat in the teacher's lounge biting into a sandwich—chicken, cheese, pastrami, what? Was his wife behind the sandwich? What was she like? Curvy? Homely? Shrimpy? Plump? Would he wink at me today? Would he grab me again? Would he take me in his arms and crush me?

I felt dead to everything else but him. I couldn't sleep. Or I slept ten hours and dreamed we were flying, in underpants and sandals, over the needle of the Chrysler Building. I woke up crying. I lingered under the shower, soaping and resoaping. I put on my favorite pants (with pleats), hoping he would notice, imagining they would please him, endlessly repeating his name in my head (Loobling, *liebling*, Aaron, rabbi) with his face across my fantasies like a purpling sunset, a ghost in the stars, it was depressing and terrific and unsettling and strange.

I was waiting for something to happen.

It was third period, just before lunch, and Rabbi Minkowitz was teaching us the birthright story, in which Jacob puts on goat skin sleeves so his blind father Isaac will feel his arms and think he's his hairy brother Esau and mistakenly give him the birthright. (Which reminded me of Loobling's arms, covered in hair and wrapped in tefillin.) (Goatskin leather?)

Rabbi Minkowitz may've been a favorite with the boys but he couldn't control his class. Everyone was talking, and not in whispers. Someone was blowing bubblegum bubbles, someone was bragging about his father's brand-new Lincoln Continental, someone was playing the radio for God's sake *("There is a blue one! Who can't accept the green one!")* like it was recess and we were out in the schoolyard.

Exclaiming above the commotion, Rabbi Minkowitz asked if someone would go borrow chalk next door. (He asked this while smoking a cigarette, right there in class, using the chalk ledge as an ashtray.) He must've thought that by scribbling a little Hebrew on the board, the class would come to order. "I need a volunteer."

Thing is, Rabbi Loobling's Jewish history class for sophomore and junior girls was right next door so I shot up my hand.

I knew Irwin Werblowsky would taunt me about it later, call me *tukhis licker* again, but how could I say no to the chance to talk to *him* (even four little words, "Do you have chalk?") at a time when I wouldn't normally be talking to him? I'd breeze on in and walk right up, and the classful of girls couldn't help but perceive how I delighted their teacher.

When I entered the classroom, Rabbi Loobling was up near the blackboard, smiling kind of dopily and swinging his arms with a clap in front, a clap in back, as his captive lasses watched. "So the Sadducees asked Jesus," he said, "if he believed that there was sex in heaven. And Rabbi Christ said, 'Whatever! You'll be turned into angels at the time of the resurrection so what does it matter?' And the Sadducees were astounded by his wisdom."

A couple of the girls looked giddy and swoony but most of them seemed antsy.

"Ahem," I said. "Excuse me? Rabbi Loobling?"

His smile got bigger.

"Andrew" Front clap. "Baer." Back clap. "What can I do" Clap. "for you?"

"Rabbi Minkowitz sent me to borrow chalk."

"You don't mean borrow." Clap. "You mean pilfer."

Some of the girls looked amused by their teacher's playfulness. The others ignored him or did not look amused.

The bell rang.

"I am but a messenger," I said.

The girls started to leave.

"But a messenger! *Ha!*" Rabbi Loobling came toward me, arms still swinging, swept out a hand and hit me in the face. (I heard a girl gasp.) "You rude young man!" I busted out laughing. "How dare you interrupt my class!" And before I could respond, the other hand came sweeping around and hit me on the other side.

The rabbi did this a few more times, full of good cheer, whack, smack, whack.

A couple of the girls continued to watch but most of them shuffled out.

I said, "Stop, or I'll have to report you," but he knew I didn't mean it.

I remembered my mother's cracks in the face, particularly the last one, the day Rabbi Landy had come back from Israel. ("How dare you not come in and embarrass me like that!") It had hurt all right, but the nastiness behind it was worse than the facial impact.

Rabbi Loobling's slaps were nothing like that. They were affectionate. They were love slaps. I laughed and laughed.

Then I glanced toward the hall and the principal, Rabbi Nass, was stroking his rolled-up beard and watching.

He stepped into the classroom. "Rabbi Loobling."

Rabbi Loobling acted like nothing was wrong.

"What are you doing?" said Rabbi Nass.

"I am teaching this perspicacious lad a bit of sign language for the deaf."

◆ ◆ ◆

"'If he undresses his slave,' Rabbi Loobling was teaching us, "if he bathes him, rubs him, dresses him again, puts his shoes on him or lifts him, thus he acquires him. If he seizes the slave and he goes to him, he acquires him. If he merely calls to him and he goes to him, he does not acquire him.'"

I raised my hand. "That doesn't make sense."

His eyes went wider. "Why not?"

"Because. Either way, the slave winds up going to him. If he goes to the master, that pretty much means he wants to *be* with the master."

"Well then. Let's investigate!"

◆ ◆ ◆

A week or so later.

"These, gentlemen, are the ovaries."

Rabbi Loobling shaded them in with chalk.

"And these." He squiggled. "These are the fallopian tubes."

The class was breathless.

"It's essential that you know these facts. No one else in this.........institution is going to teach you what I'm teaching you now."

He was right. The cigar-smoking health teacher had lectured us boys about eight hours of sleep and a balanced diet livened by basketball. That was about it. And the biology teacher talked our ears off about how tree cells resemble human cells which was nice to know, but what about sperm cells?

"These are the sperm," Rabbi Loobling said, chalking in the squiggles. They looked like bean sprouts. "And the female reproductive system." Like a split avocado. He sketched in a lady shape—parentheses for the hips—to enclose the female parts.

Irwin Werblowsky said, "Who cares?"

Jerry Leshinsky had his mouth open.

Irwin scoffed again—"Tuh"—in case we missed it the first time.

Rabbi Loobling chucked a nub of chalk in his direction and it skimmed Irwin's yarmulke.

Irwin pretended to hyperventilate, but no one reacted.

The drawings helped. I wasn't completely sure about the ovaries till then. I'd still kind of figured they were lower down on the body, like the balls.

Nobody ratted on Loobling. (Principal Nass would've ruptured a gasket if he'd known about this.) But there was controversy among us boys. Irwin Werblowsky called him Rabbi Lubricant. Horowitz called him a kook and a non-conformist. One of the new boys, Herman Ziggleman—I hardly knew him, he was the one with the dangerous bangs who'd graduated Birnbaum and swung his hips like a girl when he walked—said, "Wouldn't you like to know?" but refused to give details.

◆ ◆ ◆

Later that day, a Friday, after lunch, stuck in American History, windows open on the shimmering parking lot, Mrs. Lefkowitz held a class on the Virginia Colony as I listened for the ignition of Rabbi Loobling's car.

"Sixteen-o-eight was a hectic year in Jamestown."

Nothing. Not a peep.

"They were running out of supplies," Mrs. Lefkowitz said. "Everyone was hungry."

Jewish classes had ended, and I pictured Rabbi Loobling packing his briefcase, waving goodbye to the Spanish teacher, smiling at the janitor, off any minute in his sky-blue Fiat for the rest of Friday, all day Saturday, all day Sunday, into the early part of Monday...hours and hours with his wife. Without me.

"Two-thirds of the colonists would die that winter," Mrs. Lefkowitz was saying, "before the supply ships arrived."

Soon the engine of his Fiat would start out the window. I tried not to breathe because the sound of my breathing might drown out the vroom. I imagined disappearing and slipping into his passenger seat, riding away with him to his castle in Beechwood, and reappearing in his throne room where he'd take off his shoes and socks and pants. I'd heard that he lived in those beautiful Tudor Warwick apartments across from Wetson's, a burger joint where I'd gone as a boy, and this seemed like fate, as if we'd been close to each other across generations.

Eventually I'd hear him drive away, and there in American History, as the classroom hummed with the purr of Mrs. Lefkowitz (one of the school's few decent secular teachers), everything in me would drive away with him.

"It was feared at this point..." Mrs. Lefkowitz said.

One day, I thought, I'd be with him in that car.

"...that the Virginia colony would literally die out."

◆ ◆ ◆

When the same thing happened the following Friday I thought, What's with the moping? Raise your hand. Ask to be excused. "May I be excused?"

Mrs. Lefkowitz nodded.

I hurried to the third-floor boys' room, convinced I'd run into him before he left for the weekend. I'd position myself beside him at a urinal and get a cockeyed smile or a wink for the road. Which would be plenty of compensation for the stretch of time without him.

But he wasn't in the boys' room.

I scurried downstairs toward the first-floor boys' room, knowing I had to slip past Rabbi Nass's office (I hated running into him; I was starting to think he was sinister) and as I hurried past the office, I glimpsed Rabbi Loobling in a discussion with the principal, behind a wall of glass, inside a smaller office and another wall of glass. Neither of them looked happy—not happy in the least. Rabbi Loobling was glaring with tragic exaggeration and Rabbi Nass's face (the half that wasn't bearded) looked triple-bypass red. I wondered if they were fighting about the drawings on the blackboard—so uncalled-for, so un-yeshivalike—because someone had ratted on Loobling after all.

◆ ◆ ◆

Later, I was headed home from school in the back of a public bus, thinking Rabbi Loobling must've followed this route home earlier.

Maybe his sky-blue chariot was stalled up ahead—fan belt snapped, motor smoking, something like that—and he'd been bent over the engine trying to figure it out, totally clueless, at last he gave up, and now he was waiting to catch this bus.

Then a man about Rabbi Loobling's age with an unwashed haircut boarded the bus and walked toward the back, ignoring the empty seats.

He sat right next to me.

Not across.

Next.

We were practically leg to leg.

His pants were snug and, from the glance I got of his potato-gray skin, he needed a shave.

I wriggled toward the window.

He wriggled in closer.

I gripped the bar on the back of the seat in front of us.

The man gripped it too.

He moved his hand closer. Not pretending not to. His thumb grazed my pinkie. My heart flapped around like a pigeon in a crate.

He spread his legs wide and sotto-vocce'ed salaciously, "These long bus rides can sure get you horny," though he'd been on the bus for maybe forty-five seconds. He glanced out the window. He rubbed his fly. I couldn't believe it.

    He
        rubbed
            his
                fly!

No shame. No stopping.

I thought I'd drop dead.

I couldn't answer back.

He looked out the window, upping and downing on the front of his fly.

I jumped to an image of Thornton Vanoosten when we were new to spurting semen and the fun we used to have.

This guy was not fun.

I should've been watching for bus-stop shelters, worried that some passenger might bound up the steps and hurry on back here and catch us together. I forgot about Loobling and his broken-down car and the image of him stranded on the roadside, waiting.

Then an elbow angled into me and the wiseguy pinched the tip of his zipper, about to undo it and let the contents tumble out. I was so excited I thought I'd throw up.

The bus stopped.

A woman got on.

She paid her fare and raced straight back to where the man and I were sitting—just what I should've been worried about.

The man popped abruptly out of his seat and darted out the back before the bus pulled away.

The woman took a seat and cut her eyes at me. She was nervous and dark, with a little head. She wore a wrinkled coat and her shoes were scuffed and though I'd looked at her for only a second-and-a-half she struck me as familiar. Classmate's mom? Checkout at Shop-Rite? Friend of Mrs. Garr's?

Then I remembered. She was one of those women I'd noticed at temple, *Yum Kipper* services, gawking at Rabbi Landy. I thought I even remembered her name, Toni Di Prima, because my mother had said it a couple months back. "New gal at temple, Toni Di Prima." Or was it Deirdre da Palma? "How can she be Jewish with a name like that?" And here she was, on the 26 bus.

I wondered what she'd witnessed between the penis rubber and me. Who did she know that she could gossip about this with? Was she more than just someone my mother sort of knew? I was sure she hadn't seen anything.

21

Then the buses went on strike.

I ran into Rabbi Loobling in the second-floor hall lined with lockers which were slamming.

"Strike," he said. "It's official. Starts tomorrow."

I pretended I hadn't heard. "Really?"

We walked together, although I should've been walking in the other direction, toward *dikduk* (Hebrew grammar).

I could feel the eyes of the students on us.

"What are you going to do?" he said, not looking at me.

"I don't know. Take a bus to New York, I guess, and another back to school. Three hours each way."

Still not looking at me, Rabbi Loobling tilted his glasses forward, in that demented way that made me adore him. He had hundreds of flyaway papers under his arm. "I could take you," he said. "It's along my way. Don't you live near 46?"

"A few blocks over."

"Meet me under the underpass. You know which one. Tomorrow. At seven. No sense in your..." His voice trailed off as he veered toward his classroom.

"Thank you," I said.

He pretended not to hear.

◆ ◆ ◆

"Large cattle are acquired by delivery, small cattle by lifting," Rabbi Loobling read from the Talmud that morning.

◆ ◆ ◆

Next morning I ate in the dark—blue Kix from a blue bowl on a blue kitchen counter—because I didn't want the lights on, which would wake up my family.

My breathing was off. My chest felt tender. I ironed a shirt. I dawdled under the shower. As I toweled myself dry, I made a list in my radiant head: toothpaste, mouthwash, deodorant, underwear, socks, shirt. Countdown to the underpass.

I bumped into my mother as I tiptoed out of the bathroom. She was stumbling half asleep, headed for the can, tramping so heavy you'd think she was a communist weightlifter and not a lady in a nightgown.

"Time is it?" she said.

"Six forty-five."

She grunted into the bathroom.

It felt like I was pulling one over on her. Secret meeting. Secret crush. On secret rabbi. Out-rabbiing the queen of the rabbis.

◆ ◆ ◆

In the shadow of the underpass, before the ramp onto 46, I was confident and tall and let the day gush through me. The sky sparkled over me. The rundown houses, the two- and three-families of the families I never talked to, tilted over the sidewalks, the pavement exploded by out-of-control tree roots, as the smell of somebody's toast and coffee blew through the breeze. I'd run into the milk store and bought a miniature cherry Hostess pie just to bite into all that thrilling sugar. Why should I be nervous? The manhole cover in the middle of Pascack Road seemed to lift a little, a fraction of an inch, a supernatural howdy.

Not nervous, not me. Just alone and waiting like a sailor for his captain with a stream of traffic passing.

A slideshow of Rabbi Loobling clicked in my head, closeups mostly, smiling, pondering, shaving with a cordless razor, tossing back a tomato juice. He was sometimes in a tie and jacket, sometimes in a towel, always deliberating what was best for my welfare. I had looked up "narcissistic" after he used the word to describe one of the ancient Talmud scholars (Reb Elazar ben Shimon—supposedly obese) and I was worried the word might apply to me too, but it still felt good to ponder the meanings of the words my teacher used. No one I'd ever known—not Myra Schwartzberg or Jerry Leshinsky or my own lousy father—had given me so much pleasure just to think about them.

Click.

Click.

The pictures flipped by.

Him.

Him.

Him again.

Him.

Then the sky-blue Fiat appeared up the road, at the end of what I saw, after a hundred false alarms, a chip of the sky broken off at the horizon, and I realized I hadn't been truly awake since I'd gotten up that morning. That I'd never been completely awake since the start of my existence.

The car zoomed up. Rabbi Loobling was driving—brooding, indestructible, mightily manly. He reached across to lift the lock (his hand was the size of a seder plate) and I slid in beside him like he was letting me into his self somehow, his actual body.

Violins were playing, right out of the speaker. I thought radios were limited to top-40 songs or the swing band music my mother was partial to, not violins and cellos.

Rabbi Loobling's hard "Good morning, Andrew" seemed to come right out of the speaker.

In awe, I pulled the door shut. "Good morning, Rabbi Loobling."

"Buckle up," he said.

The car purred out toward the welcoming sky as I fumbled for the seatbelt, grateful for the suggestion. (The Bomb did not have seatbelts.)

There were swooning waves of fog on the Meadowlands and seagulls rising in spirals out of the waves.

Rabbi Loobling said, "We're listening to Bach."

"Oh," I said.

"Hear that? Listen. Two distinct melodies. Two majestic tunes at once." He gracefully waved a hand back and forth. "On this gorgeous October morning."

"Yes."

Neither of us spoke as the music went twirling around like a gymnast. Over and under and up and around.

Just the hum of the engine and the Bach and our silence.

Tick tick tick.

As smokestacks poured music into the poison-proof morning, in time with the harpsichord.

"Brandenburg Concerto Number 3," he said.

"Ah. Nice. How many concertos in total?" I asked.

"Six."

"Aha."

I was burning to talk without effort, the easy back-and-forth that adults are so good at, as smooth as the strings blending upward with the keyboard. Yet ordinary chatter wouldn't do. I wanted our talk to reconfigure our futures, to thrill us and depress us with its meaningful astuteness. I wanted to know his philosophies—the precepts and motivations that got him through a day. I wanted to know what he was feeling exactly—at just that moment—and if he thought of himself as happy.

But my teacher got there first. "Are you a Bach fan?" he asked.

"I might be."

"Explain."

"I might be a Bach fan and not even know it."

"Are you familiar with his work?"

"No."

"Well see what you think."

Ten-foot cattails spread to the west and the world's tallest buildings shot up in the east, in counterpoint to the music. I thought I liked Bach so much I could cry. Then I remembered the questions I was too confused to ask. Like, Where did you go to college? Do you get along with your parents? How often do you think of me?

But a nonsense question came tumbling out of me. "Do you speak another language?"

Rabbi Loobling looked at me.

"Besides Hebrew," I said. "And Yiddish, I'm assuming."

His eyes went back to the Turnpike. "Spanish. And a couple words of German. But I don't speak Yiddish, if that's what you're thinking. Wasn't spoken in my home." He took another look at me. "You feeling all right?"

"Sure. Of course." I looked out my window. I opened it a crack.

"You're wondering what to say to me, aren't you?"

I rolled the window up again. "Oh I don't know." It felt like he could see right through me.

Rabbi Loobling frowned. "Well fret not, *boychik*. Just listen to—here. You'll like this part."

Melody one tumbled down, as melody two tumbled up. Like the seagulls rising and hovering in the cattails. Then a burst of agitation erupted into happiness but it didn't feel bombastic—which doesn't completely explain it. If only I could tell him how I felt about him. And be sure that he would tell me that he felt the same way back. But instead I blurted it out: "Are you happy, Rabbi Loobling?"

The Fiat swerved—I was shocked that I'd shocked him—but then I realized the car was exiting the Turnpike, at the Secaucus toll plaza. A veer, not a swerve.

"Don't ask questions like that unless you're willing to hear the answers." The rabbi rolled his window down.

"I'm willing," I said.

"You most certainly are not." We were cruising into the exact-change lane. "Just listen to the—oh. It's over."

The announcer came on to confirm that it was Bach and to offer us the temperature: 51 at 7:13 under plenty of tri-state sunshine. Then he read an ad for spreadable cheese.

"And if you're compelled to say anything," Rabbi Loobling said, "restrict yourself to simple declarative sentences." He threw a quarter out the window, right in the basket, gassed the engine and rolled up the window.

I sulked and pouted, confident that sulk and pout could communicate to the rabbi how offended I was, as every make of unwashed heap came merging on either side of his car.

"You're too young to act so troubled," he said, yanking on the stickshift.

"I'm not acting."

"And whatever your mother's up to in that imaginary world of hers, making a spectacle of herself, all lovestruck over some peacock rabbi, it shouldn't concern you. Who cares what people think?"

"How do you know all this?"

He looked at me again. "Word gets around."

"Oh geez, this is horrible."

Traffic was coming toward us from miles around, from out of the swamps and up from Newark Airport, brake lights throbbing, everything teetering, every driver a couple feet from the driver in front and the driver behind.

Rabbi Loobling sighed. "Look." He touched my arm quickly and returned it to the wheel as my stiffness went flying out the cracked-open window because he'd *touched my arm*. "You think we have something important in common, being unhappy," he said. "Well maybe we have something even better in common, being happy right now."

◆ ◆ ◆

The lesson a little later made no sense. I couldn't connect the fragments:

"...a Jewish slave works day and night..."

"...two hairs on the body of a nine-year-old boy constitute puberty..."

"...nine years and a day is the minimum age at which a male's intercourse counts as intercourse..."

22

There was no end in sight to the bus strike. I couldn't be happier.

Every morning at seven, Rabbi Loobling picked me up in his jovial car, with its masculine vroom and its grill like a waffle iron.

"How was your weekend?" he asked as he steered us into traffic.

Unbearable, I thought, without you. "Great. Terrific. I saw eight movies. Babysitting money. Broke my old record."

"Eight movies? In a weekend?" he said. "Name them."

I hesitated. "Let's see." I didn't want him to know I'd seen five of them on *Shobbis*. But then this wasn't your average rabbi. "Friday night I saw a double feature around the corner from our apartment. *Bob and Carol and Ted and Alice* and *Easy Rider*." Both rated R. I hoped I sounded sophisticated.

"Two groundbreakers," he said. "What else?"

The radio music was sophisticated too. Stravinsky. I could tell. Rabbi Loobling had been exposing me to every kind of composer.

"Saturday I went to another double feature. At the Elgin. In the city. *The Fox*. You know it? From the book by D. H. Lawrence." (Which I'd read, by the way. Mostly because it was short.) "And *Who's Afraid of Virginia Woolf*? Not exactly *Mary Poppins*."

"Pretty grisly. The both of them. Though *Virginia Woolf*'s rather tender in the end."

I was sure those two would've gotten him to scold me, like a fatherly protector.

But no.

"After that I saw *The Prime of Miss Jean Brodie*. Up near Lincoln Center. The teacher in the movie reminded me of you."

the window, right in the basket, gassed the engine and rolled up the window.

I sulked and pouted, confident that sulk and pout could communicate to the rabbi how offended I was, as every make of unwashed heap came merging on either side of his car.

"You're too young to act so troubled," he said, yanking on the stickshift.

"I'm not acting."

"And whatever your mother's up to in that imaginary world of hers, making a spectacle of herself, all lovestruck over some peacock rabbi, it shouldn't concern you. Who cares what people think?"

"How do you know all this?"

He looked at me again. "Word gets around."

"Oh geez, this is horrible."

Traffic was coming toward us from miles around, from out of the swamps and up from Newark Airport, brake lights throbbing, everything teetering, every driver a couple feet from the driver in front and the driver behind.

Rabbi Loobling sighed. "Look." He touched my arm quickly and returned it to the wheel as my stiffness went flying out the cracked-open window because he'd *touched my arm*. "You think we have something important in common, being unhappy," he said. "Well maybe we have something even better in common, being happy right now."

◆ ◆ ◆

The lesson a little later made no sense. I couldn't connect the fragments:

"...a Jewish slave works day and night..."

"...two hairs on the body of a nine-year-old boy constitute puberty..."

"...nine years and a day is the minimum age at which a male's intercourse counts as intercourse..."

22

There was no end in sight to the bus strike. I couldn't be happier.

Every morning at seven, Rabbi Loobling picked me up in his jovial car, with its masculine vroom and its grill like a waffle iron.

"How was your weekend?" he asked as he steered us into traffic.

Unbearable, I thought, without you. "Great. Terrific. I saw eight movies. Babysitting money. Broke my old record."

"Eight movies? In a weekend?" he said. "Name them."

I hesitated. "Let's see." I didn't want him to know I'd seen five of them on *Shobbis*. But then this wasn't your average rabbi. "Friday night I saw a double feature around the corner from our apartment. *Bob and Carol and Ted and Alice* and *Easy Rider*." Both rated R. I hoped I sounded sophisticated.

"Two groundbreakers," he said. "What else?"

The radio music was sophisticated too. Stravinsky. I could tell. Rabbi Loobling had been exposing me to every kind of composer.

"Saturday I went to another double feature. At the Elgin. In the city. *The Fox*. You know it? From the book by D. H. Lawrence." (Which I'd read, by the way. Mostly because it was short.) "And *Who's Afraid of Virginia Woolf*? Not exactly *Mary Poppins*."

"Pretty grisly. The both of them. Though *Virginia Woolf*'s rather tender in the end."

I was sure those two would've gotten him to scold me, like a fatherly protector.

But no.

"After that I saw *The Prime of Miss Jean Brodie*. Up near Lincoln Center. The teacher in the movie reminded me of you."

"Oh?" He shifted gears.

"But of course you're not as crazy."

"I like to think of myself as not at all crazy."

"And Saturday night I went to the drive-in across the river."

"With your family?"

"By myself. There's a fence you hop over."

"How can you go to a drive-in by yourself?"

"I loiter outside the refreshment stand and eat popcorn like I belong there."

"In other words, you're a hooligan."

I laughed. "*Justine* and *The Minx*." I was really hoping to shock him with these. *The Minx* was rated X, and *Justine* was about a nun who becomes a hooker.

"That's seven," he said.

"And yesterday." Come on already. This one would surely floor him. "I took the bus back into New York. I saw *Midnight Cowboy*." With its sensational glimpses of effeminate men and bulging crotches.

"You saw that?"

I shrugged.

"How was it?" he asked, switching into the fast lane.

"A tour de force," I said. (I'd seen that phrase in a newspaper ad.) "Superbly acted."

"So I hear."

"The theater was packed."

He dropped it. He wasn't even curious how a 14-year-old was admitted into an X-rated movie. (Nobody checked.)

"I used to go to movies all the time when I was your age," he said. "But not as much as that."

"Harmless fun. An escape, that's all. Nothing to be concerned about."

Rabbi Loobling smiled. He wasn't much of a smiler. "The movies I went to were different when I was your age. Sal Mineo. Anna Magnani. There was sex and sensuality but there wasn't any nudity. We're in a totally different position now."

I pictured us in the dark, in a totally different position, eating Jujubes that stuck in our teeth. I imagined our fingers gripping our ticket stubs as two dreamy actors—one tall, one short—Jon Voight, Sal Mineo—held on to each other in desperate love on a thirty-foot projection. *Midnight Cowboys Without a Cause. Rebels in the Naked City.* They looked in each other's eyes and kissed. They pledged their troth under a flashing light with a heartbreaking song playing out of a window. (Maybe that was why Rabbi Nass disliked Rabbi Loobling. He could tell how much I wanted to kiss him.)

"Can I ask you something?" I said.

"What now?"

"Why does Rabbi Nass despise you so much?"

His eyebrows went down. He blew in and out. "Because." He adjusted the rearview and studied himself. "Because he knows I don't like him."

"I don't like him either. He's too puffed up."

"Look. Andrew. Rabbi Nass is my boss. And I am your teacher. We both may appreciate what a pompous phony he is, but this isn't something we talk about, okay? Now what were we discussing?"

I felt wounded and frustrated. What was this all about? Something to do with the anatomy lesson he'd chalked on the blackboard? Or the secret from his past that Herman Ziggleman refused to let us in on? Whatever it was, I didn't want Loobling scolding me again so all I said was, "We were talking about the movies."

"Right. I'd spend my Saturdays at the spectacular Loew's Valencia, over in Queens, one of those 1920s architectural extravaganzas."

"You went to the movies on *Shobbis*?"

"Like the Winter Palace in Leningrad. Always a double feature plus a travelog and a newsreel and a couple of cartoons. Daffy Duck was my favorite."

"Really?" I would have guessed someone craftier. Bugs Bunny, say, or Tweetie Pie.

"My parents weren't religious." He looked at me a second. "I take it you disapprove."

"I wouldn't care if you went to a Nazi rally in Munich on *Yum Kipper*."

"Don't joke like that."

"Sorry."

"That's in very bad taste."

"I said I was sorry."

He assaulted the stickshift. The Stravinsky picked up. Scrape-a-scrape skritch over syncopated timpani mallets. "My parents weren't ecstatic when I chose to become a rabbi."

"Why not?"

"They'd hoped I'd become a dentist. My father was a dentist. Still is, in fact, out in Garden City. You know where that is? His brother's a dentist. His cousin's a dentist. But the notion of soaking my fingers in *warm spit* all day did nothing for me."

I felt honored to be receiving such personal private info from him. I winced sympathetically. "Maybe—" I said, "—maybe you had an aversion to following in your father's footsteps."

"Ye who just happens to know everything about everyone," he said.

I'm certain I blushed. "No no. I'm a dope."

He changed the subject. "And what about you?"

"What *about* me?"

"Do you ever see *your* father?"

"No."

"Don't you miss him?"

"Uh-uh."

"Does he call you?"

"Nope."

"That's awful."

"He's a shit-head. We were never close to begin with. Even before my parents split. Not in the least. We weren't at all close."

Scrape-a-scrape boom; watt boom, went Stravinsky.

Rabbi Loobling snapped the radio off. "You don't expect me to believe that, do you?"

"These things happen."

"Every day. But I'd see more evidence of—I don't know—*something*—if you were that cut off from your father."

"What do you mean?"

"Is your mother still in touch with him?"

"He's married again. He's in Florida. No one's still in touch with him. Except for my sister."

"And what does your sister have to say about him?"

"Oh she hopes he'll come back and save her some day, that he'll wake up one morning a wonderful father and ditch the new wife and rescue her from the clutches of my mother. They're not exactly love birds, see. My mother and Naomi. I'm more realistic."

"About your mother?"

"About my father. I accept the reality that he'll never come back. That's all there is to it. It's a fact."

"And a shame. I'm upset for you, *boychik*."

"Don't be."

He touched my arm quickly and put it back on the wheel. His touches never scared me. "How's that business with your mother? With her and her—Rabbi Landy, is it?"

"You even know his name! How do you know his name?"

"I told you. Grapevine. Now what's going on?"

I remembered what he'd told me that first day on the roof. *It'll take a lot out of you to be my friend.* Which at the moment seemed to translate as "enough with the questions." "It's only getting worse," I said. "I think she's so obsessed with him that she can't even sleep."

The rabbi sighed. "Well remember, dear boy. Horrendous as it is. It's not your problem."

"Sometimes she doesn't sleep for days as a result of her crying. I'm beginning to think there might be something wrong with her. Some kind of serious mental problem."

"You're not even listening."

We were walled in by a fleet of trucks. And in front and behind by a caravan of buses.

He was right though. I wasn't listening. All I'd heard was "dear boy."

◆ ◆ ◆

During the Talmud break one Monday, when Rabbi Loobling was out of the classroom, that annoying Herman Ziggleman, the one with the swinging hips and the Moe Howard bangs who'd come from the Birnbaum yeshiva, was sitting with me and Jerry and saying, "You want to hear the dirt about Rabbi Loobling?"

Jerry and I just looked at him.

"He took off his clothes in one of the senior classes and ran screaming through the halls, 'I'm Jesus. I'm the savior.' He had a full-blown crackup in the middle of a school day. A totally naked crackup. Then they carted him off to the loony bin. Down by Toms River."

I didn't believe him.

Jerry just gawked.

A few days later, over breakfast after minyan, I heard a similar story from a senior with a mustache who had also gone to Birnbaum and who was eating a chocolate donut and saying, "removed his shirt and ran down the hallway shouting, 'I'm hairy, I'm hairy.'"

I didn't know what to think. What if Rabbi Loobling had done such things?? It was hard to be objective. I was bursting with curiosity. He might be a psycho. He must be in pain. And why was he stripped and claiming he was Jesus in Herman Ziggleman's version, and shirtless and hairy in the other guy's version? It was shocking and bizarre and amazingly sexy. So what if he ran around naked and screaming? I'd've loved to've seen it. It meant he was daring. Exhibitionism might sound foolish to some, but to me it sounded courageous.

Unless he was just a fool.

Fool or not, he came to mind as I read this part of a poem by Walt Whitman, a poet he'd encouraged me to borrow from the library:

> *...The curious sympathy one feels when feeling with the hand the naked meat of the body,*
> *The circling rivers, the breath, and breathing it in and out,*
> *The beauty of the waist, and thence of the hips, and thence downward...*

❖ ❖ ❖

Rabbi Loobling started a choir for the girls at the yeshiva. He could do this, being married (unmarried men couldn't listen to singing girls, according to some ludicrous law) and on top of it he played the piano. (I'd never known anyone as talented as he was, not even Thornton Vanoosten.) The choir met in the gym on Fridays, right after lunch. And all through American History, tortured that I wouldn't see him again till Monday—sixty-six endless hours away!—I could hear him banging out Hebrew songs in the gym below, heartsick tunes to accompany Mrs. Lefkowitz's talk about Washington's surrender at the Battle of Fort Necessity.

There was one tragic song that pounded away in the walls of the school and vibrated up through the legs of my desk, a Hebrew tune that could've doubled as a sad French ballad and translated as something like "I prayed for God's help and my cries reached his ears but God wouldn't help me."

23

About a father's obligations, the Talmud teaches: "A father is bound to circumcise, redeem, teach Torah to, take a wife for and teach a craft to his son. Some say, to teach him to swim as well."

◆ ◆ ◆

The yeshiva made an arrangement with the YMHA to offer swimming class to the student body, girls on Thursdays, boys on Fridays.

The morning of the first Friday swim, I shoved a bathing suit in my backpack and waited for Rabbi Loobling under the underpass. I figured splashing around with my classmates on a Friday would delay the despair of American History, piano vibrating up through my desk with its lovelorn lament, reminding me of my interminable two-day weekend without him.

Rabbi Loobling pulled up and I opened the door. There was a brown bag on the passenger seat with a drawstring peeking out. He tossed the bag in the back and I got in beside him. I felt a titillation electroshock, thinking *There's a bathing suit in that bag, he'll be swimming with us today*, but then I figured I must be seeing things. The rabbi couldn't go swimming with us. He was teaching two classes after lunch these days. That couldn't've been the drawstring of a bathing suit. It was clothesline. Or packing string. Or knitting yarn. Or boiled linguine.

I spent the morning in classes as usual (but with a secret ache, poised on a trip wire) until morning classes ended and we walked to the Y, led by Principal Nass, with his skeptical eye and his rolled-up beard and his bossy Canadian fatness.

Rabbi Loobling wasn't with us, just as I'd expected. Why kid myself into thinking I'd catch him naked in front of his locker—as naked as he'd been during his infamous Birnbaum crackup? Of course he couldn't swim with us. He had classes to teach and girls to rehearse at the lunchroom piano.

I walked with Jerry Leshinsky.

"So what's with you and Myra?" he said. "You two split up?"

"How'd you know?"

"I have eyes, Andy."

"It wasn't working out."

"How do you mean?"

I slapped a lie together. "She's in love with someone else."

"Jesus Christ. Really? Who? Larry Altman?"

"Yes, that's right."

"I knew it. I'm psychic. That girl is a cocktease."

Jerry did the rest of the talking. He said "Jesus Christ" repeatedly. The walk was depressing. We passed through a square that had been glitzy in the fifties. There were two grand movie theaters with flaking marquees and block after block of extra-wide pavement, all of which was crumbling.

We turned a corner and the trees on the block looked like broken antennas.

Jerry said, "...and to tell you the truth, people notice these things."

I said, "Notice what things?"

Jerry made a face. He'd been talking about something Myra-related, or so I figured, but I wasn't paying attention. He said, "I'm sorry. Hey. I know this must hurt. Jesus Christ."

We were passing a church with crosses over the doorways just as he uttered the famous name again.

He put his arm around me. "It really doesn't matter, And." He liked to call me And.

I didn't ask him to repeat what he'd said. His arm around me made it feel like I hadn't wrecked things.

Later, we were hustled into the locker room, about fifty of us, and we changed real fast with our backs to each other before heading to the pool in a line like geese.

Then I noticed him. At the far end of the lockers. Standing from a bench, fitting his rear into something stretchy and turquoise.

Rabbi Loobling.

I stopped.

Irwin Werblowsky walked into me.

"Hey!"

"Sorry."

Irwin walked around me.

I kept on looking. Rabbi Loobling smiled. "Afternoon, Andy."

I cursed my luck. Three seconds earlier (three seconds faster to slip on my flip-flops or tie up my trunks) and I'd've seen him naked.

"Hi," I said.

I had to keep moving. I couldn't just stand there.

His body left a burn on my eyeballs however, his sexy shape in an afterimage negative, hairy torso, beefy thighs, butt bending into a turquoise suit.

("Feeling with the hand the naked meat of the body.")

Soon my classmates were yelling in the echoes of the pool. And Rabbi Loobling did laps. I kept thinking that at the end of the period I'd get my wish—I'd see him naked. My heart sped up like a plane before liftoff, as I watched Rabbi Loobling crawl across the water, magnificent arms slipping in and crawling out, windmilling rabbi, floating on the cushions of his chest, hips, testicles, thighs.

But a whole half hour before swimming class was over, Rabbi Loobling touched the wall at the end of a lap, dragged himself panting out of the pool and, dripping from his suit, headed for the locker room. Just like that.

I absorbed the punch. I wasn't meant to get my wish. My wish was stupid. I felt washed-out and swindled.

But then anything that got me as excited as this must have some kind of good in it, I thought to myself.

♦ ♦ ♦

Still, I felt embarrassed to be so focused on his nudity. It embarrassed me in my private thinking. It was all my fault for hating sports and crying like a girl and reading Walt Whitman. I wished I lived alone so I could think my thoughts in freedom. I wished I were stronger. I wished I were older. I imagined there were places across the river—living rooms? bars?—where men stood around and looked at each other as they chatted and chain-smoked. Could love start up in places like that? I looked up *homosexuality* in my mother's two-volume encyclopedia of sexual behavior (which I imagined she'd stolen from her therapist Rabbi Landy's bookshelf) where I read about the Kinsey Report and anal sex and the risks of wearing your jeans too tight. There was never any mention of the kind of love I felt. What did that mean? That nobody respected it? I remembered the shock of the womanish man in the bar in *Midnight Cowboy*, swinging his purse and calling Dustin Hoffman "Ratso" with a mean-spirited cackle. What about the desire for togetherness, and vacations in a tent with the man you loved?

♦ ♦ ♦

The rabbis taught: "There are many kinds of acquisition. If the slave loosens his master's shoe, if he carries his baggage for him to the bathing place, if he undresses him, bathes him, rubs him, dresses him, puts his shoes on or lifts him, thus he acquires him."

♦ ♦ ♦

Two Fridays later, after two more occurrences of Rabbi Loobling's early dripping exits from the pool, I decided to take action.

Rabbi Loobling heaved himself sopping out of the water a whole half hour before the end of swimming and slapped into the locker room. My eyes followed him out. He caught my eye and smiled. At least from what I could see without glasses.

I waited a minute, watching the secondhand sweep around the giant competition clock suspended above the pool, and heaved myself out. The shouts of my schoolmates bounced off the tiles. If anyone asked, I was going to take a leak.

A second before I went, I imagined not going, I imagined the crush of defeat and despair and the sting of my cowardice. I pretended I was hopeless and desperately self-destructive.

But then everything solider braved its way into me—and there I was, whapping along the tiles with the chlorinated chorus of the boys all around me, forgetting my flip-flops but not my glasses (which I'd hidden on a ledge), picturing Rabbi Loobling in front of his locker, yanking down his bathing suit. I was trembly with excitement—hatchet in my heart. I thought I might trip and break my head.

What I didn't expect was that passing through the showers toward the lockers up front, I'd see him under a spray head, soaping his stomach, slurping the water, head hair streaming, pubic hair bursting, everything showing on a regular meaty slab of an animal, michelangelic, beautiful, bouncing, abdominally, shoulderly, cockily, scrotally, in oblivious shower happiness.

"Oh," I said.

He stopped mid-bounce. He lowered his hands. The water was hissing. He said, "Hello there, Andrew," no longer oblivious. "It *is* Andrew Baer I'm addressing, correct?"

"Uh, yuh."

"Can't see a thing without my specs, I'm afraid."

"I—um. Do you happen to know what time it is?"

"Sorry, silly. I haven't got my watch on either."

My toes gripped reflexively, ineffectively at the tiles. "That's okay," I said and continued to walk.

But he continued to talk—"Of course it's okay"—so I stopped abruptly and wobbled minutely. "Now there are lots of free showers," he said. "Take your pick."

"I was only trying to—"

"Don't be a mealy mouth. Remove your suit."

I did as instructed, like he'd whispered a prompt two days ago, after hypnotizing me, and here he was with the prompt again. I pulled down my suit, hung it on a hook and started the shower next to him. The power of his command was so arousing, however, that my penis stood out. I couldn't control it, didn't expect it. I turned away.

He said, "Why turn away? It's your nature, young lad. Your nature is a wonder. Remember Walt Whitman. 'Divine am I, inside and out.' Celebrate your youthful divine, and prove thereby 'no more modest than immodest.'"

I said, "What about—oops—I mean—"

He had an erection too. It was sticking straight out. His entire body seemed to be celebrating—smiling even—if a body can be said to have a facial expression.

But how could a rabbi's hard-on stir a ruckus this immense in me?

Then the whap-whap of one of the other kids approached and we turned our showered-on backs to each other.

◆ ◆ ◆

A few days later, this doofy kid with crooked teeth from another class came over to me at one of the donut tables and said, "Rabbi Loobling mentioned you in class the other day."

"You're kidding."

"He was talking about sex—about society's sick approach to it, something like that, you know how he gets, all pervy and stuff—and he mentioned how during swim last week you accidentally walked in on him, naked, taking a shower, and how natural you seemed, so natural and relaxed that you could ask him what time it was without even flinching."

Sugar Sugar
1972

24

I hadn't been to temple in a couple of years because I resented the rabbi's hold on my mother and his contempt for his wife and his hambone sermons, so I just stopped going, I could do what I wanted, let them act out their epic flirtations without me. I was past the age where I thought of my mother's recklessness as related to me somehow. I didn't care. I wasn't her captive. No reason for me to go.

But then one Friday night I *did* go. The night they were honoring Mr. Rothstein, the Backseat Rabbi, because he hadn't missed a Friday night in 35 years and I was the only one in the synagogue who liked him.

I sat all alone in the back and watched. I'd been in yeshiva for five years already and no longer felt it was my duty to act as number-one upstanding boy representative of the Jewish community.

In the back.

All alone.

Sat I.

I had lost all interest in the Torah and temple and praying and God. I hated the concept of the Jews as the chosen people and all those lame-brained rules about pork chops and lobster. All I cared about was the Talmud and the rabbis who made it interesting.

I smelled coffee in the vents.

I watched as the templegoers smiled at the rabbi. I wasn't surprised to see my mother smiling too, beatific beamer, smudgy with eye shadow (jungle green), her prayer book closed on her dress-and-stocking lap as she recited by heart:

> *"Do not be abashed! Do not be ashamed!*
> *Why are you disheartened? Why do you complain?"*

She recited with that look-at-me mischief in her eye, same look as ever—*Aren't you proud of me, folks, for knowing my prayers without even looking?*—as if she were eight, and I wondered if she'd ever stop humiliating herself like this.

Not until the rabbi told her not to.

Which would be...

...never.

But the crazy thing was, as I looked around the temple, noticing all the regulars, like Phyllis and Ef and the rabbi's sons and the mighty Nona Tower...

...I noticed another woman—brown hair and choker, chocolate-chip eyes and a cracked plastic pocketbook—doing the same thing my mother was doing. Straining toward the rabbi. Praying by heart. Eager for us to notice her. Eager for *him* to notice her—*Oh Rabbi,* her lingering look seemed to say, *you marvelous hunk of manhood you!*—with a big jumping bust and a tight head of curls and a choker like you'd see on a saloon girl.

"*And the city shall be rebuilt on a hill.
And your despoilers will become your spoil.*"

Her smile was clipped, her head was back, her eyebrows penciled, lost in a dream—chronically depressed and trying to hide it. Where had she come from? Who brought her in here? Sad and pretending and secretly loco. With a highly effective choker. (It definitely caught your eye.) And a mouth that seemed gentile.

I let my gaze wander, catching yawns and grins and yarmulkes all around me, as surpriseless as any temple in Jersey.

I checked out my mother, other side of the aisle, to see if she noticed the lady in the choker.

Didn't seem to, no. Or if she did, she didn't show it. Didn't consider her a threat, in any event.

I checked out the Papperniks, seated behind my mother, reading glasses half down their noses. (She was sweet. He was sour.)

I checked out Benjie Rak, accountant in the city, with his King Tut beard, in the row behind the Papperniks. (He never prayed a word, nonbeliever like me.) And his olive-skinned twins, Nanette and Renée.

Same old temple.

Same old people.

Same old reassuring Friday night sameness.

But then—over there—toward the yarmulke box—farther back in the sanctuary—my eyes caught another one whose face I didn't recognize, with a familiar fawning glint in her eye—a worried-looking lady with a frizzy mop and the gray roots showing, no prayer book in sight, reciting by heart, blinking at the rabbi, blinking and blinking. (*Oh rabbi!* her washed-out eyes seemed to say. *Forsake me not in my hour of need!*) She had an overanxious stupefied look that probably had its roots in the gloom of the shtetl.

> *"Shake yourself free, rise from the dust!*
> *Dress in your garments of splendor, my people!"*

Was she friends with the lady of the heaving bust and saloon-girl choker?

Two strange women, flushed and staring, one buxom, one blinking, waiting for the rabbi to shine his face upon them, waiting and staring, insolent and shameless, sending ripples of dismalness into the temple.

But whatever.

So what.

What did I care?

There was Mr. Lipper. Must be a hundred. Evelyn Trenk of the UJA with her big front teeth and weepy peepers, the Steefles, the Blankrots, the Zimmers, the Karps.

Whoa.

Wait.

There.

Three o'clock.

Another spacey nuthouse type with stringy hair and blotchy skin and a look like she'd been drinking. Distended belly. Dingy skirt. Mooning at

Rabbi. Reciting by heart. Spiritual sister of the other two catastrophes (the choker lady, the blinking lady), and now the bloated boozer lady.

"Rouse yourselves!
Your light is coming!
Rise up and shine!"

All three of them by themselves, no husbands, staring at Rabbi, reciting like showoffs, messily lipsticked, undistracted. And none of them seeming to faze my mother, who looked straight ahead and recited her prayers exactly as always, like there was no one on earth but her and the rabbi.

No way was this a coincidence. No way could these women appear out of nowhere and just happen to be gaga for the same bad rabbi. Maybe he treated them in his therapy practice and got them to come to Friday night services as a form of pastoral treatment. Because temple got you to put on heels and a dress (instead of slippers and a robe) and mingle for a change.

But it couldn't erase the hurt in their faces.

Plus, as I was saying, they recited by heart. Meaning they couldn't be new. It'd take quite a while to memorize the service. Maybe they'd been regulars for years and no one told me. I'd been out of the loop. How would I know? They were simultaneously bold and pathetic. With that questing ecstatic deliver-me look out of the corners of their eyes. Where the eyeliner tapered. *See how he notices me? He's nuts about me. See?*

Wishful thinkers.

Lonely pilgrims.

Empty shells.

Just like my mother.

I turned my head and there was another, a last one, in a dowdy twin set. Toni Di Prima! The one who'd boarded the bus that time, when I was sitting in the back and that seedy greaser massaged his crotch in the seat alongside me. Toni Di Prima. With her baggy eyes and her hacked-at Joan of Arc crazy-lady haircut, hypnotized by the rabbi, hypnotized like the rest of them.

"Come in peace and jubilation
Amidst the faithful of the treasured nation.
Come O bride!
O Sabbath bride!"

❖ ❖ ❖

After services I headed downstairs to the reception for Mr. Rothstein—I loved the kosher grape juice and the apricot rugelach—but the cantor's son Bobby stopped me on the steps.

"Hey," he said. "Haven't seen you in a while."

For a second I didn't recognize him, he'd gotten so muscled.

"Bobby. Hi. You look very different."

"*You* don't. Didn't you start at that yeshiva or something?"

"Five years ago, yeah."

People were passing us on the steps.

"I'm on the wrestling team at Colgate," Bobby said. (Jeezo, I would've loved to've seen him suited up for that.) "I'm a poli-sci major. Man is it hard. I'm sure you heard about my accident. Lucky for me, I only broke a rib."

I hadn't heard a thing.

The rabbi interrupted. "Andrew Baer!" He smiled wide and took my hand. "Excuse me, Bobby. Long time no see. We've missed you around these parts." Before I could respond he dropped the smile, took back his hand and went to someone else.

Bobby moved on too.

I finished my descent and zigzagged through the crowd until I found myself near the rabbi's new (well, new-to-me) gaggle of hoodwinked females (they stood in a group, bedraggled and avoided) and I hovered in the vicinity, attempting not-so-subtly to eavesdrop. (None of the longtime temple normals dared to go near them, as if they had cooties.)

"...he was telling me just yesterday..."

"...he was telling me this morning..."

"...a form of worship..."

"...a form of enlightenment..."
"...not with his wife around..."
"...emotional expressiveness..."
"...I know that..."
"...angry..."
"... the hound dog..."
"...that's dirty..."
"...you mean he left you in the dark...?"
"...you mean he didn't clue you in...?"
"...magnetism. I told you. Utter he-man magnetism..."

They were Landy addicts, rabbinical love slaves, resistant to the truth that he'd been married forever (despite the on-again, off-again whispers of divorce or separate bedrooms) and he couldn't possibly worship them as much as they worshiped *him*.

"...Rabbi..."
"...the rabbi..."
"...Rabbi..."
"...Rick..."

I could tell without much thinking that they were a bunch of deluded husbandless have-nots.

Then my mother showed up at the bottom of the stairs, swinging her beads, smiling and fizzing and emphatically chattering—something to do with "later after services" and "follow-up coffee"—and the sad-looking, pretend-happy, new-to-me ladies closed in around her (she knew them after all) in their skirts and tops, shaking their earrings, squeezing their smiles, peering beyond the Maybelline war paint, talking all at once but deferring to my mother.

They drew in even closer.

She spoke for a bit and they nodded and bobbled, they were all a little charmless, like a flock of Yoko Onos.

◆ ◆ ◆

The rabbi made a speech about Mr. Rothstein at the reception, using phrases like "most valuable player" and "the soul of humble piety" and "de facto backup rabbi" but I would've preferred something blander, such as "You may not like him, I know he's a grouch and he smells really old plus he's irritating and arrogant, but you've got to respect his commitment to this place," but that woudn't've gone over.

Mr. Rothstein seemed pleased with the rabbi's words anyway. He didn't make a speech himself. He just raised his cup and bowed.

I shook Mr. Rothstein's woody hand afterwards and told him I appreciated how nice he'd always been to me and he hugged me out of nowhere, with his coffee-and-cigarette breath on my neck and a choke of old-man woe in his chest.

Then I swallowed a lot of honey cake and bowtie cookies and rugelach and grape juice and left to walk home. I wouldn't catch a ride with my mother. It was a two-mile walk but I didn't mind. I preferred to hurry along on my personal horsepower.

It had rained during services. I could smell the wet dirt. There was a median down this avenue and the soil had just been turned. This was the upscale part of Montevideo with its canopy trees and wraparound porches. Walking in the dark I peeked into the houses and admired their orderliness, living room after living room, table lamps and breakfronts and the flickering lights of TV sets on oblivious strangers' faces. Obliviously calm and focused. With their two-parent families, the love of those families and their domestic contentments. Invisibly observing, I remembered the dreams where I could make myself invisible and visit Rabbi Loobling in his living room in Beechwood.

That all quieted down after we'd looked at each other naked in the showers and I realized that nothing would happen beyond that—no kisses, no romance, nothing, ever—but also that he wasn't my only option. I could respond like this to someone else, someone more willing. I no longer had any classes with him but he was still at the yeshiva, teaching other students, coming and going, saluting me in the hallway, the ghost of my crush which was really, when I thought about it, much more than a crush, due to the agony he'd caused me.

So the funniest thing. Just that week.

Rabbi Loobling: "Andy."

Me: "Oh hi."

We were just outside the lunch room.

"Andy my boy. I was wondering. *We* were wondering. Sarah and I. If you'd like to spend Shabbat with us in a couple of weeks."

"Really?"

"Weekend of the twenty-third."

"That would be fine."

"You want to verify with your mother?"

"No no. I'll come. Let's plan on it."

"Sensational."

It's not that I didn't like the idea, it's just that the invitation was three years late. Imagine if he'd asked me when my feelings for him were jacked up to the stratosphere. I would've collapsed right in front of him before he landed on the question mark. I would've reacted by having a heart attack.

But I had a new love interest—new kid in school—son of Rabbi Gottschall the moyl—transfer student Gabriel who had wide-apart eyes, long limp hair, John Sebastian glasses and a skinny waist. He was the coolest boy in school—all of the sudden—no one came close—who loped when he walked, slung a backpack over his shoulder and spoke in a seductive mumble.

And I'd seen him naked.

At Friday swim, in front of our lockers. There he was, next locker over, a little older, a little shorter, with the lumpy nose of a Roman soldier, yanking his tie off, pulling his shirt off, undershirt, sneakers, slacks, socks, methodical, inattentive, till he was down to his briefs, cerulean blue, so close I could smell him—baby powder and grapefruit—and he let out an "ah" as he slid down his briefs and the packing sproinged forward (pubic hair and jittering dick). I didn't think it was possible to be that easy with yourself. I didn't think it was possible to be so aroused by another person.

And that includes Loobling. I had waited around forever for my teacher to make his move, to follow up on the shower scene and show me the ways of love, and he had wound up disappointing me. (Of course!) He would never become my boyfriend. I'd been naive to ever wish for it, naive and self-bewildered. I was determined not to repeat my mistake.

So even though Gabriel was naked, I talked to him. "You're friends with Rabbi Loobling, aren't you?"

Because—and this was amazing—irony of ironies—he was friends with Rabbi Loobling. You'd see them alone in a classroom, talking, or mid-discussion down the second-floor hallway. He'd been a student of his at Birnbaum Yeshiva, where Loobling had had his nervous breakdown. You'd see them with their heads bent, Loobling and Gabriel, relating like grownups, like the Kennedy brothers, a far cry from our starstruck talks a thousand moons ago, when the relationship was fatherly rather than brotherly, one-on-one on a rooftop.

"Yes," the naked Gabriel said. "Loobling's talked about you. You're Andy, aren't you?"

"I am."

He shook my hand and I smiled idiotically (only fleetingly glimpsing below his waist) and that was the end of it. For the time being.

But so I was thinking about the two of them, back and forth—Loobling, Gabriel—Gabriel, Loobling—as the streetlights glowed in the wet of the asphalt and I hurried home from temple. Here I'd known Rabbi Loobling and craved him like food and seen him naked, naked with a hard-on, which was one kind of love. And now I'd seen Gabriel naked as well, right off the bat, but he didn't know me, not in any real sense, and apart from the moment when he yanked down his underpants (no hard-on in this case) and put out his hand, we'd never socialized. Yet he lived in my thoughts and posed in my dreams and that was another kind of love.

So it was during this walk back home, as I peeked into the blue tint of other people's happiness, that I saw the upper portion of a kid my age in front of a TV, lost to the moment, lost to a sitcom (I could hear the canned laughter), though he wasn't remotely smiling. He was lulled by day and time and channel as organized by TV Guide. I wondered whether happiness was the word for a kid like this. If I was going to make any progress with Gabriel it wouldn't happen with me sitting on a sofa and vacantly watching.

25

When I showed up at home, the door was unlocked and all the lights were going and that jumble of zombified Rabbi ladies I'd observed back at temple were gathered around the dining room table, gossiping and drinking coffee.

There was the sexy one with the choker.

And the blinking one with the frizzy gray roots.

And the drunk one with the belly.

And Toni Di Prima.

Clones of my mother.

Not at all like my mother.

She was the original. That's how she saw it. You could see it in her posture. What could the rabbi possibly see in these cheapo knockoffs?

"Oh there he is!"

"Who?"

"My son."

"Your son?"

"Who knew?"

"I knew."

"Me too."

"The elder."

"The middle."

"Numero dos."

"The yeshiva *bachur*?"

"The prodigal son!"

"That is not a Jewish expression, Toni."

"How about the prodigal shlub?"

I didn't smile.

I went to my room.

Where Toby was in bed already, practically asleep.

"Who are those ladies?" I said.

"Temple."

"Why are they here?"

"Dunno."

He lost consciousness in seconds, snoring and wheezing, out and in, along the edge of the bed, about to fall out, his arm dangling down like the arm of a dead guy. It was his usual sleep position.

I stripped in the dark (I never let Toby see) and slid between the freezing sheets (though it was already spring) and plotted my future. Stage a meeting. Target Gabriel. Be strong and brave and present and manly.

But our bedroom bordered the dining room and I couldn't block out what the women were saying. It was impossible not to eavesdrop on the zombies. The only voice I could pick out for sure was my mother's—Bea's.

She said, "His sermon was very satisfying."

"Illuminating."

"Entrancing."

"On a very high plain," my mother said, "whatever you care to call it."

"Meaning too high for the likes of us?"

My mother said, "Of course not."

"I guess we just aren't groovy enough."

My mother said, "Christ."

"No no, come on now, serious question. What did he mean by substitute atonement?"

"*Substitutionary* atonement," my mother said. "It's exactly what it sounds like."

"Why do you insist on playing the dum-dum?"

"Defense mechanism."

"And the scapegoats," my mother said.

"Hush."

"They're the centerpiece of the story," my mother said.

"The rabbi thinks I'm brilliant."

"Unless otherwise instructed."

"He said that?" my mother said.

"I never knew there were scapegoats in the bible."

"Exact words."

"Which is completely far out."

"Well they had to come from somewhere," my mother said.

"Who knew it meant an actual goat?"

"I thought they were from that Steve McQueen movie. You know, the Great Escape Goat."

My mother said, "Here the one goat is killed—"

"You're a kook!"

"Sacrificed!"

"No no, I'm a waif."

"Sacrificed," my mother said, "and the other goat, the scapegoat, is spared."

"I thought your husband left you."

"I said waif. Not wife."

"Why don't you empty this ashtray?"

"Aha."

"But only after the sins of the community are transferred onto said bovine," my mother said. "Onto the poor defenseless scapegoat."

"How convenient."

"Isn't it?"

"Hell, I'll empty it myself."

"Then they release him into the wilderness," my mother said.

"To take his din-din among the camels."

"Here?"

"Lots of meanings."

"There," my mother said.

"So many meanings."

"Such as?"

"Such as forgiveness is within our grasp," my mother said. "Such as nobody has to apologize for shit."

"Tuh. So it's the old goat's fault."

Silence.

I wondered if they were thinking about the old goat Rabbi Landy.

"I had to memorize snippets of the Torah when I converted."

"Like a bar mitzvah boy?"

"Like a bar mitzvah *goy!*"

"Wait. You converted? What are you saying?"

My mother said, "You didn't know?"

"I thought your old man was Italian."

"He was. I divorced him."

"Oh that part I knew. Rabbi told me. But I thought you were Jewish."

"I am……now."

My mother said, "Does that face look Jewish?"

"My maiden name is Malta."

"I didn't know that."

My mother said, "I did. Rick told me."

"Well, so I memorized the tale of Jethro, a major-league idol-worshiper…"

"Memorized!? In Hebrew?!"

"…who converts to this faddish new phenomenon known as Judaism. He even winds up circumcising himself."

"Now that's what I call a *schlemazel*," my mother said.

"I doubt Judaism was faddish at this point in history."

"And there's a party that night where his son-in-law Moses—"

"I wonder what they serve at a bris in the desert."

"Oh I just love 'The Ten Commandments.'"

"Bagels and rocks," my mother said.

"Wait a minute. I'm only just getting this. You had to memorize the story of the convert? Because *you yourself* were a convert?"

"Bingo. No Hebrew. And so his son-in-law Moses lowers himself to the level of servant so he can wait on the convert—his father-in-law—at his do-it-yourself bris."

"I don't remember that from the movie."

"There's a lesson in that. In the honor of the convert."

"Oh. So Rabbi converted you?"

"Where have you been?"

"Yeah, see..."

"That's how she got to know him so well."

"I told you. No."

"So very very well."

"I find that offensive."

"You weren't even listening."

"Extremely offensive."

"Inside and out."

My mother said, "Can you believe Lou Rothstein?"

Silence.

"Every Friday night," she said, "for thirty-five years."

My mother apparently discombobulated the group by changing the subject.

"Ahem."

"Ahem yourself," my mother said.

"Would you ever have an affair with *ahem*?"

"Don't remind me," my mother said.

"Is Rabbi, you know, okay with *ahem*?"

"Why wouldn't he be?" my mother said.

"What difference does it make?"

"Rick's okay with everybody."

"He ever try any funny stuff? Lou? On you?"

My mother said, "Welp. I had to literally chop his head off once. Very *handsy* with me, if you know what I mean."

"What a nerve."

"What a snake."

"One particularly scurrilous pinch on the tukhis," my mother said. "After services. It was right in the social hall."

"I thought you said it was right in the tukhis."

(Mr. Rothstein? No! I couldn't believe it.)

"I hope his old lady didn't witness that goose."

"I saw Ricky-doo chatting her up at the kiddish."

"Who?"

"Stop calling him that."

"Not an hour ago."

"Mr. Rothstein's wife. Cecile."

"Who the heck cares?"

"But so which of the men would you have *wanted* to goose you?"

"What a question!"

"Of the men at the temple?" my mother said.

"Your questions'll land you in jail someday."

My mother said, "Ike Blaustein."

"You mean the one with the psychedelics?"

"He has an enormous penis," my mother said.

A few of them snickered.

(I cringed in the sheets.)

"Rick flirts with me."

"How do you know?"

"Just watch him sit down," my mother said.

"Rick digs me."

"You're terrible."

"What's his first name again?"

My mother said, "Ike."

"Bigdick Blaustein."

"How about the women?"

"Did you hear what I said?"

"Which of the women would you care to get it on with?"

"Why Marilyn P. Have you gone lezzie?"

"Is it really such a surprise?"

"Jesus," my mother said. "Let her talk."

"That's right. No judging. I heard Rick say that."

"All right already. Let me just shut up."

"I would never get it on with a woman."

"Me neither."

"Please do."

"If I were a man? No question. Tehila."

"She's a fox. Admit it."

"Who's Tehila?"

"Rick obviously hates her," my mother said.

"We can all admit she's a bitch, *n'est-ce pas?*"

My mother said, "The rebbetzin."

"What does that mean?"

"You have to admit she's smokin'."

My mother said, "The wife of a rabbi."

"Yeah, she qualifies. She's a downright beauty."

My mother said, "It's a hard beauty though. Nothing sensuous about her. I'm sure she doesn't make him happy."

"Where was she tonight?"

"Haven't seen her in a while."

My mother said, "Well, if you must know. They've separated." Everyone gasped. Me included. "As in separate dwellings," my mother said.

26

But as I was saying. I was in love with Gabriel Gottschall. He'd replaced Rabbi Loobling in my fantasies and daydreams. In pajamas on a boardwalk. In boxer shorts with a raggedy waistband. In a mud bath. In a hot tub. On a waterbed. On a go-go stage.

The images made him pop all over at the height of my excitement.

Which traced to his striptease in front of the lockers.

You could say it was an insignificant high school attraction and leave it at that, but it wouldn't explain the berserkness of that attraction. The feelings made me crazier than I'd ever been about Rabbi Loobling, though what attracted me wasn't crazy. It was grounded in the facts of his high forehead, jaunty walk, premature calmness and faraway romantic staring. How could anyone not be attracted? But I was more than attracted. I was in love. And it freaked me to think that I was that much in love with someone I didn't know yet.

I was sure I'd have a chance at grownup romance if I only figured out how to let him in on my secret. Because Gabriel might respond in kind. You never knew. He never had a girlfriend. I wasn't overconfident. I just remembered how relaxed he'd been when he talked to me with his dick out. That had to mean something. I should stage a conversation. Talk to him again. About something besides our friendships with Loobling.

But someone was in my way. Gabriel's friend Simon, the son of another rabbi. There was no way to casually stumble onto Gabriel at the bus stop or at lunch and start up a conversation because Simon was always with him.

Big fleshy Simon Mandell with his fat lips and sausagey legs about to burst their dungaree casings. His ass rolled around like cantaloupes when he walked and his fingers were as thick as pickles. I would've otherwise been drooling over all that yeshiva-boy lusciousness, but he was too jerky for me to venture past that. He was always telling moronic jokes or responding with a string of *whys* to whatever you said to him. (*It's chilly out. Why? Because it's cloudy out. Why? Because there's rain in the forecast. Why?* Et cetera, et cetera.) You could understand his behavior because his brother was a genius studying math at M.I.T. and his sister had Down syndrome so, guaranteed, the Rabbi and Mrs. Mandell had little attention left over for Simon, but he still was pretty annoying.

Necessity drove me batty.

One morning I walked right up to them.

"Hi, Simon. Hi, Gabriel."

"Do we know each other?" Simon said.

We were stopped in a busy hallway.

"That's Andy, you wombat," Gabriel said.

Simon said, "Eddie?"

"He's Andy and you know it," Gabriel said.

Simon scratched his head, screwed up his eyebrows, rubbed his chin. Then his mouth sprang open and a laugh flew out. "Haw, haw!! Fooled ya. Of course I know. Give me your phone number."

"Why?" I said.

"Just give **IT TO ME!**"

"Jeez, Simon."

Gabriel said, "Don't mind him. He's generally speaking a douchebag."

"Fuck you," Simon said.

"See what I mean?" Gabriel turned to go. "Gotta head to the head before chemistry class. Good luck, my boy." (He called me *my boy!*) And Gabriel was gone.

But Simon wasn't.

Damn that Simon.

"Your phone number! Step on it!"

"Why?"

"So I can ask you out on a date." Pause. Stare. Crossed eyes. Donkey laugh. "Haw haw!! Just pulling your leg. I have a car, Eddie." One of his eyebrows went up. "A Dodge Charger. We can go to the movies. Let's make it Sunday."

"Okay. Sure. Great. Terrific. But don't call me Eddie."

"We'll see *Heartbreak Kid*."

"No, yeah, of course, fine."

"It's at the drive-in in Highpoint Corners."

Drive-in implied a late night on a school night, which I definitely didn't go for. "Excellent," I said.

"I take all my hot dates to the drive-in," he said. "Haw haw haw!"

I wasn't sure how going to the drive-in with Simon Mandell would lead to the expression of my love for Gabriel Gottschall, verbally and physically...to Gabriel himself!...but there had to be a way and this felt like an inroad.

Thinking it over later, I had to wonder why Gabriel was friends with obnoxious Simon Mandell in the first place.

◆ ◆ ◆

Simon smoked a joint in the car after he parked us in a spot at the drive-in. I'd never seen anyone smoke pot before. I was gobsmacked. I was riveted. He tried to get me to join him in the crime but I said no. He asked me several times. I had to be persistent. He wandered over to the refreshment stand a bunch of times during the course of the movie to get popcorn and soda and Goobers and Razzles.

Meanwhile, *The Heartbreak Kid* was a downer. I hated the husband's nastiness to his pestering wife (she couldn't help being so Jewishly Jewish) yet I related to the sleazy hero's fanatical attempts to subdue an elusive object of beauty (Cybill Shepherd).

After the movie Simon and I went to Johann's Fountain which had to look bad for a rabbi's son because they served bacon cheeseburgers in addition to sundaes and the owner worked for the SS in Deutschland, or so the rumor went. Simon didn't wear his yarmulke, not even at the movies beforehand, which was additionally daring for a rabbi's son.

I figured the only way I'd get the skinny on *my* object of beauty was by seeming not to ask for it. So I waited.

We ordered a couple banana splits (Simon's eyes were glassy from the pot he'd smoked) and he told me about his girlfriend Shifra who was in Israel on kibbutz and making a sucker out of him with some brute in the Israeli air force.

"Does she write to you?"

"No. And I really can't take it. It's making me insane. You can't imagine what it's like. I haven't been sleeping. It's excruciating torture. It's like they pulled out all my wisdom teeth. It's like a slow-motion firing squad. I know I must look awful." You could see how insecure Simon was by the way he rubbed his face, as if he hated his nose and lips, which made me like him better but not by much.

A waiter brought our ice creams.

"Do you write to her?" I said.

"What do you **THINK!**"

"Hey!" I said. "I don't appreciate being yelled at after everything I say to you."

He sighed a humongous put-upon sigh, popped the cherry in his mouth and pulled out the stem. "Every day. Okay? I write her every day. Mail it after dinner. Wake up after midnight and start a new letter. Tell her everything in my heart. That my heart is full of passion. That my balls are full of semen. I have a couple dozen air-mail stamps right here in my wallet." Another sigh. "But she doesn't write *me*." He began to attack his multiple mounds of mint chocolate chip and butter pecan.

"Sounds difficult," I said, attacking my vanilla and strawberry cheesecake. "But you know. She's far from home doing all these new things..."

"Doing all of the Israeli air force."

"...doing all these new things so who has time to write you back?"

"That's what Gabriel says."

"Gabriel?"

"My best friend. You've seen him. Little skinny-ass twerp with a—say, you all right?"

I'd started to cough. "Nut went down my—*kek, kek, kek*."

"Here. Take a sip." I took a sip of Simon's water. "You sure you're all right? Must've been all that pot you smoked."

I wheezed out the words, "I didn't smoke, remember?"

"Oh right. That was me. You know, I might've been exaggerating when I said she doesn't write me. She does in fact write me. On occasion."

I sipped more water. I cleared my throat. "Did you tell Gabriel?"

"What?"

"That Shifra writes you every now and then?"

"I said on occasion. She writes me on occasion. Weren't you listening? What does Gabriel have to do with it?"

"He's your best friend, isn't he?"

"Since kindergarten."

"I figured you guys must talk."

"He's quite the schnook when you get to know him."

"Oh come on. Gabriel?"

"Awkward as hell. No luck with the ladies. None whatsoever. Just look at him. What a pansy. Only thing unpansylike is, he smokes with me."

"You mean pot?"

"Yeah."

"Gabriel Gottschall smokes pot?"

"I said yeah. But who cares? What are you, a narc? Why are we even talking about him?"

"I didn't mention him. You did."

"Yeah and otherwise a pansy. You gotta see him naked. Total worm. Like the wimp on the beach—you know the type—back of the comic books? The one they kick sand at?"

I couldn't come out and say *I've already seen him naked, in fact. And you're obviously blind. I mean, really. He's a beauty.*

But again, I waited.

"We went to Birnbaum together," Simon said.

"Oh. Right."

"We started there in kindergarten. From way back then until Loobling's class." He was shoving more than half of the banana-split banana into his mouth. "You know about Mistress Loobling, don't you?"

"What do you mean?"

He made the crazy sign around his ear.

"Oh yeah, I've heard. Couple different stories."

"Of course you've heard. You guys are, like, what? Lovers?"

"You better shut up about that."

"L - O - V - E - R - S lovers."

"Just shut the fuck up!"

"Jeeps, Andy."

"I mean it, Simon."

"I'm kidding, Christ. Kidding, kidding, kidding. Don't you get that by now?"

"Not everything's a joke, Simon."

"Why not? Lighten up."

"Not everything's a goddamn joke."

"I know. I get it." Simon shoveled banana and ice cream and fudge sauce into his mouth. "You and Loobling are, what? Just sleeping together? Side by side with the covers up? Maybe a handjob, hm? No strings? No commitments?"

"He's my friend."

"Your *friend*."

"In fact, he invited me to stay with him in a couple of weeks for *Shobbis*. May twenty-third."

"Is that Memorial Day weekend?"

"Huh. Might be."

"You're kidding!"

"What?"

"Rabbi Loobling invited Gabriel Gottschall to come for that *Shobbis* too."

"**WHAT????!!!!**"

"Hey! You all right?"

"Sorry. Ouch. I hurt myself. Under the, yow, I banged my knee." It wasn't much of a cover but Simon didn't say anything.

He drove me home, talking about the cuties in our secular classes, the gorgeousness of Cybill Shepherd and the faithlessness of Shifra. Plus he offered to sell me pot. I said, "No way José."

Before I knew it I was back in the sheets at home in my bedroom, with my brother at the edge of his bed and snoring.

I was scared to think. I dozed for half an hour and dreamed about giant Rock Hudson robots stomping across the countryside but I was awake for the rest of the night. I kept thinking *Gabriel*. Gabriel Gotschall. Gabriel naked. Rabbi Loobling had invited us. Same *Shobbis*. Same room. Same overnight in adjoining cots. (Was this a scheme of Rabbi Loobling's to get us together? Had he noticed how much I'd been mooning over Gabriel? Why hadn't he asked me if I minded Gabriel's coming?) Pajamas. Pillows. Darkness. Nightlight. Stretching. Scratching. An opening in the pajamas. An opening into Gabriel. The excitement was unbearable. What if my insides exploded apart?

I understood that night that, for all of my time in yeshiva among the rabbis, I'd never believed in God, even though God was what made the rabbis rabbis. When I was praying to God it was just a form of wishing. *Grant me more confidence. Grant me new shoes. Grant me Gabriel Gottschall.* And now that my greatest wish had been granted, I wondered if I'd've been better off believing in Jesus. With his lank hair and scrawny physique, he was Gabriel Gottschall's double.

Then it occurred to me. Marijuana. Of course. Gabriel smoked it. Misery solved. I'd have to tell Simon that I'd changed my mind and I wanted to buy a joint.

27

They were here again on a Friday. I was naked in bed and listening. As usual, Toby was snoring.

I couldn't understand why they kept coming over. My mother couldn't afford to entertain nicely—no quiche or lox or fondue or cheesecake—but the women were there in the dining room anyway, smoking and yapping and munching on potato chips. And I thought to myself, As bad off as it was for my mother and us, between the welfare checks and eviction notices, these depressed, demoralized lead-balloon ladies might've actually been *worse off than we were.*

"I didn't really like it."

"Oh I did."

"Me too. I dug it completely."

My mother said, "It was bliss. Sheer heaven."

"But all that touching."

"It's touching as healing."

"I forgot where I was."

"I knew where I was for the first time ever."

"It made me feel open," my mother said.

"Open. Yes."

"Open and vulnerable."

"Did I mention I was a flower child? Couple years back?"

"And welcoming."

"Exactly," my mother said.

"I felt like a flower child again."

"I wish I could have known you then."

"I was worried that someone might hurt me."

"Me too."

"But hey," my mother said, "nobody did."

"Never knew you were a flower girl."

"A flower *child*."

"Everyone fed me."

"The vibe was so groovy."

"I thought I'd get my eye poked out but instead I got caressed."

My mother said, "That's the whole point. It only registers when you welcome it."

"Some asshole went for my tit."

My mother said, "That wasn't supposed to happen."

"I think it was Manny Moldivan."

"That is so *not cool*."

"I pushed him away but he wouldn't back down so I mashed his balls."

One of them tittered.

"You shouldn't be laughing," my mother said.

"That wasn't a laugh. That was a titter."

"How should she be?"

"I peeked."

"You did?"

"Respectful," my mother said.

"You gotta report that motherfucker."

"I did."

"To Rick."

"Okay. Enough."

"Are you serious? You mean you actually cheated?" my mother said.

"On and off, yes, through the whole, you know..."

"...encounter."

"Encounter."

My mother said, "You weren't supposed to peek. This isn't nursery school."

"It was Manny. I'm positive. Now that I think of it."

"Well I peeked too."

"His sideburns felt like pubic hair."

My mother said, "Why?"

"I'm sure you peeked at some point."

My mother said, "No. I did not."

"Me neither."

"Not once," my mother said.

"I mean, that's how I knew it was Manny."

"Well I did, and so what. I don't appreciate your lecturing me."

"Confession?"

"This isn't Catholic school either," my mother said.

"I peeked too."

My mother said, "Wait. You mean all of you peeked?"

"I told you already. I did not peek."

"So then the three of you," my mother said, "peeked."

"Aw, what's the big deal?"

"She's right. We cheated."

"Must be grand to sit in judgment like this, especially when you're teacher's pet."

"Don't start," my mother said.

"I know a teacher's pet when I see one."

"Now ladies."

My mother said, "Stop."

"We all know who his favorite is."

My mother practically shouted, "I'm serious. Stop!"

It got quiet all the sudden. Pin-drop quiet.

One of them coughed.

"I really do relish these sensitivity sessions. They teach me so much. So much about myself and even more about the participants."

"We're too competitive."

My mother said, "And so what if I'm his pet? Hypothetically speaking. Everyone has favorites. It's ridiculous to think we come without judgments."

"I thought you wanted to drop this."

"Entirely too competitive."

"Not everyone has favorites."

"Group psychosis. Contagious hang-ups."

"You're right," my mother said. "Let's drop it."

"You're the one who keeps bringing him up."

"He told us this experience was personal and private."

My mother said, "He did. And I'm sorry."

"Are you listening, Toni?"

"And what does it matter anyway? He isn't here."

"She said she was sorry."

"What's with the look?"

"Does he even know we're rapping here tonight? Eating potato chips and smoking?"

My mother said, "Now you're the one who keeps bringing him up."

"Time to move on."

"Yes. Agreed. Let's be anything but predictable."

"It might help if you tried to masturbate."

"What a thing to say," my mother said.

"Not you. Her."

"What do you mean?"

"I'm only suggesting."

"This is exactly what I'm talking about."

"Is there any more coffee?"

"Right on."

"Who do you mean?"

"Samantha."

"Welp," my mother said. "We all have our perspectives."

"And our vibrators."

"How 'bout I make us more coffee?"

"Only instant left," my mother said.

"'Release from Sexual Tensions.' You aware of that book?"

"Revelatory."

"Life-changing."

"He got me to read it ages ago," my mother said.

"He actually lent me his personal copy. Signed by the author."

"I'm telling you. This is the diametric opposite of what he told us we should feel."

My mother said, "And what, oh flower child, did he tell us we shouldst feel?"

"Yes, if you would be so kind as to illuminate."

"Gratefulness."

"For what?"

"I would've remembered that," my mother said.

"Gratefulness. Plain and simple."

"I ain't got nuthin' to be grateful for, pumpkin."

"Except him."

"Except Rabbi."

"Except Rick."

"Yeah, Rick."

28

My mother dropped me off in front of the Warwick Apartments. "Bye, honey."

"Bye."

The heat was like a punch in the head.

My mother rolled her window down. "What time am I picking you up tomorrow?"

"Nine-forty-five. We talked about it. Thanks for the lift."

I put a yarmulke on and shouldered my backpack as her car pulled away in a cloud of cigarette smoke.

Rabbi Loobling's apartment building loomed up above. It was imitation Tudor, with beams in the façade and high brooding gables, a castle over Inverness Road in Phyllis's town of Beechwood. It made sense that he'd live in something Henry VIII because he went through life as if wearing a crown, mighty and pompous, with additional torque in his shoulders and spine to keep the crown from falling off. (I wondered if his pay was so yeshiva-teacher measly that he had no choice but to live in an apartment building instead of a moated castle, which was what he deserved.)

I looked straight ahead, and there he was, Gabriel, already yarmulka'd—permanently yarmulka'd?—about to buzz 8B.

(*Just this much,* I said to myself. I didn't know what it meant exactly but it seemed to mean everything that stifling afternoon. Be stronger? Braver? *Just this much.* Get Gabriel talking? *Just this much.* Get Gabriel to unassumingly remove all his clothes?

Just.

This.

Much.)

"Hey there, Gabriel."

His shoulders jumped. I'd startled him. He turned around. "Andy! Where did you come from?" He eased into a smile, sweat down his sideburns, pink in his cheeks. He wore a backpack over his shoulder too and a vented ivory polyester *Shobbis* suit.

"My mother just dropped me. Sorry I scared you. You want to walk a minute?"

"Sure. Where to?"

"Little over here."

I put an arm around his shoulders, surprised by my bravery *(just this much)* and by his bodily serenity, but I didn't let it linger. It was just

too

hot.

"Some temperature," he said—no shudders, no flinches—my move was only natural—and the pressure left a shimmer along my forearm. "I saw ninety-six degrees on the side of a bank just now," he said, "as I made my way over."

"You walked?"

"I did."

"Oh right. I forgot."

"I'm seven blocks that way."

We were almost at the back of the building. "Just a second of your time," I said. "We've got—" I looked at my watch. "—four whole minutes." I had an overheated suit on too, likewise polyester, though mine was fossil gray (see label). We were nearing a grass patch in front of a dumpster.

He said, "So Simon told you."

"What?"

"That I'd be here."

"Yes."

"Some coincidence."

"And how."

I put my backpack on the grass, bent to unzip a pocket and pulled out a joint and lighter. I smiled halfway and lit up the spliff.

"Oh man. You're kidding."

"This ain't no Salem 100," I said. I puffed on the joint about four or five times and exploded into a cough. "Cough-cough, cough-cough, cough-cough, cough-cough."

"Hold it in," Gabriel said. "That's right. Keep holding. Wait. Not yet."

"Cough-cough, cough-cough. Cough-cough, cough-cough."

"Easy there, bucko." He hit my back. He hit it again. He swirled his hand in a circle around the shoulders of my jacket then took away the hand.

"Out of practice," I rasped. It was my first time smoking pot. I didn't want him to know. I could still feel his hand in the middle of my back, like I had one-sixth of his love. I passed him the joint.

He turned it back and forth. "You get this from Simon?"

I nodded yes.

"I recognize the paper." It was cocoa brown with silver sprinkles. He took a couple tokes and held his breath, then released little syllables of exhaust in my direction, settling on my suit. He made a heep-heep sound as he re-inhaled some of the smoke then passed me back the joint.

"I am *not* out of practice," he said. (Huge smile.)

I was thrilled to be breaking the law with him, to be kissing where his lips had kissed, to be mingling our smoke. Which I held in my lungs. Which I'd learned to hold quickly. Which tasted like ashtray.

I let out the smoke in a chokeless gush. I was letting myself go. I was proud of being chokeless. But the pot seemed defective.

"I don't feel anything," I said.

"Not yet?"

"It's my first time buying from Simon, you know."

"His product is always quality, Andy. Don't worry. Relax. Your tolerance must be fierce."

"My tolerance? Oh yes." A flower fell. "Did you see that?"

"What?"

"A flower fell."

"Rhododendron," he said. "We've got tons of them in our garden. Only seven blocks that way."

An airplane rumbled.

A pigeon cooed.

A car stopped short, a Plymouth wagon. Tan on the outside, red on the inside.

"My mother's *jide* and *proy*," Gabriel said.

"Plymouth wagon?"

"Rhododendron."

"Where'd you get those?"

"Whats?"

"The freckles. Where'd they come from?"

"Milkman."

I snorted. "Never noticed them before."

"Never *had* them before."

"You're funny."

"I am."

"Those trees. So tall. Do you know what kind of trees they are?"

"Only that they aren't rhododendrons."

"I wish I knew the names of the trees," I said. "I mean, I know the names. Hickory, chestnut, cherry, elm. Sycamore, poplar, cedar, beech."

"Don't forget maple."

"Maple. Of course. But I couldn't pick them out in a lineup. Well, maple I could. As long as it had its leaves on."

"Don't forget oak."

"Okay. Oak. As long as it had its leaves on too."

"And weeping willow."

"The sky's pretty hazy."

"And pine."

"Is it lavender?"

"Wow."

"Look."

"It *is*. It's lavender. You think it'll rain?"

"Not until Sunday. Are there other names for sky? The heavens of course, and the wild blue yonder but. Oh. We're late." I looked at my watch.

"What else do you see?"

"It's more what I feel. My body's a footbridge. My mind is a river. We're lost in the woods and we've got to get to grandma's."

"You're wigged."

"I am."

We smoked back and forth.

We smoked forth and back.

I said, "What were we saying?"

"Bupkis," he said.

I stubbed out the joint on the bottom of my shoe and put it in my pocket.

"Now take. Take two." With a wizardly flourish he presented me with a packet of Fruit Stripe gum, like this was a magic trick. "We don't want Rabbi Busybody smelling it on our breaths."

I took two sticks, peeled off the wrappers and shoved them in my mouth. "Supposing he does?"

"Not very likely. Just being cautious. Dear rabbi's a might, well. Self-involved." He shoved two gums in his mouth as well.

I said, "Oh I've seen worse." The gum was delicious. It tasted like cake. I stuck the wrappers in my pocket. "I've had plenty of experience with self-involved rabbis."

"Oh right. Rabbi Landy."

"You know about him?"

"Rabbi Slick-Rick Landy of Montevideo, New Jersey."

"Seems like everyone in the universe knows about him."

"You go to his temple."

"Not anymore. How do you know about him?"

"Word gets around."

"And what pray tell is the word that's in circulation?"

"Hambone."

"They say that?"

"That he puts on a show. Like a holy-roller preacher."

"I didn't know that was public knowledge."

"Sure. What do you think?"

We were headed around to the front of the building without any prompting. We were telepathic synchronistic chewing-gum comrades.

He said, "Jeepers, it's hot."

And I said, "Atrocious."

"Loobling tends to blast the a/c. You'll like it. Come on."

"So you've been here before?"

"Couple times, yeah. We're practically neighbors."

I was surprised by my easiness. I was surprised I was relaxed around Gabriel Gottschall. I hadn't even considered I'd feel anything close to relaxed around him. But I was playing the part of my own good friend. Trying something different. Marijewana. Arm around shoulders. Casual chitchat. *Just this much.*

He buzzed the buzzer. We were buzzed in fast. "He can't wait for us," Gabriel said, grinning goofily, using a shoulder and hip to push the door in.

Then with deft theatricality, he stuck his nose in the air, smushed his pretty lips sideways and strode around the lobby with his arms up like a matador—"Gather round, insipid youngsters, and partake of my magnificence!" I snorted again. His Loobling imitation was hilariously accurate and we couldn't wait either and besides we were high.

We are high together, I thought. Gabriel and me. We're high as a unit. We're wedded in smoke, combined in titillation, refrigerated noodles, entranced by the lobby, entranced by the entrance.

I said, "We've walked into a palace."

"And lucky for us," Gabriel said, "it's cold enough for an emperor penguin."

It was all tall walls and tall stained glass and a statue of a man in an air-conditioned pelt holding a great stone book.

"Look at his jaw," I said. "Look at his lips. His nostrils. His eyelids. So realistic. Even the stockings, look, they have actual wrinkles."

"Beautiful," Gabriel said.

"It's like we were dropped down in Camelot."

"And King Arthur's up on eight."

We found ourselves in a box, zooming up.

Gabriel couldn't meet my eyes.

I said, "Don't."

"What?"

"Worry."

"I won't. I don't. I'm not. You worried?"

"A little."

"Just remember," Gabriel said. "Rabbi Loobling adores us."

An apartment door was directly in front of us. Rabbi Loobling swung it open before we could ring. It was true, he couldn't wait. He was out of breath like he'd just done push-ups. Or jumping jacks. Or a line of coke. He looked at us, one to the other, Gabriel and me. I reflected back the look. He had a bathrobe on and black shoes and socks and *possibly nothing underneath*.

"Shabbat shalom, gents." He touched our shoulders—Gabriel's; mine—and shook our hands. "I'm in the middle of getting ready. Excuse my *dishabille*. Turns out Sarah couldn't make it this weekend."

"Why not?" I said.

"Spending Shabbat with her sickly *eemah*."

Gabriel looked at me. "Her mother's a hypochondriac."

I grinned for no reason.

Then Loobling defaulted to his signature stare, boring holes in my forehead, in Gabriel's too, all molten eyes and maximal eyebrows. When I'd first gotten to know him and he looked at me like this, he was the rabbi of my dreams, breathing life into my meager existence. Now it just seemed like he wanted something from us. And he wanted it bad. But it was something we didn't have.

I turned to look at Gabriel.

Gabriel said, "That mother of hers. An absolute kvetch. They should put her in a home already."

Rabbi Loobling said, "Yes," then ducked his chin and perused his corpus. "Gotta put on some pants." But he didn't move. His chest hair sprouted out of the top of his robe—he was still a good-looking manly man—and a knee poked out of the slit up his thigh.

If he was trying to turn us on, I didn't get it. He was married. He was burly. He made references to a woman's womb ("it's shaped like an avocado") and her mons veneris ("a velvety artichoke"). Gay guys didn't talk like that. At least I didn't think they did. But the so-called wife—did she even exist? And what about his boner under the shower when I was a freshman? Was I remembering that right? He looked too vague, in any case, to be plotting a seduction. Maybe he was off kilter tonight because of his wife and not us. Because she wasn't around to cook the dinner, lay out his clothes, greet the guests.

Still masticating gum I said, "I'm sorry Mrs. Loobling bagged. I'd've loved to've met her."

"Well she's here in absentia," Rabbi Loobling said. "She cooked the meat."

"Very nice of her."

"I'd reserve my judgment."

The place smelled of brisket and the rabbi's shampoo. His hair was combed. His chin was chiseled. He said, "I bet you'd enjoy her. She's a very social animal. Unlike Yours Truthfully." His lips squooshed sideways.

What, I wondered. What if this weekend were his last-ditch effort to win me back before I graduated high school and slipped into the future? Why else had he answered the door in a robe with possibly nothing underneath? At one time, after all, we had shared something intimate—not easy to define but definitely sexy—including smacks in the face.

But why bring in Gabriel?

He masticated too.

There was geometric white and orange wallpaper in the hall, with snazzy arabesques of sizzling golden filigree lacing that twirled against the wall like the headdresses of a showgirl lineup on a stage in Las Vegas.

The wallpaper stopped at the start of the living room where Aaron was leading us toward still more dazzle: White recliner, white sofa, white pillows, white curtains, white credenza, white light. The adultness, the perfection, the style of white.

"Gee," I said. "This place is something!"

"It is," Loobling said. He motioned for us to sit on the sofa. "Shall we only speak Hebrew?" He sat in the recliner. *"L'dabair b'ivrit?"*

"Not happening, Loobling," Gabriel said, as the two of us sat.

I laughed.

Loobling sniffed.

And finally, the carpet. A lawn of white shag. Like something out of Double-o-seven.

The gum lost its flavor.

Gabriel said, "I've known Rabbi Loobling since I was seven years old. Can you believe it?"

"Oh right," I said.

"Oh right what?" Rabbi Loobling said. "How would you know that?" He crossed his legs with a cross of impatience, causing his bathrobe to open so high up his leg that you could see **half his scrotum!**

I swallowed my gum.

"Because he adds two and two," Gabriel said. "Don't listen to Rabbi Crab-ass." He clearly hadn't noticed the testicular peepshow.

I didn't know what to focus on so I focused on the shag. "I never pay attention to Rabbi Loobling," I said.

Rabbi Loobling said, "You used to."

I was dying to holler *Your balls are out!* and snicker at the dorkiness of black shoes and socks with naked legs showing, but my wish to snicker irked me.

Gabriel said, "What were we talking about? Just before? I can't remember. Oh. Um. Hey. Ahem." He pointed two fingers at Rabbi Loobling's nuts and said, "Criss-cross applesauce," like this was behavior he was used to.

Rabbi Loobling surveyed his outstretched body and closed his robe with a flick. He didn't fluster. He picked up a book.

◆ ◆ ◆

Later, Rabbi Loobling led us into the guest room.

"Relax a bit," he said. "While I put on my pants." He went back out.

Two army cots glowed in the dusky light that ricocheted off the parking lot a hundred feet down. The covers were folded open at angles, showing the sheets. My heart was banging. I slapped Gabriel's back. I said, "Ain't this peachy?" and flopped on a cot.

"Like summer camp," he said.

"Yeah. For sure." I'd never gone to summer camp.

"How's the head?" he said.

"Silvery. Shivery."

"Excellent," he said. "Rebbie's hot to trot tonight." He flopped down on the other cot and jiggled his knee.

"You think?"

"That's some samurai horndog outfit he's wearing."

"We caught him in the middle," I said.

"Yeah in the middle of jacking off. You notice how he was panting when he came to the door?" Gabriel threw a pillow at me. "You get a glimpse of the testis? World's biggest alley cat."

"Ha ha ha. But don't you think there's something, I don't know, a little cold about Rabbi Loobling?"

"Hot and cold is how I'd put it."

"What's that about?"

"Early dementia. Dementia praecox."

That made me laugh too. "And what's with the wife?"

"You heard. Sick mother."

"Have you stayed here overnight before?"

"Couple times."

"Really?"

"Jealous?"

"Not in the least. And Mrs. Loobling was always here on those occasions?"

"Sometimes yes, sometimes no."

It was a funny situation, a rabbi's relationship with his classroom favorites. It was always okay in the world of yeshiva—no questions asked, no whispers of anything—for a student to spend a *Shobbis* at his teacher's.

"You never told me any of this," I said.

"We hardly know each other, Andy. And why are you so fixated on Sarah Loobytunes anyway? I thought your focus was Aaron."

"It is. Well, it was. But not anymore."

"I get it. Believe me. No need to explain."

I thought: We'll be together in these cots tonight. Close enough to reach. Close enough to touch. To put our tongues in each other's mouths. (Although the thought of the tongues was sort of disgusting to be frank.)

Rabbi Loobling called us, "Ready, men?" and we went to meet him. He was standing at the door, adjusting his glasses in an entryway mirror. He said, "*Allons-y!*"

And Gabriel nodded.

And I said, *"Oui,"* thinking People behave automatically, with charm and grace, and their peoplehood enthralls me.

◆ ◆ ◆

Spring was like summer after tons of rain and a freezing April. We walked under trees in comestible colors—green-grape, parsley, iceberg lettuce—and though regret and reluctance and pine-green envy might be lurking around the corner, it was all just blank-slate insouciance now. The humidity had dropped. And it hadn't even rained.

We walked past chateaus and Cape Cods and ranches and houses with clapboards. The windows were eyes, the doors were mouths and all of them opened into immigrant bellies regardless of where the immigrants hailed from (Poland, Egypt, Biafra, the Mayflower) with children in driveways on scooters with squeeze pops.

Rabbi Loobling was bending a few steps ahead of us, into the twilight, shading the pavement, blue slate buckling.

"What are you thinking?" Gabriel said.

"The houses have faces."

"Exactly. What else?"

"Nothing."

"Come on. What's the condition of your soul?"

"Oh my soul. Oh that. I've been thinking about my soul. That I've let my soul flounder."

"All that's missing is the butter sauce."

"Plus some cut-up lemons."

"Sure but that's it."

"Recipe's simple." (Just this much.)

"We've got plenty of time."

"'Cause in the end we're just kids."

"You got that right."

Rabbi Loobling turned around and said, "What are you criminals philosophizing about?"

"The conditions of our souls," I said.

"Good."

◆ ◆ ◆

During services in a makeshift shul in a cardiologist's basement, I thought: Rabbi Loobling's soul is a pilot light, blue and even, always on. Gabriel Gottschall's soul is the incense sticks my sister burns when she bongs marijuana. And my soul is lickety-split and crunchy.

I didn't pray a word. I shuffled around, watching the *daveners*, men and boys, one of whom reminded me of myself as a boy, with squaresville specs and a baggy suit and a couple of hands he didn't know what to do with. He looked lonely and oppressed as he muttered to God and I wanted to pinch him.

Rabbi Loobling and Gabriel stood at opposite ends of me, blurring my edges, extending my radius.

◆ ◆ ◆

"Aaron's always talking about you," Gabriel said. "You're his number-one pet."

"He's right," the rabbi said into his soup.

"I tell him he ought to kidnap you," Gabriel said. "Or adopt you at least."

"Adopt," the rabbi said.

I said, "What else does the rabbi say about me?"

"That you're a living terror," Gabriel said.

"That's what I say," Rabbi Loobling said, slurping extra-thin noodles into his mouth.

Quickly, outrageously, I squeezed Gabriel's knee. Did it leave an impression, like a hand in a slab of kindergarten clay?

"He says, 'Gabriel,'" Gabriel said, "'I don't know what to tell you. That Andy's impossible.'"

"You are," Rabbi Loobling said.

"I can't be," I said. "I outgrew that a couple years ago. I'm no longer impossible. In fact, I'm quite possible. But Simon Mandell. Now he's what I'd call impossible."

"Oy," Rabbi Loobling said. "Simon."

Gabriel said, "Simon lives pretty close to here, you know."

"Yes," I said. "I know."

"My family's friends with his family," Gabriel said. "We used to vacation together. Both of our families. In the Catskills. In the sixties. Two rabbis and their families."

"And it was my wife," Rabbi Loobling said, "who brought us all together. She knows every rabbi who's ever had *smeecha* in a suburb in America. From Venice to Verona is how I like to put it." He lifted his bowl and slurped the remaining broth.

"From Venice, California to Verona, New Jersey," Gabriel said. "He's used that line before. Sarah's father's a rabbi too."

I said, "Everyone's connected to a rabbi but me."

"Oh you're connected," Rabbi Loobling said.

"Rabbis in Suburbia," Gabriel said. "Sounds like a cover story for National Geographic."

"But so Simon," I said, wanting to pick on Simon for some antipathetic reason.

"Bit of a pill," Loobling said. "But hey," he said to Gabriel. "He's your dearest friend, isn't he? I'm sorry for being a bitch."

Gabriel smiled. "Well ol' Andy and I might be better friends already."

Heaven's spaghetti.
I'm feeling unsteady.
Lots of nonsense in my confetti heady.

I mean, how could we be friends when we'd never really talked?

"Actually, I'm dating Simon's cousin," Gabriel said. "I've been dating her for a couple of months now. She goes to Ramaz."

"In the city?"

"Besh."

"Boodee boogly?"

"Nazz. Suppa tuppa."

The words made no sense.

Simon's cousin. That explained it. The girlfriend you never saw him with. The cousin who was his girlfriend. And she lived in the city, that was my guess, because Ramaz was in the city.

Everything I'd hoped for went swirling down the toilet.

◆ ◆ ◆

Gabriel used the bathroom first.

I stood pajamaed in the study, thumbing the bristles of my worn-down toothbrush, among a thousand spines of a thousand books—Maimonides, Jung, Buber, Emerson, Wilhelm Reich, Khalil Gibran, and of course Walt Whitman—in awe of Loobling's scholarship, in awe of the nearby fold-away cots and their visible topsheets, their tantalizing closeness, imagining Gabriel's preposterous girlfriend, overweight and hardly brilliant, pleading for his kisses on a fold-away cot.

The study ticked like a timebomb. The light from a lamp put a bull's eye on the ceiling.

Then Gabriel appeared in pajamas, barefoot, thumping his stomach, smelling like mouthwash. "All yours," he said, and he grinned as I passed, headed for the bathroom. (He threw out a force field that threw me off balance.)

Rabbi Loobling was out in the hallway, meanwhile, opposite end, belting a robe, pajamas underneath, brooding and huge in the dim of the apartment. You couldn't touch lights for twenty-seven hours so there was nothing we could do about the levels of darkness.

He said, "Come with me first," so I turned away from the bathroom and followed him into the living room where a lamp was set at its lowest setting.

Rabbi Loobling sat in the big white chair.

I sat in the circle of light on the sofa, toothbrush in my lap.

He wasn't the type to ease into things. "Are you frightened of me? Because if you are, I understand."

"I am not frightened."

He took a slow breath. "Well I am. Of you." He let out the breath.

Now I felt frightened. "How could you possibly?"

"Your arrogance, *boychik*. All that supposed brain power and you don't see shit. It's scary."

"I'm sorry. Really. I. Is this about the pot?"

He smiled stiffly.

"The marijuana," I said.

"What are you talking about?" He took off his glasses and rubbed between his eyes. "Your lack of self-awareness, that's what I mean. You're unaware of who you are. It's common at your age. You don't know your feelings. You're all corked up. I just thought you were further along than that. Sorry. My mistake."

Annoyance gurgled up to my throat, like horseradish and potatoes. "You don't know what you're talking about. I'm further along than just about everyone else in my class." The part about being all corked up made me flash to Rabbi Landy and his similar observation. Were these smart-aleck rabbis in cahoots somehow?

He squinted past my words, like they hadn't just clipped him. "And I know the whole story so let's not dance around it." He put his glasses on again. "You loved me with all your heart. Once upon a time. You expected me to save you. To rescue you like a handsome prince on a fairy tale sojourn to the fortress of our love. But that's impossible, Andy. Even a nine-year-old understands that he'll never be rescued by *anyone*." He tugged on the spot between his chin and his lower lip. "So I failed to live up to whatever you held me up to. And you threw in the towel. You jilted me. You had your reasons. You thought I didn't love you. But in truth, you had no choice. When you factor in that mother of yours."

"What's my mother got to do with it?"

He looked at me hard. "Because I loved you too."

He was going too fast.

Loved me too?

Handsome prince?

Expecting to rescue?

"Another few months and she'll be out of your hair," Rabbi Loobling said, like he hadn't just confessed his love for me, a confession I'd remember till the day I died. "Oh, and a word of advice about Misery Mama. Are you listening, Andrew? Because this is the *one thing* I'm telling you that you need to pay attention to." He looked at me ever so slightly cross-eyed. "She should sue Rabbi Landy. She's got a lawsuit against him. She's too far gone to see it, but she's got every reason to sue that Jew. And it's your responsibility, regardless of how you feel about her, regardless of how you feel about *me*, to persuade her to pursue this. It's the thing to do, the moral imperative, but she doesn't understand that. This is your first official adult obligation. To do something difficult that you're not exactly sure about."

"I've done plenty of things I'm not exactly sure about."

He wouldn't stop going. "Another few months and she'll be out of your hair." He smiled like a fatcat condescending to a panhandler. "Just don't end up dead in the gutter to spite her."

"What's that supposed to mean?"

He fidgeted one of his bathrobe cuffs. "You uh. You stirred something in me that I thought I'd gotten rid of."

The sofa cushions were rising around me. I longed to return to three years back when I could've altered how our friendship went by keeping my distance.

"It isn't ethically wrong," he said. "My only transgression was in almost—*almost*—taking action on those feelings." He looked at me. "With you, I mean. Andy."

I fingered the stiffened toothbrush bristles.

"Oh Andy," he said. "Thank God I didn't."

I looked at him courageously. "I wouldn't have minded."

He examined his hands. "Stop talking. Please. You don't know what you're saying. You no longer love me. That's all I know. You can't pretend otherwise." His face got dark, all eyebrows and chaos. "I tried it myself. I had a boy lover. Long before Sarah. Way back in college. But it just wasn't worth it. It was morbid. It was horrid. All that testosterone. All that hair. You mustn't judge me harshly. Sarah knows everything. We don't have secrets. There are things about her that'd shock you too. But Andy." He extended his hand, not for the taking, it seemed, but to tease me. "Don't do it. I'm warning you. You'll end up dead in the gutter. Trust me." Rabbi Loobling got up.

I said, "Don't do what? I don't understand."

He stopped. He sighed.

I looked at him looming in the caramel lamp light. He might've been grimacing or grinning or scoffing, it was difficult to see.

"Watch out for the roughnecks, that's all I ask."

"I don't know any roughnecks."

"Don't be naive. You know what I'm saying."

His phrases cut like hedge clippers.

...you don't see shit...

      ...I had a boy lover...

           ...I loved you too...

                  ...dead in the gutter...

"Rough trade," he said. "Ever hear of that expression? Cruisin' for a bruisin'? Bondage and discipline?"

I wondered if Rabbi Loobling had brought me home for *Shobbis* just to horrify me like this. I said, "What does that have to do with me? I never met any people like that."

"You will. It's inevitable."

My heart was clanging like a broken bell. He was a person I didn't know anymore, someone frightening and frightened. Where had this come from? I made myself courageous again. I said, "I don't like how you're talking to me."

The lamp went off. I smacked my chest. Rabbi Loobling had a *Shobbis* clock. All those rabbi types had them. Timers to make their rooms go dark.

"Just a friendly warning. That's all this is."

"You don't sound friendly."

"Then call me a vicious queen," he said. And he walked away, gone in the dark.

I felt sideswiped, disappointed, pissed off, confused. I'd never heard the expression before but it was easy to guess its meaning. What did he have to be vicious about? Why did he think he was a feminine queen? I'd never imagined him as anything but masculine.

I decided right then that I'd take off my clothes, including my underpants, and leave the covers down in the cot next to Gabriel's. I'd seduce him that night, wake him if I had to, moaning and turning. Who cared if Simon's cousin was his hard-up girlfriend? I was sure he was ready. Rabbi Loobling was a chicken. And Gabriel, it turned out, was a cooperative dog.

Mirror Mirror
1972

29

Diabolically hot and humid conditions lasted sixteen days in a row that July, and I had nothing to do but bask in front of the air-conditioner (in the living room icebox, containing the only a/c in our dismal apartment), reading *The Exorcist* and *My Name Is Asher Lev* and watching movies in installments like *Bye Bye Birdie* and *The Snake Pit* on the Million Dollar Movie. My mother hounded me a few times a day to get a summer job (which I eventually got—although not until the last-ditch last half of August—selling magazine subscriptions door to door). But in the meantime, I had plans to hound *her* about the task Rabbi Loobling had suggested I hound her about.

I just had to find the moment.

"Hiya sweetie," she said as she entered the living room after her drive home from work. She dropped her bag and keys with a thump and a jangle on a worn-out sofa cushion. She lit a cigarette.

"Hi," I said.

"Nice and cool in here." She looked at the TV, blowing smoke. She came a little closer, then backed away slightly, like she was parallel-parking her carcass. No matter the situation, she was always—at least a little—putting her body on display. She had on a lightweight periwinkle shirtdress because she couldn't wear shorts or capris on the job. "Oh," she said. "*BUtterfield 8*. I'm surprised it's on in the daytime. This in two parts?"

"Three."

Elizabeth Taylor was looking miffed in a flamboyant lynx-and-cashmere concoction as she perused a fan of callgirl cash that Laurence Harvey had left her, along with a snotty note. It was odd to see a woman festooned in a fluffy fur-collar fantasy in the middle of our actual heatwave.

"What's for dinner?" I said.

"I bought Chicken Delight. A chicken and a shrimp." (Naomi was out with her guitar-strumming boyfriend, and Toby was overnighting at a pal's with central air.) "Don't get up," my mother said. (I hadn't made a move to get up.) "I'll bring it. We can eat in here. The dining room's a furnace. Want Pepsi?"

"There isn't any."

"I bought some, silly," she said, going out.

Commercials were on when she came back in with a big brown bag, plastic cups and a paperboard cylinder of soda. The cigarette was jittering in her mouth and the smoke was stinging her eyes. She put the dinner down on the coffee table and twisted the cigarette out in the supersize Gulf Oil boomerang ashtray that no one had emptied in weeks.

"Which would you like? Chicken or shrimp? Or you want to just share?"

"Shrimp," I said.

I heard sudden hard plops of rain on the air-conditioner. Thunderstorms had been forecast and they were about to roll in.

My mother lifted the lids, passed the containers, poured out the soda and said a little angrily through a margarine commercial, "Would you lower that thing?"

I turned the TV off.

"Wha'd you do that for?" she said.

"I want to talk to you about something."

Maybe the plops of rain were too loud for her to hear me, because she acted like I hadn't said anything. "Dig in," she said. We had to lean forward to accommodate the coffee table. The room smelled of deep-fried animal and vegetable. "Oh." She felt around and then tossed me a packet. "Tartar sauce. You'll need more than that."

"I never use tartar sauce."

"You do. I've seen you."

"You're thinking of someone else."

She waggled her fingers, as if to wave away the distraction. "God, that office. Such a madhouse today. All because of that leak in the rectory. You'd've thought they were patching a hole in the Sistine Chapel. All that arguing and screaming, not to mention the kvetching about the heat and humidity." She continued to work half days, answering phones and typing homilies for the pink-faced priests at Immaculate Conception. "Father Quinn can be such a class-A priss."

I expressed no interest in her hard day at work. (Her hard half-day.) Or her hint that Father Quinn was less than a Real Man.

"So," she therefore pivoted, squeezing ketchup out of a packet onto her pile of french fries, "did you work today? Did you try to look for work today? Did you try to look for work the day before yesterday?"

The sky had turned purple. The heatwave was breaking. The rain exploded into a rattle on the air-conditioner.

I took a quick breath. This wasn't the time for her comedy. "It's about Rabbi," I said. I couldn't pull the breath down deep enough to fill my chest. "That's what I wanted to talk to you about."

"Rabbi? Really? You mean he's helping you find a job?"

"This isn't easy to talk about. I think you know what I'm going to say."

She smiled. "I don't." She held a ketchup-covered fry in front of her mouth but waited to put it in.

"He abused you."

"Who?"

"He's a monster. He's horrible. And I'd say you have the right, maybe even the *obligation*, to sue that creep."

"What are you talking about?" She popped the fry in her mouth. "Rabbi Rick? Gee, Andy." She chewed it and swallowed it, then popped another in her mouth. "Rabbi Rick is a wonderful person. You know that. He's done only wonderful things for me. Ever since I've known him. He's helped me so much. He's helped *us* so much. The whole damn family. He's even helped you in terms of being a boy. How dare you talk such gibberish."

The rain turned abruptly torrential, like jackhammers breaking up sidewalk.

I said, "What he's done to you is criminal."

"What he's done to me. How do you know what he's done to me?"

"You're going to have to deal with this at some point. You're already starting to deal with it, I can tell. Otherwise you'd've left the room."

"Enough, Andy. It's dinnertime. Put the movie back on."

"He's a rabbi. And a therapist. Both of those jobs have codes of ethics. And you were his patient. He has to pay for what he's done to you. Including monetarily." I began to gobble shrimp, like this was a shrimp-eating contest, shrimp after shrimp, pulling out the tails. At last I'd broached the topic and my appetite was surging.

"I'm not going to sue Rabbi Landy, come on now. What are you, crazy?"

"I have a duty to speak the truth about him."

"Close your mouth when you eat."

"No one else is prepared to do it."

"You have no idea what you're talking about. Rabbi Landy never hurt me. I said close your mouth, it's disgusting."

"You can sue him and get his license revoked."

"Oh no. No sir. Never. Ridiculous. *You're* ridiculous. I couldn't do that to Rabbi."

"What about what he's done to *you*?"

"Oh shut up about that. Enough. I'm serious."

"Just think about it."

"No."

"You have to."

"I won't."

"Why not?"

"Because."

"Because why?"

"Because."

"Because *why*?"

She shouted—"Because!"—out of nowhere. It must have been building up in her. Then, more quietly: "Because." And even quieter: "I'd lose. Okay? All right? You satisfied?"

"What else?"

"You're a nosy shit, you know that? My dinner's getting cold." She put her fingertips on the chicken. "It has in fact *gotten* cold." She slid the dinner away from her, bleeding grease on the cardboard platter.

"What else?" I repeated.

"Just leave me alone." She wiped her fingertips on a stiff little napkin and put the napkin on the meat. "I refuse to discuss this..."

"Why so stubborn?"

"...especially with you."

"Why especially me?"

"Because." She sniffed, cleared her throat, lowered her head maybe twenty degrees. "I can't afford to lose your respect."

"That's a new one," I said.

"You're the only one who knows me. You have that insight."

"Naomi knows you."

"Naomi hates me. If you hate me, you don't know me."

"Naomi knows the rabbi story as well as I do. No. She knows it better."

"She doesn't understand me. You do. Because we're...similar. You and I."

I hated that Siamese mother-son crap of hers. I'd hated it forever, dating back to the time when my father ran off. I said, "Most of the time I hate you too."

My mother sighed. "Not as much as Naomi does."

"And the rest of the time I'm pissed at you."

"Andy—honey—"

"Just think about it," I said.

"I won't. I told you. Now leave me alone."

"You really can't lose."

"How do you know?"

"I know quite a bit."

"He's the one with the power. It's my word against his."

"No, it isn't. You have those, well." As repulsive as the topic was, I had to bring it up. "Those transcripts."

"Those whats?"

"Of your sessions with him."

"Oh God."

"You left them out in the open."

"I most certainly did not."

"Be that as it may."

"Where do you get the chutzpah to mention those pages?"

"It was you who left them lying around like the damn Reader's Digest."

"I could murder you, I swear to God. You meddling son of a bitch. You snotty little know-it-all."

"You snotty little know-it-all…"

"And it's a moot point anyway."

"…I'm so tired of hearing you call me that."

"It's moot because they're gone."

"Gone?"

"Stop it already. You sound like a parrot. I burned them," she said. "I burned them a million years ago. Now get out of my way."

She stood up, pushed me aside and left the room.

First there was the thunder. Which was followed by the lightning.

"Oh shit," I heard her say. "All the windows are open."

30

Three Years Later

At her dining room table with the ketchup-stained tablecloth, dusted with Frito crumbs and cigarette ash, my mother said, "There's going to be a trial. Two Mondays from now. I thought you all should know. A suit against the rabbi." She fidgeted with her skinny-banded Twist-O-Flex wristwatch, nearly breaking it in two.

"Holy cow," Naomi said. "When did you decide this?"

"Finally," I said. "I'm proud of you, Mom."

"How can you bring a suit against a rabbi?" my brother Toby said.

"Which rabbi are we talking about?" Naomi's husband Nate said. "There always seem to be so many."

We were gathered at my mother's for an early Saturday dinner of takeout Polynesian. It was her forty-fourth birthday. We were onto the dessert course, wedges of Entenmann's Louisiana crunch cake that had been topped with a single candle, now blackened like a fuse and lying on its side in the cake box. My mother had waited till dessert to drop the bomb, so she could avoid a big discussion.

"I hope you win a ton of money," Naomi said. "It's time you got your revenge on that gutless asshole. It's time you got your dignity back." She had platinum streaks in her fluffed-up hair, which made it look like a coconut mousse bomb. "Your dignity and your sense of humor."

I said, "I knew you'd take my advice at some point. I'm glad you broke down and listened to me."

My mother said, "This has nothing to do with you, Andy." Her hair, on the other hand, was flat and dyed black, like the soy sauce in the packets still strewn across the table.

I said, "I must've had a teeny bit of influence."

My mother ignored me. "They're telling me the trial should run to four days tops."

I left it alone. Her self-esteem was shaky. She couldn't accept the indignity of such a major life decision (court case targeting powerhouse rabbi) having come from someone else (me). Well, that's how I saw it.

Toby said, "Will somebody please explain to me what the heck is going on here?"

Nate said, "Is this that rabbi you're always talking about?"

Naomi said, "Yeah. Rabbi Rick."

I was renting a room in the city at the time, a sophomore at Columbia with a shelving job at the library, and Naomi was a waitress on Restaurant Row, married for a-year-and-change to her high school boyfriend Nate Malinowski, an attractive, thick-waisted magazine typesetter and part-time guitarist with an interest in astrology. They were also in the city, in a Murray Hill highrise, with a partial view of the Empire State Building. Toby was in the seventh grade at a Montevideo middle school with a rotten reputation and had lost twenty pounds, lifting weights and skipping desserts, because there were girls on the horizon.

(Both he and Naomi were a hundred percent unsqueamish about my gayness. My mother was ninety-five.)

"Four days tops," Naomi said. "That's not very long for a case this consequential."

"Yeah," I said. "And why are you only just telling us now? Less than three weeks beforehand?"

"Are you telling us because you want us in the courtroom?" Naomi said. "To kind of paper the house?"

"You'd better not come," my mother said. "I'm warning you both. I'm warning all four of you."

It was easier for us to focus on her eleventh-hour disclosure business than on the details of the rabbi's sex crimes.

"Why do you all keep talking about a lawsuit?" Toby said. He had a plate of uneaten cake set in front of him because no one had remembered not to serve him something sugary.

"Either you want us in the courtroom," Naomi said, "or you want to piss us off. Unless you want us to talk you out of it."

I said, "You don't have to do it if you're reluctant to, Ma. No one would blame you for dropping the charges."

My mother said, "Christ almighty."

Toby said, "Would you all please be quiet for two fucking seconds and tell me what's going on here?"

There was a minor shock of silence.

Naomi said, "Take him home with you, Nate. I'll get the bus back later. Go play knock-hockey with him or something." Toby had arranged to stay the night with Naomi and Nate in Manhattan. He'd been finding it increasingly difficult to be alone with our mother, in her rarely cleaned apartment, for longer than a Monday-to-Friday.

Our mother said, "He's not a little boy. He's twelve."

"Thirteen," Toby said. He actually looked eleven, with his cleaned-up nerdy astronaut haircut and all the flab sloughed away from his middle and dewlap.

"He's old enough to figure out what went on between me and Rick," my mother said. "You must've had *some* inclination."

"Oh that," Toby said. "I'm not old enough, you're right. And I'm not interested enough either."

Naomi said, "Take him."

Nate ignored her. "If this is about what I think it's about, then it all makes perfect sense, Bea. It's typical of Libra with Mercury in retrograde. This is a time for transformation. A season of self-care. And a return to neglected projects."

"No kidding," my mother said.

"I looked it up for your birthday."

"That was sweet of you."

"And when you throw in the lawsuit—wham. No surprise. Libras are big on vengeance."

Naomi swatted his shoulder.

Nate said, "Ouch," though he wasn't hurt.

"Well, here's the story," my mother said. "And this has nothing to do with my horoscope—no offense, Nate—or any kind of birthday realization or the onset of early menopause or—" She looked at me. "—your wise and witty influence. I'm pursuing the suit because of that stink over Toby's bar mitzvah."

"I already told you," Toby said. "I never wanted a bar mitzvah."

"Of course you did," Naomi said. "You could've had a party. A very big party. In *your* honor. With all your friends at little tables and all those fifty-dollar savings bonds worth thirty-seven fifty."

Toby said, "Not everyone gets excited about a party in their honor."

"Not to mention the finger sandwiches," Naomi continued, "and the cantaloupe balls and the chopped liver sculpture in the shape of the Ten Commandments."

Toby said, "I don't enjoy Hebrew and I dread giving speeches."

"Oh no one enjoys Hebrew, baby boy," Naomi said.

"In any case," my mother said, "*I*, for one, wanted you to have a bar mitzvah. Or the option to choose not to have a bar mitzvah."

I wondered if she hadn't wanted the bar mitzvah for herself, so she could prove to Sisterhood hotshots like Nona Tower and Felicia Flamm that she wasn't a worthless penniless nympho.

"But I lied to you," she said. "It wasn't because I couldn't afford it. That was my cover-up excuse. Because Father Quinn had said he would pay for it. I couldn't believe what an angel he was. And I was all prepared to accept his offer. I even asked Rabbi Kornspan which Saturdays would be good for him. But instead of consulting his calendar and saving the date, which is what Rabbi Landy would've done, he said I'll get back to you in a couple of days."

Rabbi Landy had left the temple in '73 to pursue his private therapy practice and teach more classes at Unami U. And so the temple ended up with Irving Kornspan.

"When I didn't hear back from Kornspan," my mother said, "I called him again. He sounded uncomfortable. I asked him what was wrong and he said, 'Oh, um,' like a milquetoast petunia. 'The powers-that-be would prefer it if you didn't *utilize their facilities* for your son's bar mitzvah.'"

"Why not?" Toby said.

Naomi said, "Think about it."

My mother said, "I was blackballed, just like that. Because of. Well."

"Don't tell me," Toby said. "I don't want to know."

"Because of the rabbi situation. Because of what *I* had done to Rick, not what *he* had done to me. I was forbidden the use of their sanctuary and social hall, when all I wanted was to celebrate the ritual passage into manhood of my youngest child. That was the final straw."

I looked at my brother. He was pulling a piece of tattered paper out of his wallet.

"I was furious," my mother said. "And still am, damn it. That's why I'm siccing the law on him."

"Let's go, Nate," Toby said, with a finger on the schedule. "There's a bus in exactly seventeen minutes."

Nate winked at Toby—they were excellent buddies—and said, "I bought a Liberty quarter I've been meaning to show you. Let's blow this ice tea stand."

I said, "You shouldn't take it personally, Toby."

My mother said, "Right. I'm the one those hypocrites wanted to crucify. You were just a stand-in, a scapegoat. And when I understood how hungry they were to exploit *my son* and make *me* the scapegoat, I remembered what you'd said, Andy. Long time back. That I had an *obligation* to sue that schmuck. A mother can only take so much."

Toby said, "Interesting story. You ready, Nate? We better get going."

Naomi said, "See? You've upset him so much he doesn't know what to say."

"I'm not upset," Toby said. "I already knew I never wanted a bar mitzvah. Right now, I've got a bus to catch."

"This is no longer just about you, Mother," Naomi said.

"Of course it isn't just about me. That's what I've been trying to explain to you kids. That's what I've gotten so pissed and enraged and litigious about."

"This is about Toby," I said, "Naomi's right, and what you thoughtlessly deprived him of. This is about the fallout of your over-the-top self-centered behavior."

"Why are you two ganging up on me? And on my birthday, for Christ's sake?"

Toby broke the ensuing silence by getting up and saying, "Well folks, gotta go." He hugged my mother, said see-ya to Naomi and me (mouthing "thanks for sticking up for me"), grabbed his jacket and ran for the bus with Nate.

After the door slammed shut, Naomi said, "Huh."

My mother shook her head in bewilderment. "What?"

"Just huh," Naomi said.

Dead air.

Decimated air.

I said, "I would've expected a civil damages trial. Where a judge made all the decisions."

Naomi said, "Me too."

We were thrown off balance. We'd banged our heads against a bunch of sharp corners: the shock of the blackball, the shame of the scandal, our brother's humility.

Naomi said, "What a doozy of a birthday present."

"Indeedy doozy," my mother said.

"Yeah. And anyway. Even if you wanted us to sit in the audience," Naomi said, "I couldn't possibly get off work."

"And I've got class every day except Friday," I said. "All through the semester."

"I don't want either of you to come. I believe I've made that clear. And it's a gallery, not an audience. This isn't a performance of *Hello, Dolly!*"

◆ ◆ ◆

Next day I caught this in the *Times*.

THE NEW YORK FUCKING TIMES!

SEX TRIAL AGAINST MONTEVIDEO RABBI STARTS IN TWO WEEKS
By Caroline Schumacher

In two weeks, a Montevideo rabbi and marriage counselor goes on trial in Mackinac County Court after being charged with using questionable methods in his psychotherapy sessions with a female patient.

Rabbi Richard Landy, 48, is accused of gross malpractice with the patient between 1966 and 1970. He allegedly pressured the patient (whose name is being withheld by the court) to remove her blouse and allow him to touch her sexually, and to engage in masturbation, oral sex and sexual intercourse with him. The suit claims that the defendant insisted that the patient have extramarital sex with him and as a form of "surrogate love."

Within the first several psychotherapy visits, the petition claims, Landy "made comments of a sexual nature and told the patient that if he put his hand inside her blouse and touched her breasts she would no longer feel emotionally cold."

In subsequent visits, the petition says, Landy hugged the woman "in an intimate fashion," began to "touch her sexually" and ultimately engaged in "sexually intimate touching, masturbation and oral and penetrative sex."

In addition, the petition claims that Landy told his accuser that "she had a beautiful body and he would like her to pose in the nude someday, so he might photograph her." He allegedly urged her to have regular intercourse with him, saying it would help "overcome her fear of men."

Finally, the petition states that while Landy often referred to himself as "Dr. Landy," his doctorate in philosophy comes from a West Virginia university not recognized by the New Jersey Education Department.

Landy faces additional scrutiny from his religious peers, although Rabbi Joshua Sanford, executive vice-president of the Rabbinical Foundation in Manhattan, the international association of conservative rabbis, confirmed that Landy is still a member in good standing. Rabbi Sanford said he had heard nothing about the allegations.

❖ ❖ ❖

I read the story over the phone to Naomi who wasn't a newspaper reader.

"What a slime," she said. "What a scumbag. I can't wait to see him completely humiliated, convicted to the fullest extent and gunned down by a firing squad. It's an open-and-shut situation, Andy. Just listen to what he did to her."

"*Allegedly* did to her. I don't think these cases are so easy to prosecute. It's Rabbi Landy for Pete's sake."

"Oh. Right. Mister Pretty Boy Mezuzah-witz. This'll be hard on her, Andy. I know I said I wanted to be there for the trial, but I don't think I could stand it."

"Me neither."

"Now that every fucking body on the whole fucking planet's going to know about Mom and Rabbi."

"But she isn't named in the article."

"That doesn't mean the Sisterhood vultures won't figure out who she is. Oh, and while I think of it. Don't tell Toby."

"No, you're right. It could scar him for life."

Naomi mumbled, "Like that woman hasn't already scarred *me* for life."

The two of us were close again, for the first time since we were little, because we were both paying rent in Manhattan—one uptown, one downtown—and it was easy for us to meet in the middle—for coffee and a danish, for three-dollar seats to Bette Midler at the Palace, for a budget-busting dinner at Mamma Leone's—leading to hour-long phone calls (eventually daily) and no holding back on opinions and kinship. Naomi's husband Nate was so easygoing, he never got in the way. Plus he worked weird hours due to the typesetting.

"My concern right now," I said, "is how to follow this thing. It isn't likely the *Times*'ll publish a summary every morning of the previous day's proceedings."

"Yeah, it isn't Watergate. But why are you so nosy for details?"

"Aren't you?"

"All I'm concerned about is seeing that that degenerate gets his—hey. Wait a second. Wasn't it you who encouraged her to proceed with this suit in the first place?"

"Yeah. So? You knew that already."

"Long time ago, right? Telling her how important it was for that rat to be brought to justice? And to pay her a juicy settlement? What made you so astute back then?"

"One of my teachers."

"One of those holy-roller beard-o boys?"

"No no. Rabbi Loobling."

"Oh. The one you had a crush on."

"I didn't have a crush on Rabbi Loobl—"

"Andy. Please. Not at this stage of the game. What did he say? Come on now. Tell me."

"Oh only that he'd heard some kind of gossip through—now *you* wait a second. How do you know about Rabbi Loobling?"

"What do you mean, how do I know? You used to talk about him."

"No I didn't. Not to you. You and I didn't talk to each other in 1969."

"Okay. Well. How should I put this? I used to rifle through your diary on occasion."

"You what?!"

"You used to rifle through mine as well. I could tell from the disarrangement. And the Scooter Pie crumbs. Don't get all hypocrite on me."

"Oh God. This is so—so—"

"Ridiculous?"

"Cringe-worthy."

"Ridiculous and cringe-worthy. Like Shelley Winters in *Poseidon Adventure*. Now come on, brother. Tell me. What did Loobie Lovebug say?"

"Oh I don't—let me—you truly are the worst, you know. What were we saying?"

"Loobling."

"Loobling."

"That he seemed to know about Landy."

"Yeah, that there was some kind of nasty rabbinical gossip. That they knew he was a showman. And a charlatan. And a holy roller."

"Elmer Gantry type," my sister said.

"Exactly. Turns out this secretive little rabbi world is shockingly incestuous. Rabbi Landy might've been gossiped about for years."

"Meaning they already knew about his monkey business with Mom, no doubt, no question."

"I really couldn't say. Rabbi Loobling didn't go that far."

"And what are your current thoughts about Loobling? Still starry-eyed after all these years?"

"That was high school, Naomi. We stopped being close a couple years ago."

"Lovers' quarrel?"

I sighed exaggeratedly.

"I'm sorry for being obnoxious," she said. "You did Mom a good turn by encouraging this lawsuit."

"I'm not so sure anymore."

"Why not?"

"Over one million people read the *Times* every morning."

◆ ◆ ◆

Funny thing was…just that night, after three years of silence, after the horror story he'd scared me with, three Shavuoses earlier, about his traumatizing homo-criminal college-age dalliance, Rabbi Loobling called me up.

I answered the phone in the hallway of the musty apartment where I rented a room. "Hello?" Small silence. "Who is this?"

He spoke as if we'd talked just yesterday. "You see the article in the *Times*?"

"Rabbi Loobling! Hi. How did you get my number?"

"Your brother. Sweet fella. So your poor old ma's going through with it. Finally."

I hesitated. "Yes." So this was how it started. With the whole fucking planet knowing the whole fucking story. "My mother is in fact going through with the case."

"Thanks to you, *boychik*," Rabbi Loobling said. "Or rather, thanks to me. You would never have had the wherewithal to encourage her to do this if I hadn't encouraged you first, if I hadn't stressed the imperative—the moral imperative—of seeking justice for his crimes."

Whatever, I thought.

I hadn't revisited the idea of a lawsuit over the past three years because she'd told me flat out she had no interest in legal remedies. And it wasn't my concern to begin with. The concern was Rabbi Loobling's. He was the catalyst, he was right. And yes, it was a milestone for me to do as he'd suggested and act like an adult without self-interest and pressure my mother into suing Rabbi Landy. But I was still after all a self-interested teen with a lot of other things on my mind.

I said, "How did you know it was my mother bringing the case? She isn't identified in the article."

"Self-evident, comrade," Rabbi Loobling said.

I muttered, "This is awful."

"One of the pitfalls of being the progeny of scandal. You'd better get used to it. Anyway. To the point. The soon-to-be defendant? I know all about him."

"What do you mean?"

"I worked at his summer camp, back when I was in college. Little setup in the Finger Lakes, Camp Nefesh Yehudi. I was a counselor there for the summers of, let's see, '59 and '60. I saw him every day up there. At flagpole, at breakfast, at general swim."

"How come you never told me this?"

"And it was common knowledge that Rabbi Landy was having affairs with a bunch of the female counselors. Sixteen- and seventeen-year-olds. All underage. Stautory rape. And he was executive director of the camp for fuck's sake. He'd go skinny-dipping, regularly, with one of the female counselors—a teenager, Andy. Name of Jennifer Teplin. And I saw him in bed once, in one of the bunks, with another teenage female counselor after lights out—porking her. Schmekel in pussy. Sixteen years old. Name of Reena Zabarovsky."

"Why do I need to know this?" I said. "And how did you witness such a scene in the first place?"

"I was O.D. that night—on duty—patrolling the camp with a flashlight. I heard noises in the bunk. Sounds of a struggle. I was obliged to investigate. And there in the high-beam I saw his empurpled rabbinical pintle battering the twat of an underage counselor."

"Okay. All right. You established that already."

"Right there in the Finger Lakes."

"Did you tell Rabbi Landy what you witnessed that night?"

"I did. Twice. First time he told me to mind my own business. My own *fucking* business. Second time he told me if I mentioned it again I'd be fired from the camp. Rabbi Landy, if you please. With his spouse by his side on the rusticated premises. I am telling you now to assure you, dear Andy, that your mother has a case. A winnable ethics misconduct case. Rick's misdeeds did not occur in a vacuum. This is not a lost cause."

"Thank you............I guess."

"What do you mean you guess?" Rabbi Loobling sounded chapped.

"Because I honestly don't know now. I'm feeling like I probably shouldn't have encouraged her in the first place. I'm having second thoughts, especially after that *Times* thing, God."

"The truth is the truth. It's got to come out."

"But so public. So embarrassing. Makes me wish I'd never planted the idea in her head."

"So in other words you blame me."

"Why would I blame you?"

"Because I was the primal planter."

"I don't blame you, of course not."

"In any event." He sounded pissed.

"You're not even listening. I said I didn't blame you."

"The lawsuit is following its natural course. When it's this far along, the brakes don't work on the wheels of justice. But remember. Rabbi

Landy leaves a trail of moral villainy that features statutory rape, Andrew, a felony in this state—and your mother ought to exploit that."

"What good is it if you just tell *me*? The only way your story'll make any difference is if you testify at the trial."

"Oh. Well."

"Kind of last minute, true, but I'm sure you could finagle it. You're very persuasive. Probably just a phone call or two."

"I couldn't swing that. No. No sir. Sorry Charlie."

"Why not?"

"Ah. See. A rabbi could never do such a thing. Not to another rabbi. He could never bear witness against a fellow professional."

"Come on. I studied the Talmud. I studied the Talmud with *you*. Rabbis were always doing whatever they wanted to other rabbis, mocking them, discrediting them, like those wiseguys at a Friars Club roast."

"So in other words I'm a wuss."

"I didn't say that."

"But you were thinking it. And before this phone call's over, I'll be a coward in your eyes for refusing to take the stand. A coward and a wuss and, while we're at it, a perjurer."

"Why are you talking like this?"

He inhaled deep and exhaled deeper. "Because you don't understand one iota of what I'm going through. It's always been the same with you. The same bloody thing all over again. You claim to see everything when you don't see shit."

He was getting under my skin in that way I'd learned to resent. Self-aggrandizing and manipulative. He really was a weirdo.

And when had I ever professed to *See Everything*?

So I let it rip with the first thing I thought of. "What I don't understand is why you talked to me the way you did, that last time we were together, about ending up dead in the gutter." If he didn't watch what he said to me, why should I watch what I said to him? "I realize it was a very long time ago—old news already—but it had a terrible effect on me. It was like all of the sudden I had this redneck for a father, a queer-bashing John Wayne asshole type, and he was casting me down into the fires of hell."

I could hear him open his mouth and close it. Was he holding back from scolding me? Wondering how to defend himself? Trying not to blow his top? His mood swings were always so hard to predict. "First of all," he said. "I am not your father. Second of all." His tone was practically normal now, no defensiveness, no scolding. "You may have heard about this. About my tenure at Birnbaum. From which I was abruptly dismissed for allegedly running naked through the halls of the yeshiva, exclaiming inarticulately."

"I—yes. I heard about that. Well, something like that. Different variations. I never knew what to think. It made me sad for you."

A gay thing, I thought. (Not the first time I'd thought it.) His forbidden desires had been piling up inside him, in his heart and in his penis, and resulted in a naked freakout. Was he about to let me in on his crushing inner struggles? Would he proceed from these particulars to his intimate feelings after I'd left him my love note in 1969, and the fascinating story of how those feelings scared the shit out of him? No wonder he'd told me gay life was deadly. He'd been twisted and perverted. And now all he wanted was to ask for my forgiveness.

But instead he said, "I'm afraid that behavior could come back to bite me in a courtroom situation."

"Wait. Really?"

"They'll discredit my testimony by bringing up that incident, my full-frontal crack-up, and my subsequent stay in the loony bin. Only a couple of days, but that won't matter."

"Look," I said. "If you want to testify, testify."

"You don't understand. I suffered a nervous breakdown."

"So what. It wasn't a crime."

"Question of character. Question of witness reliability."

"You've always been well-regarded as a teacher. That's not nothing."

Of course he had a point. Of course he wanted to protect his reputation, despite what the gossips had done to it. But he'd reawakened an anger in me that I'd forgotten about. Dating back to his slur about gay people winding up murdered at curbside.

"Yes, I always scored high in the excellent teacher department," he said.

"Then what are you so worried about? Why are you such a coward?"

I imagined him throwing his hands up on the other end of the line. "Didn't I tell you you'd end up calling me that? Andy! Andy. Have pity on me."

"Look. What Rabbi Landy did to my mother isn't all that removed from what you almost did to me. You're not as villainous as he was, sure, but imagine what would've happened if we hadn't been interrupted during that shower scene when I was a delicate, innocent yeshiva-boy freshman. When I was all of fourteen." (I actually would have loved that. And I wouldn't've been damaged psychologically, I know it. But all I wanted right now was to guilt him.)

"I refuse to accept that," Rabbi Loobling said. "That was a period of kindness and a special brand of closeness. Your thoughts are indecent. Your libido's half-baked. You haven't progressed beyond the infantile stages. But you know what? Hey." I heard his fingers snap. Or his ankles crack. "I've got it now, yes. I figured it out. Just this second. I'll contact the bailiff and the lawyers and the judge and tell them what I witnessed in Rabbi Landy's summer camp." Like I hadn't just suggested this. "His orgiastic three-ring circus. Two summers in a row. Fifty-nine and '60. It'll buttress your mother's case when I do this. If anyone deserves to be punished, it's Rick."

I wound up the call pretty quickly after that.

What a screw-up, I thought. Why had I stooped to discussing *anything* with him? He was and always would be certifiable, bananas.

Like my mother, when I thought about it. Certifiable. Bananas. I'd gotten so used to her emotional bananahood—especially when you tossed in a rabbi—that my obsession with Rabbi Loobling had been practically preordained. I was glad, at least, that the obsession had dwindled. Essentially disappeared. All he seemed now was cracked. Even a little freakish.

And what about my mother? Look where she was headed. Her bananahood was so out of whack that her story might spread to additional papers—her name revealed eventually, inevitably—as one of those cuckoo cultish saphead nutjobs. And there was nothing I could do about it. It was her own dumb fault for following Rabbi Landy around like an urchin in rags in a silent movie. Nobody had forced her to become his love slave. It was *her* life, not mine.

And unlike Rabbi Loobling, I had never married a pretty woman who could fricassee a brisket just to prove I wasn't a homo.

◆ ◆ ◆

My mother called me later and reinforced this feeling of indignant indifference. I wasn't in the mood to yak away the night with her. Yes, the story in the *Times* was an earthquake of a development, but if she wanted to process her feelings about it, she ought to consult with a professional or a girlfriend, not me. Plus she'd been calling me too much for a couple of months now, inconsiderate of my schedule. I had papers to write, *Ulysses* to read, a life to create that was a hundred-and-ten percent separate from hers. But what did she care?

"The noose is tightening," she said. "It's about to turn ugly. I wanted to warn you. I've got to be more honest with you—a lot more honest—with regard to what's about to go down."

"Don't worry about being honest with me. As a matter of fact, enough with the honesty."

"Okay. No problem. Although, truth be told, I'm still a tad preoccupied with that article in the *Times*—and that's completely justifiable. I'm not proud of it, Andy, but please understand. I go into this courtroom with a new self-awareness and that article's been a part of it. That article's pretty accurate. It took away all my hiding places. All that's left now is the truth. And another part of the self-awareness comes from my talks with the public defender, Kitty Fonseca. Sensational gal. Kitty keeps reminding me I have nothing to be ashamed of and I'm starting to believe her. I'm starting to feel a little better about myself. And I like how that feels. And it's partly *your* doing, yes, yours. Because you encouraged me to proceed with this, to sue Rabbi Skunk, and you never passed judgment. I appreciate that."

"Okay, great, listen, gotta go."

Her vulnerability and openness touched me in spite of everything. Here she was, talking frankly and unselfconsciously about a topic she would never have even thought about a year ago—and being surprisingly composed about it (no sobbing, no screaming) despite the strangeness of having the specifics of her (still anonymous) sex life broadcast around the world, or at least around Mackinac county, for the salivating hoi polloi to puzzle over.

Still, she never let up on the ratatat chatter, and I didn't feel like yessing and uh-huhing through her endless unedited self-justifications.

But on the other hand, this was juicy.

She said, "I admit I made a spectacle of myself. I admit I repeatedly denigrated myself by giving him license to do whatever he wanted with my one and only precious body."

"Okay, all right, I get it, goodbye."

"I just want to prepare you for the possibility of even more salacious reports coming out in the coming weeks."

"Yeah. I heard you. Enough. Jeez. You have no understanding," I declared with some heat, "of the damage you do with your total lack of boundaries—normal protective motherly boundaries—and the long-term effect that's had on me and Naomi and all of us really, including yourself, with your avoidance of even the most basic self-discipline. I mean, look what it's come to. A criminal court case. With all this hoopla in the paper. It really is kind of sick."

"Oh come on, Andy. Cool it. I just wanted to let you know that I take full responsibility for every one of my disreputable actions."

"Are you having this same conversation with Naomi? Are you having this same conversation with Toby?"

She might've needed a hearing aid. "And yet *full responsibility*," she said, "doesn't exempt Rabbi Rick from his share of the blame. It's pretty much fifty-fifty."

"So you take *half* the responsibility," I said. "Good to know. I have a midterm tomorrow. Talk to you later."

31

I was at college, as I said, with classes Monday to Thursday, and discos every weekend. In discos I was starting to behave like an active participant in the world of attraction (I wasn't just a hapless yeshiva-boy mooner—not anymore) which is a topic to write about elsewhere, maybe in a sonnet. ("To the Heartthrob in the Muscle T on the Ice Palace Dancefloor.") Along with odes to gay bars, and haikus to gay beaches.

The routines of my life in sum weren't a burden. Too much reading that semester, true, but none of the professors expected you to read every word and I already knew from experience that whatever papers I handed in, in whatever condition, I would never get less than a B+.

So apart from school and pickups at discos and friends who sold pot and friends who knew whiskey and the job shelving books and Truffaut at the Thalia and Garbo at the Regency, my mind was free to speculate on the upcoming trial (just two weeks away) and to wonder how I felt about Rabbi Loobling.

Because like it or not, he was back in the picture. And if he'd actually gone ahead and signed himself up as a prosecution witness with his tales of Rabbi Landy's felonious quest for underage poontang, he was stronger than he'd been a couple days earlier. He would've called the courthouse, recounted his racy summer-camp stories and risked his reputation so he could protect the world's weaklings (represented by my mother) with their fragile self-opinions and obsessional love lives.

But what did I really feel about him? All that attraction, all those fantasies and filthy prayers and imagined confessions of love everlasting—where had they gone to? I could think of him objectively, with his lumbering physique, his tree-trunk legs, his hairy arms entwined in tefillin, and still pop a boner and jerk off in minutes, but it wasn't him himself I pictured. Just a two-dimensional photo spread. Because he was who he was—he couldn't escape that—which was exactly who they said he was behind his back in the high school lunchroom. Rabbi Lubricant, Rabbi Weenie, Rabbi Crackpot, Rabbi Hoity-toity.

And whatever he was struggling to tamp down inside him was only making him more of a crackpot.

◆ ◆ ◆

Back here on earth, back here at college, I was suffering through an embarrassing crush on Chris Maragliano. He was one year older than me, in a class one year behind me, and a beautiful blend of smart and humpy, with meaty rolling football haunches and a sexy receding hairline. He also had a room in the apartment I lived in. We had met in an imaginative writing class. And I was constantly imaginatively writing poems about him while disguising his identity (though not his gender) because the professor was always calling on us to read out loud.

I was miserable. I was mopey.

This latest occasion of pining catatonia lasted four-and-a-half months and isn't central to this story but shows how I continued with my self-destructive romantic attractions (from Thornton to Loobling to Gabriel to Chris), cribbed from the infatuation game plan (I'll admit this now and take it back later) of my lovelorn mother. That my crush on Chris lasted only four-and-a-half months was a sign of my improving mental balance. Or so I hoped. Ten bonus points: He wasn't Jewish.

◆ ◆ ◆

Speaking of fellow college students.

Rabbi Rick's son Avi was at Columbia too. A coincidence that cast a shadow across my carefree trajectory. If I found myself at a big friendly party in Ferris Booth Hall or in a busy pub near 110th Street or at the frat house of my Art-Hum classmate Harrison Congreve, I would often worry (beforehand and during) that fate might usher the bastard into the middle of the get-together to provoke me with his vicious mouth and possibly slug me.

I was a year and a half into my bachelor's and hadn't run into him. His specter was fading. He was a year ahead of me anyway. So I had only three semesters left in which to worry about our possible meeting. But things felt worse with the advent of the lawsuit. More than ever, I dreaded running into him—charter member of the cult of his father. What would I do if I saw him again? I imagined him on College Walk or lounging with classmates on the library steps, cutting class and swilling ripple from a brown paper bag. My worry collided with the rage I'd unleashed after yelling at my mother for her lack of motherly boundaries. I imagined running into Avi all right, literally running into him, and knocking him down.

◆ ◆ ◆

He appeared the next day at the back of the Lion's Lair, a bar full of undergrad long-hairs a couple of blocks off campus. I was there with some friends for beer and darts. (I hated playing darts. I was laughably uncoordinated. I usually just drank and kept score at the chalkboard.)

It looked as if Avi had emerged from the pool-table section, back of the joint, like a sheriff in a western, to stare me down across the saloon. He was easy to I.D. because of the Landy height and that fuzzy caveman face of his, though he looked a lot older than he'd looked a couple years ago, more thirty-six than twenty-one. He had a plaid flannel shirt on and wasn't wearing a yarmulke.

He scared me and he shocked me. Scared me because he had always been scary. Shocked me because I had just been thinking I'd spent all this time in his likely vicinity and had never run into him—and now I'd run into him. (What would Nate have to say about the alignment of my planets?)

Avi shocked me in addition because of how hot he looked—disheveled, scowling, uni-browed, fatty—but hot nonetheless, with a cocky cock of the hip. And now that I was away from home and meeting men and assessing their sexiness, I realized I'd never gone deeper than Avi's jerkiness. His temperament might've been different from his father's—combustible rather than suave—but they both had a charismatic semitic physicality that compelled you to look at them and follow their movements.

And he was looking at *me*, with his head thrust forward in a threatening, messy, Molotov-cocktail manner.

Without a word, I put down the chalk—ditching my friends—and went the other way, toward the bar up front. I thought about continuing out the door and onto Broadway but I stopped myself, re-centered myself, and felt out-of-the-blue emboldened—who was this twerp to chase me out of my favorite bar? (my favorite *straight* bar)—and decided to order an *actual drink* and not let this shit-head upset my equilibrium.

The bartender was busy at the opposite end of the stick, working one of the taps, so I leaned on the bartop to get her attention. I was thinking Tequila Sunrise.

Then an elbow in a rolled-up sleeve appeared at my periphery.

"What do you want?" I said before turning to look.

"Your mother's in trouble," Avi said. "Some very deep shit. She has no idea what she's in for."

I turned to look but was scared to lock eyes, so I focused on the V of his shirt, at the jugular notch, where the hair sprang out. "This trial has nothing to do with me," I said. "Why are you harassing me?"

"She's your mother, isn't she? She's a jezebel and a tramp, is she not?"

He was trying to intimidate me by way of my mother. Plus he was clearly enmeshed in some kind of macho pact to ride shotgun for his father.

But, as I continued to remind myself, this had nothing to do with me.

"What is wrong with you?" I said. "Please leave me alone. Why are you bothering me?"

He grabbed his crotch—"Because I can"—and joggled it aggressively. There was a creepy queer-baiting lewdness in the gesture and in his cagily lowered eyelids. Plus something a little ridiculous. And of course, a lot hot.

I forgot about the Tequila Sunrise and returned to my friends. I asked them if they would go across the street with me to Billy Midnight's where they also had darts. They said okay. They could see I was edgy. We glided past Avi on our way to the street, but his face was down on the bar like he was crying or passed out or disgusted with himself or laughing his head off.

32

My mother drove into the city to take me to lunch at Waldblatt's Deli. She liked to treat me to a meal on occasion though she couldn't afford it and—self-involved me—I never said thanks.

After placing our orders for sandwiches (pastrami for me, corned beef for her) with extra pickles and two cream sodas, my mother lit a cigarette and studied the placemat with its full-color photos of cocktails and their recipes, calling on every liquor in the alcoholic's lexicon. (Like all Jewish mothers I knew at the time, my mother wasn't a drinker, not even Manischewitz at the seder.)

"Did you realize there's an egg in a pink lady cocktail? I never knew poultry played a role in mixology."

"Why not?" I said. "There's egg in an egg nog."

"Good point," she said. She put the ashtray on top of the pink lady picture and flicked a bit of ash. "So. *Shayn kind*. How goes academic life in the hallowed halls and hallways?"

"I'll never make dean's list again, that's for sure. Remember that syllabus I showed you?"

"Oh I could never manage the workload they give you." Puff, flick, puff. "I mean, you know I love to read. You know I can plow through a paperback a day when I put my mind to it."

"Well that was only one of *five* fatal reading lists. My roommate Chris—you remember him—gave me a bit of advice." It was exciting to drop his name like that, with so much easy-going thoughtlessness. *"Even if you can't read everything, make sure you read thoroughly whatever you read."*

"Smart," my mother said. Then yawned. "Anyway. You're probably wondering how I'm feeling about the trial."

"In fact, I am not." I waved away her dragony exhalation.

"As I've made it amply clear by now, I don't want to talk about it either. Excuse me, darling." She gave a perfunctory wave at the smoke as well. "But I will say this. We've been provided with a list of witnesses for the defense and it's lucky we have them. Case in point. Nona Tower. Witness numero uno. No doubt her ladyship will jabber nonstop about what a saintly squire the rabbi is, versus little old *moi*, the slut."

I bristled, as usual, at my mother's trivial interest in subjects unrelated to herself (my schoolwork, for example). But I liked it, too, when she described herself with a word like "slut" because it backed up the store of similar words I'd been using to describe her (in my head at least) for the past several years, and it seemed to imply that she might be open to trenchant self-analysis at some point.

"Nona Tower isn't going to rattle me, Andy, trust me. I can handle that piranha. Plus a *farbissina* you never met, a certain Toni Di Prima from the rabbi's sensitivity groups—" I knew who Toni Di Prima was. "—will testify that those groups of his were pure and sweet and kindly and innocent, not depraved, as I've contended."

"Okay," I said. "Let's move on to something else."

"Surely." She jabbed her cigarette into the Waldblatt's ashtray, jabbed and jabbed until she finally put it out, then lit up another. "Just let me complete this one last thought. Rabbi Landy's the one I'm worried about. Because. Well. You know the story. The whole sorry saga. It was awful. Just imagine. Oh Andy. What a mess. I was such a big dope. Because to be honest with you, you don't know the half of it. To be honest with you, you don't know the quarter of it." I realized she was crying—I hated it when she cried—but this type of crying never lasted that long. Little slickness down the cheeks. It wasn't like the sobbing.

I thought about what Avi had said at the Lair the other night: *She has no idea what she's in for.* And it got me kind of worried.

"But so," my mother said. "Come on. You're right. Let's enjoy our pastramis. Where are our pastramis?" She pulled the napkin out from under her fork and dabbed at her eyes and blew her nose.

I said, "Didn't you order corned beef?"

She shrugged and smiled and started tearing up again.

I was touched yet again by my mother's surprising openness. I was starting to understand that she was probably suffering from some undiagnosed psychological disorder—we were reading about untreated mental illness in Abnormal Psychology, which I was taking to fulfill the science requirement—and I had no idea how to catalog her symptoms: instability, impulsiveness, radical up-and-downness, laughable boundaries and dead-end relationships.

"In spite of your mouthiness, buster," my mother said, "I have one more thing to tell you and that'll conclude our broadcast." She was still a bit wet-eyed as she scanned the over-bright turquoise surroundings of Waldblatt's kosher-style deli and restaurant and its chattering college carnivores. "My lawyer's been prepping me for every worst-case scenario. She contends they'll try to humiliate me and make me eat shit and clobber me into a nervous crackup, but I feel I have to do this, honey." She reached for my hand but opted not to take it. "You were right all along to encourage me to do this. Thank you, sweetheart. But Kitty's been asking—did I mention my lawyer? Kitty Fonseca? I was telling her what you said—this is awkward, sweetie—about those transcripts. Of my sessions with him. You brought them up some time ago."

The mention of the transcripts sent a shiver of nausea from my stomach to my sneakers and up to my esophagus. It was especially distressing now that *she* was the one who was bringing them up and not me.

"I'm at an awful disadvantage," she said. "I never should have destroyed those papers. It's something I'll regret for the rest of my life. But it's not irreversible. Not necessarily."

"Why? Do you have carbons lying around somewhere? Like Easter eggs?"

"No, dear. No eggs. Unfortunately not. But see, you actually read through those transcripts."

"Something I'll regret for the rest of my life."

"I'm so sorry about that, kiddo."

"I was an innocent boy."

"But as Kitty was saying. Um. If you were to talk about what you read."

"Talk about...?"

"In court. This is only if you want to, honey. Testify. Tell the court what you read. It's proof of his violations. You could swear under oath."

"You've got to be kidding."

"This is serious, Andy." She lit a fresh cigarette with the butt of another. "I know this puts you in a terrible position. But the transcripts were destroyed."

"It doesn't put me in any position. I'll never talk about what I read in those transcripts. You were the one who violated every norm in creation by leaving them around for any of us to read. I've done more than enough of your bidding. My God!"

The waitress served us our two meaty sandwiches, as big as a couple of boxing gloves. "Sorry for the delay," she said. "Kitchen's backed up." And hurried away. (I have a feeling my intensity might've frightened her a little.)

"And just to clarify," I said. "You *burned* those transcripts. Or so you claim. It's not like they were suddenly—poof—destroyed."

My mother said, "I know. I fucked up. I know it, I know. But I'm desperate, Andy. You must realize what I'm up against in the figure of Rabbi Landy."

I got up and left the restaurant.

◆ ◆ ◆

I stomped down Broadway, holding hard to the right and bumping into anyone who got in my way. All I had in my head was the trauma of those transcripts—anger, revulsion, shock, titillation—dating back to when my gorgeous friend Thornton suggested we play that snoop-around-the-apartment game and I stumbled on the looseleaf. It was all because of my rancid, tarty, pickle-brained mother. Leaving that nastiness around for anyone to read. With her defiant, frozen, bitch-vixen voice calling out from every paragraph. Unforgivable, I thought. Unforgivable and revolting.

I remembered her line at the top of one of the pages—"Don't toy with me, Rabbi"—and how disgusted I was by her cynical brattiness.

And the way she trashed our dead-beat dad. "I didn't love him. I didn't even pretend to love him." Okay, all right, he deserved her disdain, but her sourness had shocked me nonetheless.

And the absolute worst: "If I only hadn't had those kids."

Who cared if I could save her by recalling what I'd read in front of a jury? I wished I could cut the transcripts out of my brain, like the memory Katharine Hepburn wanted lobotomized out of her niece in *Suddenly Last Summer*.

The words and images looped in my thinking, over and over: transcripts, Thornton, pretended to love him, hadn't had those kids, stomping, Hepburn, looseleaf, revolting, lobotomy, Broadway, transcripts, Thornton, pretended to love him, hadn't had those kids...

Then a tune twangled under it, in a flourish of bitter guitar chords:

Doodla, doodla. Dwang dwang dwang.

Chain chain chain.

Chain of foo-ools.

Before I knew it, I was approaching Times Square, where the tourists were ideal for bumping into.

"Hey!"

"Watch out!"

"The nerve!"

"Some people!"

Oversized signage loomed overhead, pushing *Oh! Calcutta!* and *Peepholes of Paris* and "Spectacular! Strippers! Runway! Live!" and "Gaiety Theater | the Best in Male Burlesk."

You'd never see *me* like that trashy love-starved mother of mine, hypnotized into doing whatever her Ashkenazi Svengali demanded: be my patient, type my transcripts, surrender your privacy, kiss my balls. Not even at my worst with Rabbi Loobling would I have descended to such undignified wretchedness. (Although I might have kissed his balls.)

And Loobling. What a wreck. A joke without a punchline. Histrionic. Pusillanimous. When given the chance to come out of the closet to a sympathetic stalwart (me), he crapped out entirely. A worm of the wormiest order.

But who was I to talk? I had crapped out on my mother only half an hour earlier. Too chicken to take the stand for her and swear on a bible. A disappointment to Lady Justice and Kitty Fonseca, a hard-working, underpaid public defender. Because I was unrepentantly sneering and selfish.

No.

Hold it.

We're talking about *My Mother* here, I thought, who had confessed to her confessor, on paper, in transcripts, that she was *sorry she'd ever had me*. This was wicked-witch territory, snake-haired Medusa, queen at the mirror who poisons Snow White. My mother was the one who should be thrown down a well, fed to the leopards, melted with a bucket of MGM water. Grandiose, loud, always interrupting, endlessly yammering about her underdeveloped boring existence, making an ass and a fool and a spectacle of herself, encircled in cigarette smoke.

Whoa, I thought.

Get a hold of yourself. Talk about bananas. She's nowhere near as bad as that. Most of the time she's kind of a hoot. Everything she says, when you think about it, is a sassy-assed wisecrack. Maybe all she was doing in those transcripts was joking, big performance, like a guest on Johnny Carson.

And look at yourself. Practically twenty-one, making life decisions and gainfully self-supporting. The adult response is a lot more nuanced than the moralistic judgments of an overgrown baby.

I obeyed the DONT WALK sign and connected with the street. Shoppers, messengers, taxis, pigeons, aromas of hotdog, exhaust and burnt sugar. I was approaching Herald Square. Life all around me. Jaywalker, bag lady, noisy sneezer, sooty statue, flying napkin, handsome cop, mink coats on a rack being wheeled down 36th Street. Why so hostile? Why so aggressive? You want to bump instead of touch. You want to hit instead of hug. You want to punch—and keep punching.

But under the lively 3-D influences of midtown, I returned to the joys of being pissed at my mother.

33

Thursday night Naomi called. She talked about her husband Nate ("That astrology nonsense is driving me nuts") and her coworkers at the restaurant ("That waitress with the overbite got a dance part in *A Chorus Line*") and how our father had destroyed her when she was ten and eleven and twelve and thirteen ("that traitor, that loser, that contemptible fuckface").

After an hour of her free-range jibber-jabber she said, "And how about you?"

I'd buried the lead. "Mom asked me to do her a favor. An extremely humongous favor."

"Naturally," she said. "A favor from the favorite."

"Don't start with that today, honey bunch."

I told her about our mother's lawyer's request that I testify. She was stunned to learn that there were transcripts of our mother's sessions with Rabbi Landy.

"You mean you never came across them?" I said.

"No."

"You sure? Big white looseleaf behind an end table in the living room?"

"I was never all up in her stuff like you. But Andy. *How disturbing.* What a psycho that fucking Landy was. Why didn't you ever tell me any of this?"

"Too embarrassing."

"And humiliating. You must have been traumatized. No wonder you're gay."

"That has nothing to do with it."

"You sure were a snoopy little squishpot back then."

"Look who's talking, Miss Rifle-Through-Her-Brother's-Journal."

"Ha," she said, dismissing the accusation. "I can't imagine what you read about in those transcripts."

"All this stuff about the divorce, for one. How there was never any love between our father and mother. That shocked me."

"Oh I didn't need a transcript to tell me that."

"And all about her growing up. Her mother's death. Her stupid crushes. The abandonments, depressions, loneliness, weight gain."

"Sounds like a living hell. How awful."

"And the worst part?" This wasn't the worst part. Her wishing we hadn't been born was the worst part. But I couldn't lay that on my sister right now, not after her maniacal rant against our father. "Lots of specifics about her affair with the rabbi. Nothing but abuse and exploitation and degradation."

"Yick. I'm nauseous. I always knew Rabbi Rick was a pig. And here's the proof, in black and white."

(And Avi was a pig as well—though he didn't make me nauseous—for grabbing his crotch.

Like rabbi, like son.)

"So they want you to spill the beans," she said.

"Under oath. In front of a jury."

"Because Mumsy torched the evidence."

"Or so she claims."

"And what's your plan?"

"I'm not going to do it. I have very mixed feelings, but in the end, I just can't."

"Oh no, but you must. No question, little brother. It's your absolute duty."

"I shouldn't have told you."

"You can't look at this through your little-boy perspective. Not anymore. No time for that now. Forget about the boundaries she's crossed over the last three hundred years. This isn't about her. This is about him. It would be unconscionable for him to get away with this, Andy, and he's very likely to get away with this, given his status. It'd be unconscionable and unjust, when there's this testimony of yours hitting him right in the kisser, guaranteed to reduce him to smoke and ash in less than five minutes. Listen to me. Do not hang up."

34

"Hello?"

"Andrew Baer?"

"Yes?"

"This is Tehila Landy. The rabbi's wife."

"Mrs. Landy. Hi. How did you get my number?"

"Your sister."

"My sister?"

"My Avi says he ran into you the other day."

"Yes. Let's see. Must've been Tuesday."

"He said you had an interesting conversation."

"Your son has a sense of humor."

"Which gave me an idea. He didn't exactly give it to me. He inspired it. I have to see you as soon as possible."

"I'm busy with school, Mrs. Landy. I can't come out to Jersey without missing a bunch of classes. What is this about?"

"I'll come to you. I'll come to the campus. I've got to see Avi anyway. It's urgent. It concerns the trial. I can drive there now. Just tell me where to meet you."

◆ ◆ ◆

She met me at Alma Mater, a statue with her arms up, in oxidized exultation. The statue wasn't a symbol of justice—Lady Justice wears a blindfold—she wasn't a symbol of anything really—but if she had in fact been dangling scales, they'd've been tipped in the rabbi's prominent-citizen favor. And (it goes without saying) there was something I could do about it, something involving a raised right hand, as Naomi had strongly hinted. And as my mother had practically begged me.

Mrs. Landy was there already, as stiff as a guard in a bearskin hat at Buckingham Palace. (She always managed to look a little seething, even when she wasn't, even when she was singing a light-hearted Hebrew holiday song.) Today she had a rigid jaw and a perfectly sculpted sticky-bun hairdo. It was odd to see her centered in the sunny buzz of campus, students zooming in a hundred directions—the opposite of boring Montevideo.

She said, "Thank you for agreeing to meet."

"Sure thing, Mrs. Landy."

She shook my hand (she was surprisingly brawny about it) and passed me a thin manila envelope. "Deliver this to your mother's lawyer. Don't tell him where it came from."

"Don't tell *her*. The lawyer's a woman."

"Ah." A smile. "Even better." A rarity.

"What's in here?" I said.

"Don't look. Just deliver. I can't do it myself because of, well, my situation. There are conventions and customs. No other way to explain it. Main thing is. I got me a no-good shit of a husband." I wondered about her sanity. Where did the cursing and bad grammar come from? She didn't smell of liquor.

Two of my friends cruised by on College Walk (a shag cut Pennsylvanian and a pony-tailed blondie) with books under their arms and quizzical eyebrows like tildes on their foreheads. The blondie gave me a tiny wave.

I gave him a tiny wave back.

"I've got to flee," Mrs. Landy said. "No time for the bread to leaven."

"Why don't we go get a coffee or something?"

"No. This is it. Be well. Don't crumble."

◆ ◆ ◆

Of course I opened the envelope, even though the flap had been licked. Two Polaroids and a handwritten note.

> I, Mrs. Tehila Daphne Leibowitz Landy, the defendant's wife, am providing these photographs as evidence for the prosecution. I found them in the defendant's desk in the defendant's office at Temple Shir Shalom, 77 Salem Street, Montevideo, N.J., after the defendant had resigned from the synagogue in 1973. I was cleaning out his office at the time.
>
> *Tehila Daphne Leibowitz Landy*

First picture: A naked woman licking the nipple of her own left breast. The breast was large. Possibly double-D.

Second picture: A naked woman spreading her vagina, her fingers pulling either side apart. There was the bottom half of a naked man's body in the lower right corner. He was masturbating his hard-on. He was sitting on a bed or a cot. His face was outside the frame. The woman's eyes were closed. They looked like who they were, Rabbi Landy (long legs) and my mother (dusky eyelids). But his face was omitted and her eyes were shut.

The transcripts may have been hard to take, but these pictures were a whole lot harder. I didn't have the inner resources to file them away. They stayed spread out on the counter of my darkroom psychology, under lurid red lights, refusing to find their way into a drawer or a strong box or an album or a porno collection.

They would follow me around for months—naked pictures over and over—stirring anger, frustration, reluctant stimulation and assorted sickening choked-back feelings that are hard to find words for. I thought, there are certain experiences we aren't meant to have. These feelings bashed the doors in.

And what would a jury think?

I sent the pictures right away to Kitty Fonseca. It was easy to get her address from a Mackinac County phonebook in Butler Library. I sent them certified, return receipt. It was worth the extra money. I didn't want my mother involved, not in discussion and not in the middle.

♦ ♦ ♦

When I thought about the pictures later, I wondered who'd taken the shot of the two of them. Yes, one of Rabbi Landy's alleged arms was out of the frame and could've been responsible for pressing the plunger. But the awkward angle made it seem like someone else had pressed it.

Or—more likely—I was thinking too much.

♦ ♦ ♦

I came across this in the *Columbia Daily Spectator*:

> To the Editor:
>
> Regarding the charges of alleged sexual harassment against history professor Dr. Leon Zilberberg: The *Spectator's* editors have failed in their duty as neutral journalists to present a consistent, fact-based narrative about the case, and have instead done everything to poison opinion against Dr. Zilberberg before all the details of the case are actually known.
>
> It's high time the *Spectator* desisted from publishing biased statements such as, "Zilberberg is a professor who has long demanded that his students perpetually flatter him while swallowing his every insult."
>
> Says who?
>
> Avraham Landy, Class of '76.

35

My brother Toby got a tremendous kick out of hanging in the city and staying overnight with Naomi and Nate in Murray Hill or with me up in Morningside Heights. He loved to pal around with my college buddies who would shadowbox him and hold him in headlocks and drape their arms around his neck.

He'd sleep over my place on occasional Saturday nights and we'd drink cheap wine (usually with the roommates) and go to a silly kung-fu movie the following morning or a pinball arcade in grimy Times Square. All I had was a room with a bed in it, within a larger Claremont Avenue apartment, so he had to make do on random blankets spread out on the linoleum beside my bed, but he didn't seem to mind it. He actually seemed to enjoy himself, singing to himself, as he laid out the pillows and sheets and quilts.

It was a comfort to eat sardines and corn and Vienna sausages with him at the oversized windowsill, straight from the cans, and to walk with him in Riverside Park and talk in the dark as we struggled to stay awake.

"I know where I can get a motorcycle for forty-five dollars," he said.

"You can't ride a motorcycle at age thirteen."

"I already do."

"I don't want to hear about it."

"With a couple of friends."

"Stop it. Don't tell me. And how good can a motorcycle be for forty-five dollars?"

"It's secondhand."

"Do you at least wear a helmet? Wait. Don't answer."

"I'm not supposed to drink alcohol at age thirteen either."

"Wine isn't alcohol."

◆ ◆ ◆

"I used to wish I had a rowboat when I was your age," I said. "I even took out an ad in the paper. 'Boy seeks rowboat.' But I had to abandon the idea when I realized there was nowhere to put it."

"Why don't you get one now? You've got the Hudson River right down the hill. You and Chris could go halfsies." It aroused me to hear us mentioned together, going halfsies on something. It sounded so sexy.

"That's an idea," I said. I cleared my throat, as if a rumble in the chest were a sufficient transition for anything. "Hey, um, Toby. I've been meaning to ask. Are you okay with all of this rabbi stuff?"

"Oh I don't care, Andy. Truly. I don't. She's been acting like this since I was practically a baby. Rabbi this, rabbi that. What's it to me if she wins a stupid lawsuit? She doesn't care about me, so why should I care about her?"

"She cares."

"Come on."

"She does."

"She doesn't"

◆ ◆ ◆

"I'm thinking of joining another family," Toby said.

I was dozing off. "Another what?"

"I don't know if you've noticed but Mommy's not very nice to me."

"She's preoccupied."

"Don't defend her."

"I'm not defending her. I'm explaining her."

"No, I know. I realize. The lawsuit. But it's more than just now. She's been like this since I can remember. I can't take it anymore."

"What does she do?"

"Nothing. That's the problem. She completely ignores me. Like I'm just not there. You know how she gets. I've come to the conclusion that I really don't like her."

I remembered my mother telling the rabbi in the transcripts that my brother was a mistake. What a horrible thing to have down on paper. "I get it, bro, no. No need for an explanation."

"That's why I come and visit so much. Either you or Naomi."

"You can visit me as much as you want. You have an open invitation."

"Thanks, Andy." It sounded like he was shifting his pillow to accomplish more comfort, shifting then punching. "I was wondering the other day, in fact, if her battle for my bar mitzvah wasn't actually a lie. Maybe she'd never really argued for me with the synagogue hotshots. Maybe all she did was forget my thirteenth birthday—oops, I forgot!—and that was why the temple commandos couldn't make room for my stupid bar mitzvah. She asked too late. They were already booked."

"Oh Toby."

"Remember the other day when she thought I was twelve?"

"I know. I *know*. But hey. Let's be practical. How can you join another family?"

"I have a friend in my class. Kid named Shepsy."

"You've talked about him."

"They have a big house on McKinley Street with an unused bedroom. A bunch of unused bedrooms. His mother is very nice. She cooks chicken or steak every night of the week. She buys him new shoes when the old ones wear out. She keeps the house clean. And anyway, it would only be for a couple of years, until I qualify for my working papers."

"You can't just move in with another family."

"Shepsy thinks his mother'll be okay with it. She's some kind of charity lady. All that's left is convincing his father. He's kind of a grump."

◆ ◆ ◆

"Toby," I said. "Are you asleep yet?"

"Tuh."

"You can come over here whenever you want, you know. I don't even have to be here. I'll make you a key."

"Oh no. You'd need a birdcage. For Daddy Warbucks and the canary."

He really was half asleep.

"A *key*. To the outside door and the door of the apartment. So you can come and go as you please."

"What? Oh. Thanks, ha ha. But Mrs. Friedman wouldn't like it."

It was Mrs. Friedman's apartment. She was ninety with a Yiddish accent and gigantic pierced earlobes. She was as shrimpy as a ten-year-old and occupied the kitchen, maid's room and a miniature bathroom, all of which were connected on the sunny side of the building. She watched shows like *Kojak* with the volume up high and asked for my help every couple of days to open a jar of gefilte fish. She'd been renting to students for fifty years.

"She's pretty much totally deaf," I said. "And she doesn't see well either. She'll probably just think you're me."

◆ ◆ ◆

"The worst thing is the pictures," Toby said. "I shouldn't be telling you. Polaroid pictures. I found them in the desk in Mommy's bedroom—of a lady and a man. They're totally naked. Showing off everything. Everything, Andy. A lot more than *Playboy*. The guy's got a boner and his head is cut off. And the lady. You'd be shocked. I don't even want to tell you." Quizzical pause. "Andy? You up?"

I pretended I wasn't.

36

I was back at Waldblatt's Deli—I was running in for takeout, a tuna-lettuce-tomato on a sesame bagel during a break between classes—when I saw him again.

Avi.

At the counter near the bathrooms. Alone and spooning soup into his fleshy unshaven badboy face. It shouldn't have surprised me—same university, only Jewish deli (kosher *style*, not actually kosher) (not even close) and the laws of coincidence—but I was surprised nonetheless. No contact in a year and a half, and here I'd run into him twice in one week.

And he was alone both times.

And this time...eating *pea soup with what smelled like ham or bacon in it!* In other words, *unconditionally not kosher!*

He noticed me. He stared at me. (Again with the staring.) He didn't back down. I was worried he was going to walk right up to me and throw hot *tref* soup in my face.

I approached him regardless, no hesitation. Who was this mangy mutt to assume he could unsettle me? I was channeling an unfamiliar inner self-assurance. (I'd need a serious dose of backbone if I was going to take the stand at the trial, and I was leaning toward going ahead with it.) And besides, as I've mentioned, he was surprisingly good-looking. Ruggedly attractive. Though today at least his eyes looked small and his hair stood up.

He pushed his soup aside, as if ready to fight me. "Here we go," he said. "What is it this time?" A vaguely sickly alcohol smell was radiating out of him.

I didn't have a comeback. Why had I approached him minus a strategy? Why was he drunk in the middle of the week, in the middle of the day?

"Did somebody send you here?" he said.

My back and neck stiffened. "No."

"And why do I keep running into you in the first place? Are you stalking me?"

Now it was me who wanted to throw the hot soup in the other one's face.

He just kept going. "Your mother's going nowhere with this lawsuit of hers."

"You said that the last time."

He shrugged.

He burped.

"Do you even know my name?" I said.

He pretended there was lint on his shirt and flicked it away. "Dandy, isn't it? Short for Dandelion?"

I rolled my eyes. I squared my shoulders. I forced myself to slow down my breathing so he wouldn't see how shaky I was. I thought it might help to sit so I sat, leaving an empty stool between us.

He meanwhile guzzled from a bottle of Miller High Life and put it back down on the counter. "I got news for you," he said. There was also the bowl of soup on the counter and an entrée plate he'd cleaned completely and a yet-to-be-eaten chef's salad. He was always a colossal eater. "Nona Tower's the defense's first witness," he said. (I knew that already.) "They're hatching quite a plot to assassinate the character of your charming mamasita." He picked up the bottle again and tried to empty it down his throat but there wasn't any beer left. "Hey waitress!" he called without any break, raising the empty. "Kindly provide us with another."

The drinking didn't startle me as much as the chef's salad. Dairy and meat. *Pinwheels of ham!* What would his parents've thought? And why didn't he care what *I* thought?

Then he looked at me oddly, like he was taking me in for the first time ever. "Say, why are you even at Columbia to begin with? How did you get in here?"

"I was accepted like anyone else," I said. "I was admitted legitimately. You can't intimidate me."

"Ooooh. Scary-scary." He wiped his mouth with the back of his hand, suggesting the blood of a vampire. "What was I saying? Ah. So after Nona Tower places her hand on the bible, she'll place the same hand on her tit—excuse me, her boob job—and confess how she asked my devilish dad for a devious date. This is a married woman, mind you."

A subsequent Miller was put down in front of him and the empty whisked away by a woman with a long thick braid and a paper hat who toddled off disapprovingly.

He guzzled roughly a third of the beer. "Ahhh. Then Nona'll continue all precious and bashful about how he turned down the date—" Another long burp. "—claiming he could never do such a dastardly thing to his darling Tehila." He winced for a second—something about his sinned-against mother—I could've easily missed it—while all I could think was "a son's secret hurt."

Avi kept going: "So then my father comes off as too much of a goody-goody to victimize the harlot."

"The harlot?"

"Your mommy."

It hit me, then, that there wasn't any difference—he was, in fact, *exactly* like his father, with the same glib schmoozing and annoying good looks that both of them used to subjugate and dominate, just for the fun of it. I mean, he'd grabbed his crotch the last time I'd seen him, like a gorilla in the jungle asserting his supremacy.

I said, "My mother was a victim and you know it. Show some respect."

He looked confused for a second but bounced back fast. Who was this *nobody* to dare to confuse him? "Then Nona paints the *harlot*—" He spit out the word like an olive pit. "—as an unfeminine aggressor—how utterly distasteful!—who's laid boobytraps all over the place to ensnare my father. Guaranteed to turn off any jury."

"You're despicable. Every one of you."

"You got that right."

I looked at the plate alongside the soup, a landscape of mustard smear and a slimy cup of coleslaw. I looked higher up, at his werewolf face, a little puffy today and blotched in places, and was surprised to see he was no longer sneering.

"Plus there's this," he said after another slug of beer. "And don't forget to pass it along to your mom's esteemed counsel. Yes, Nona Tower led the rabbi search that selected my father. Yes, Nona Tower's sissy-poo in Bumfuck, Pennsylvania, ushered him through to our dazzled parish. But what Nona doesn't know, and will never be told, is that that very same sister had been shtupping my pops for years." I might've wondered in that moment why he was leaking this to me, for my mother's potential benefit.

But I didn't.

"And when word got around and the tongues started wagging," Avi continued, "she managed to spirit him away to Montevideo, En Jay and cover up the evidence."

"Jeepers. How do you know all this?"

He gave me an antisocial smile. "How do you know what you know about the harlot?"

37

Next day, I rang up Kitty Fonseca and told her I wanted to testify about what I'd read in the transcripts when I was a kid. Ms. Fonseca said, "Thank you. We'll get back to you later today with a time and a date, most likely tomorrow—Wednesday the latest—because we want to move fast as the judge is predicting a four-day trial."

I asked her not to hang up just yet because I also had Avi's news to impart, about Nona's sister's affair with Landy back in the sticks. For this additional nugget, Ms. Fonseca was slightly less businesslike. "Thanks a million, Mr. Baer, goodbye."

I think it was this detail that finally persuaded me to testify, because it perfectly measured the reach of Landy's 24/7 philandering—clear across the Jersey mountains and into another state.

I called my mother to tell her I planned to testify. She was grateful. She even cried a little.

I felt good about my decision. I was contributing to the cause of my underdog mother and fulfilling a civic duty. Yet I still had no desire to put myself through the torture of actually sitting in the gallery and observing the trial.

38

I tried calling my mother after the first day of testimony but she didn't pick up. I wasn't surprised. The tension had probably totaled her.

What surprised me was a call from Rabbi Loobling.

"Hey Andy," he said. As if he hadn't called me indecent on the phone the other week. As if I hadn't called him a coward. "Guess what, *boychik*? I went down to the courthouse Friday and offered myself as a witness, as an official burnt offering, in the case against Rabbi *Dick*."

"How about that," I said, no inflection, no affect.

"And more laudable still," Rabbi Loobling said, absurdly enthusiastic, "I already tendered my testimony. First thing this morning."

"How is that possible?"

"Judge Callison is hustling things along rather briskly. I'm surprised you didn't know about the occasion of my testimony. Didn't you talk to your mother?"

"Not yet."

"I told them exactly what I told you, Andy. About the serial abuse of underage counselors. About the skinnydips and the intercourse."

"What a mitzvah, Rabbi Loobling."

"You don't sound impressed. Not nearly as impressed as I am."

"Ha. Just tired."

"But so if you didn't talk to your mother, then you have no idea what happened today. And a whole lot happened. That dotty little bailiff hosted a hustle-bustle witness box. Six on the stand this morning alone. Including yours truthfully. All with some sort of ax to grind against the degenerate defendant. One of them even schlepped in from Philly. Knew him back in Hollywood. But here's the thing, *mi amigo*. I can't tell if they liked my testimony or not. Not sure if they believed me. I mean really, when you think about it, what kind of proof did I have? A couple of hysterical flashlight memories from fifteen, sixteen years ago? On the other hand, they didn't delve into my mental health history, so maybe they did believe me. Unless they were being polite. But I'm self-aware enough to know that at times I come off as a bit of an oddball."

I liked that he said that. After all, he was the first man I'd ever fallen in love with, and that shred of self-reflection reassured me somehow.

"Then this over-age vixen named Rhoda Power—"

"Nona Tower."

"Yes, that's it. Heavy breather. Thinks she's Kim Novak. Trashed your mother to smithereens. But then your mother's lawyer spooked her with the shocking revelation that Rick had had an affair with her sister. All that was missing was a couple of toots from the soap opera organ. Then King Richard himself took the stand, all afternoon, going on and on about how vile and shoddy your mother was. Must've made her feel all measly and worthless."

I should've defended her then—I'd never known Loobling to be so cavalier and tactless—but my sympathy only went so far. Yes, I'd promised to testify in support of my mother (Rabbi Loobling wasn't the only one) but it was putting a strain on my nerves and stomach. I convinced myself that I'd done all I could for her.

"So come on. You're a New Yorker now. Get with it," Rabbi Loobling said. "What's your reaction?"

"Like I said. I'm tired. And frankly. I didn't expect to hear from you again. Not after the last discussion we had. I mean, it got kind of heated."

"Not hear from me again?" He laughed pretty loudly, and I thought a little fakely. "Why would you not hear from me again? I already told you I was planning to bear witness. It was a breakthrough for me. A kindness on my part. I did it for you, Andy. You really are a character. You won't get rid of me that easily." He laughed again, almost as loudly.

"It's just. Well. Whatever," I said.

"What? Because we hadn't been in touch for a couple of years? Is that what you're alluding to? So what. Who cares? These things happen. Take another look at your *Jonathan Livingston Seagull*."

"No. It's just. I mean, listen to yourself. What you said about being in court today. So breezy about my mother's unhappiness. Talking like it was some kind of feel-good frolic in the merry old court of Candyland."

"Oh you know me. Emperor of denial. Prince of detachment. All mumbo-jumbo and cymbals crash."

It surprised me to admit that in fact I *didn't* know him. But what did I expect after ping-ponging back and forth between idolization and demonization with nothing in the middle?

He can't help being who he is, I thought.

"Oh, and just to let you know." I barely squeezed it in there. "I'll be testifying too."

"You will? Bravo. Bit of therapeutic air-clearing. Good for the soul, take it from me. But getting back to the trial," he said, with no apparent interest in how I might help my mother's case. "For just another mo. Because at the end of today there were pictures passed around. Horrendous pics apparently. Not shown to us in the peanut gallery. But from the sound of it, from the gasps of it, they were especially incriminating. Anyway. For what it's worth. And since we're both officially witnesses now. You and I shouldn't even be talking."

Truth is, we haven't talked since.

◆ ◆ ◆

Not only was I annoyed by this phone call, I was still disconcerted about Toby's reaction to those passed-around pics which he'd found in my mother's drawer and had obviously come from the same seedy photo shoot that was captured in the pictures Mrs. Landy had slipped me, and which ended up scandalizing the jury that afternoon. I'd behaved like an ostrich, pretending to be asleep when Toby told me what he'd seen, and I felt guilty.

I played hooky the next day (no Elizabethan Poetry, no Yoga at Barnard) to see a dollar double feature of *Deliverance* and *A Clockwork Orange* at St. Mark's Cinema with frat boy Harrison Congreve. Harry hid a flask of Southern Comfort in his jacket that the two of us got smashed on.

◆ ◆ ◆

I called Naomi.

"I'm going to testify," I said.

"Good."

"About the transcripts."

"I figured."

"Did you talk to Mom?"

"I didn't."

"Me neither."

"She's incommunicado."

"Understandably. All the stress."

"But congrats, little brother. You're about to take the stand. This is quite a big step in your emotional maturity."

"I don't need you validating the events of my autobiography."

"Now, now. Temper, temper. I'm not validating. I'm acknowledging. Because at long last you'll be focused on something bigger than your ego."

"You can't help yourself, can you?"

"What?"

"You have no idea how condescending that sounds. But you know what? I'm used to it. And you know what else? You aren't the only one who knows how to stand up to a bully. In fact, just the other day I ran into Avi Landy—"

"Avi Landy," she said dreamily. "I always had a thing for that beast."

"—at one of the restaurants near campus—"

"Oh that's right. I forgot. You two go to school together."

"—and I told him to watch how he talks about our mother."

"Huh. Interesting. Especially when you don't give a shit about our mother."

"I told you just a second ago that I'm going to testify for her."

"Because I shamed you into doing it."

"Think what you want."

I heard her sucking slurpily on a straw, most likely a Tab, the only drink she drank. "So Avi's going around defending his wicked daddy. But of course he is. They're birds of a feather. Jerks of a feather."

"Yes," I said. "And I gave him what for. Told him he and his father were despicable creatures. Right to his fatty face."

"That could've been dangerous. But wow. I'm inspired."

"I'm a whole lot stronger than you think, Naomi. Even Rabbi Loobling has had to wrestle with my logic. He called me after he read about the trial in the *Times*—"

"Surprise!"

"—reporting all of this damaging dish he had on Rabbi Landy."

"Seems like every Hebraic human in a twenty-mile radius knows exactly what that dickens is up to. What he was, or is, or will be up to. But hey. You sound speedy. Did you take speed?"

"Why is it you can go on and on for hours on end about whatever comes into your head, turning your two cents' worth into a hundred thousand dollars, and when I have all of this important news to tell you, you think I'm on drugs?"

"I'm sorry, honey. Please. Keep going."

"I was *trying* to *explain* that I found an opportunity to speak truth to Rabbi Loobling. About his sexual self-hatred and his all-around cowardly snooty-ass pretentiousness."

"Sexual self-hatred? Is this a closet case we're talking about?"

"Cheez, the way you put things. That isn't the point. Not today. Fact is, Rabbi Loobling has already testified. That's right, just this morning. About Rabbi Landy's summer-camp escapades with giggly jailbait." I told her about the fuckings in the Finger Lakes and it really set her off about how insufferable Rabbi Landy was.

So I left out the news about the Polaroid nudies because she was apoplectic enough as it was.

I did tell her this. "I'm worried about Toby."

"Me too. So's Nate."

"He wants to run away from home and move in with one of his buddies."

"Shepsy Spencer. He told us. Over on McKinley Street."

"What do you think? It doesn't seem like Bea has the emotional budget to deal with this now."

"No. You're right. She's completely tapped out."

"That's why I'm going to advise him to go ahead with it. Once the trial is over."

"What do you want to do that for?"

"He's almost fourteen. He's a very together kid. Nothing'll ever change in that scuzzy household of hers. Even if she gets some kind of professional help, the narcissistic profile is the most intractable of them all." I'd been learning about it in Abnormal Psychology. "You can never tell them anything. She'll never move past that."

What I was really most upset about was Toby's discovery of the rabbinical porn, and what that meant in terms of discomfort and danger in his very own home.

"You're letting your intolerance get in the way again," Naomi said, as she proceeded to try and lecture me on musts and shoulds and attitude adjustments but I tried in turn to rebut her superiority by swamping her with loudness. "Stop it! Stop. Will you stop it already? I am right about this! And you're wrong!"

But maybe she was right and *I* was wrong. Our brother was still thirteen, not even in high school.

Still, it was hard to back down in an argument like this after so much nonstop big-sister arrogance.

39

I was nervous the following evening, convinced I wouldn't sleep. I was scheduled to testify the morning after that, so I asked roommate Chris to put his Wallace Stevens aside and go to the Lion's Lair with me for a burger and a beer.

He said okay.

"I know you can't say much," Chris said, looking foxier than ever, his linebacker mitts around a Heineken, "but how do you feel about the progress of the case? And the viability of the charges?"

"Oh I can tell you whatever I want," I said, because no one had told me not to. I talked about Landy's unfair power and the harem and the hypocrisy and how it was all *so* Aristophanes. But I was still pretty solidly under the woozy spell of Chris, so I mostly imagined what he looked like naked and wondered how to keep him sitting across from me forever.

My bladder, alas, broke the spell.

And again, there he was—Avi—I couldn't believe it—that jackass was everywhere—stumbling drunk in the pool-table section, between the booths up front and the toilets in back, watching the rolling balls—the stripes and the solids—caroming and clacking.

He cornered me. He breathed on me. He was sloshing a pint of dark, holding it before him like a navigating lantern. "You doan unnerstand. You do. Not. Get it. What this does to her. What *he* does to her. Daily. He humiliates her. He treats her like shhhhhit. Goes out of his way, every day, to break her heart, to hurt her pride. Again and again. Just imagine what iss like for her."

"Okay," I said.

Not *my* mother.

His mother.

"And thass not including how he browbeats *me*. He isn't azackly sweet to me." He put a finger on my lips. "Doan tell anyone." Then took an extended gulp of the beer until the pint glass was empty.

Then belched.

I proceeded to the men's room. There was no one else in there. It was as cold as a cave and stank like the elephant-and-rhino house at the Bronx Zoo. I went to the urinal and started to piss. I could still feel the dent of Avi's finger on my lips.

The bathroom door banged open behind me.

Shocked me.

"Hurry it up," a bossy baritone barked. (Avi of course.)

I chuckled unconvincingly. "Don't rush me, man. The stall is empty. Go tinkle in there."

He mumbled, shuffled, bumbled, stumbled. The door of the toilet stall banged open. A couple seconds later I heard a torrent of giraffe piss.

I was meanwhile shaking my dick and zipping up. I was eager to get the hell out of there.

"You're dyina take a look at it," I heard from the stall, "aren't you?" It didn't sound like a welcoming offer. The river of piss was diminishing to a trickle. I imagined grabby hands, yanked-down underpants, anal rape.

I didn't reply. I didn't bother to wash my hands in the rusted sink. I was on my way out when a fist grabbed my collar and spun me around.

No sign of threat in Avi's features, only the look of a drunk who hasn't been shaving. His penis was out of his fly however, jiggling back and forth, like a bathtub toy, with some urine still dribbling.

"Come on, Andy. Look." He sounded almost pleading about it. "Look all you wann. I doan mind." At last he'd said my name.

"Hey—watch—you're dribbling on your shoe."

His dick was nicely fleshy like the rest of him and beginning to stick up. Too bad he had that awful personality.

He had his hand around it now and was shaking off the drip, directly onto the floor, like he was still above the toilet. Boy, was he snockered. I didn't want to leave because the dick dance (I'm ashamed to admit) was a pretty big turn-on. Yet I didn't want to stand there either, gawping at this bully. He could easily knock my block off.

"I let you see it," he said. "Now toush. Come on now. Give it a pull."

I imagined some violent football Bluto, even drunker than Avi, barging in. Was this how his father got his pitiful synagogue zombies going? Was this set-up nothing more than a lame reenactment of the primal scene between my mother and Avi's father? (Ew.)

He pulled me by the collar again and pushed me into the stall, shoving just to shove, and banged the partial door shut. I pretended to resist, but I was too excited to stop him. He had a solid, surprising (given the brewskis) alabaster boner, nested in a fluff of blue-black Superman pubic hair.

"This is your reward for shupporting my mother," he said.

Again with the mother—when all along I'd been thinking he was taunting me in the name of the father. But what exactly had I done for the mother? Deliver some pics? It didn't seem likely that Avi and *Eemah* would chitchat unassumingly about the X-rated candids of dear old Dad. Or maybe he thought I'd *shupported* his *eemah* in an indirect way, by hearing him out a few minutes earlier as he bemoaned her abuse by the father.

He grabbed my hand and put it on his cock. The ridge of the tip went sliding back and forth in the cup of my fingers as his hips drove the sliding and his eyelids came down like blackout shades to hide what we were doing.

And in less than a minute, bam! He came. Just like that. On the floor, on my fingers, on the wall and on the toilet seat. A spectacular squirt, a reckless splatter, no sound effects whatsoever.

I was short of breath and swoony. He was comatose and standing. Not a peep or a moan or a shiver or a thank you. An unromantic moment, as quick as the climax of a fever mosquito, but I felt I'd gotten through to him, a guy no one else in the world could get through to. And I started revising: Correction. Romantic. *Highly* romantic. I'm in love with Avi Landy. I could live in love with Avi forever.

Until I remembered he was drunker than Truman Capote on a talk show. And an asswipe to boot.

There was no room to move.

His head went heavy. His penis shrank. His hips were stopped. I unstuck my hand from the glaze of his donut and wriggled for some toilet paper. His chin was on my shoulder. I thought he'd fallen asleep. But then he whimpered like a pit bull. I was annoyed with myself for pitying him. I wiped off what I could, then put a hand on his back to steady his teeter and maneuvered his penis back into his pants.

Chris opened the stall. I'd forgotten about Chris. We'd forgotten to lock the stall.

"Ope," Chris said. "Sorry, Andy. Is everything all right?"

I smiled over Avi's shoulder and whispered, "Totally plastered. Very old friend."

Chris smiled back. "Ah. I'm headed back home. Let me settle the bill and you can pay me back later."

I whispered, "Thanks, Chris."

He stopped to take a leak on the other side of the wall, saying, "Don't forget you have that all-important court appearance in Jersey tomorrow, honey." He meant it as a joke but that's not how I took it.

"Thanks for reminding me," I said.

I heard Chris wash his hands and exit.

Two new voices entered the bathroom.

"...and command that much rent for a rattletrap on La Salle Street."

"I don't understand it."

"Hoo, what a stink."

I shook Avi's shoulders. No response. He was sleeping standing up.

One of the guys who'd just entered opened the stall, saw what was happening and chanted like a fan in the bleachers at Butler Stadium, "Ah! Vee! Lan! Dy! Inebriated! Yet again!"

I asked the guy, "What dorm is he in?"

He chuckled. "Furnald. Seventh floor."

Avi sleepwalked leaning against me as I guided him out of the bathroom and out of the bar and north on Broadway and up the five blocks to Furnald Hall.

40

An older woman in what looked like a wig that looked like a hat put her reading glasses on—they were hanging from a chain around her neck—and swore me in at ten the next morning. It irked me to think of my hand on a book of Jesus stories I didn't believe in. But then I didn't believe in the angry-God-of-the-Hebrews stories either.

My mother's lawyer, Kitty Fonseca (all bouncy curls and a plain gray suit), started things off.

After establishing who I was and what I was studying and the family connection and a dash of family history and substantiating the existence of the looseleaf binder with the transcripts in it, she said, "And what would you say was the nature of their contents?"

I was still a bit unsettled by the presence of a jury, twelve actual voting-age citizens of Mackinac County, New Jersey: seven women, five men—one of whom looked Japanese—and the rest of them squishy white bread with the crust cut off. Handbags on laps, ties around throats, eyeglasses flashing, dirty hair, clean hair, mop-top, hairspray, a jaunty pink neck scarf, a denim blouse, a denim work shirt.

I was unsettled, too, because I'd had only two hours' sleep after hustling Avi to his pigsty of a dorm room. His extreme drinking and penis flashing and instant coming and hapless crying and conflicted suffering about his impossible parents were a lot to absorb as this inquisition was about to ramp up. An inquisition entwined with the very fate of his very father.

"What would you say was the nature of their contents?"

"Psychotherapy sessions," I said, returning to the attorney's question. "In-depth discussions about childhood traumas and the breakdown of my parents' marriage."

Rabby Landy's lawyer, Nicholas Collins, a blubbery bald guy, stood up to interject: "Objection, your honor. Insufficient evidence. No exhibits have been offered to support the witness's claim."

Ms. Fonseca said, "Your honor, best-evidence rules grant that original documents must be provided as evidence *except* when the original is lost, destroyed, or otherwise."

The judge said, "Back yourself up here, counsel."

Ms. Fonseca said, "Mr. Baer, explain to the court why there's no typed-up looseleaf version of the therapy sessions."

I said, "Because my mother says she burned them."

◆ ◆ ◆

Ms. Fonseca asked me, "What was contained in the transcripts that the court might find relevant to today's proceedings?"

I talked about the affair between the plaintiff and the defendant that was referenced in the transcripts and their jocular comments about their sexual proclivities.

"Mr. Baer, you interacted with this content quite a while ago, at a very young age. How can you assure the court that what you retained from your reading hasn't been diminished or compromised with time?"

I talked about those experiences in life that you never forget. I talked about how there were details in the transcripts that scandalized me because my mother and the defendant were not only involved in a therapeutic relationship, but in a sexual relationship—while both of them were married. Which raised an uproar in the temple. And acute humiliation in me and my siblings. I was unconfused and confident. I had the truth on my side. And I wasn't the one on trial.

Mr. Collins objected to my use of the phrases "raised an uproar" and "me and my siblings," but after those insignificant bumps in the lane I was free to keep going.

I said I might not've remembered every word they said in the transcripts but I remember the most important thing. They were having sex with each other—rabbi and congregant, doctor and patient—and joking about it callously like it was this hilarious chain-smoker's ring-a-ding parlor game. And he was the criminal.

"Objection!"

Mr. Collins didn't like that last part. And the judge didn't either.

◆ ◆ ◆

"Mr. Baer, how can you assure the court that your testimony isn't colored by your bias toward the plaintiff, your own mother?"

"I have nothing to gain from my testimony. I understand that I may not be believed or that I'll be badgered by the defense, but I know what I read in the transcripts of those sessions."

◆ ◆ ◆

Before defense lawyer Collins cross-examined me, he put a neuropsychiatrist on the stand, a Dr. Lydia Marlowe of West Hartford, Connecticut, and here's the gist of what she said:

> "Childhood memories are typically remembered without emotion, owing to the distance from the events and to the need for self-protection."
>
> "It's a fallacy that the most traumatic memories are the most accurately remembered. Such memories are prone to exaggeration and inclusion of details that couldn't possibly have occurred."
>
> "Such memories can be radically altered with the input of others."
>
> "Fragments of memory may be forever broken up and never sufficiently reconstructed as an entire picture of the past."

◆ ◆ ◆

Then the defense took its adversarial crack at me.

"Before we begin, Mr. Baer," Mr. Collins said, "I want to preface this inquiry by stating that I have no intention of questioning your reliability or your integrity as a witness. My sole focus will be on the accuracy of your memory for details you claim to have uncovered roughly eight or nine years ago. When you were a child of eleven."

"Possibly twelve," I said.

"Possibly twelve."

"Not a child, exactly. More of an adolescent."

"Mr. Baer. You make a claim that you found a looseleaf binder containing transcripts of psychotherapy sessions between your mother and the defendant. Can you tell the court how many pages of content were collected in the alleged looseleaf?"

"Not really. No."

"More than ten?"

"Yes."

"Less than a hundred."

"Not sure."

"What about the possibility that you're forgetting the actual source of what you read? Couldn't these so-called transcripts have been contained in a textbook?"

"No."

"Your mother was taking a night class in psychoanalytic technique during the period of our focus." *She was??* "At Unami University. Couldn't the excerpts you're referring to have been stumbled upon by yourself in one of your mother's textbooks?"

"They weren't excerpts from a textbook. They were typewritten transcripts. Page after page of verbatim dialog. In a looseleaf binder."

"Mr. Baer, I'm sure you understand that we have no way of knowing what constitutes 'verbatim' in a case such as this. It's just as likely that every line of the allegedly transcribed therapy sessions could have been completely made up, completely concocted. Like the dialogue in a play."

"Doesn't seem *just as likely* to me."

"Be that as it may. I find this entire situation hard to swallow, Mr. Baer. That a professional of the defendant's caliber would allow such sessions to be recorded in the first place and typed up in the second place, compromising his integrity and his standing as a mental healthcare practitioner."

A thoroughly specious argument, I thought. These were transcripts used in the training of a doctoral candidate. There must've been similar records all over the world of psychodynamic scholarship.

"Objection," Ms. Fonseca said. "Counsel's opinion about the situation is speculative and irrelevant."

"Sustained."

I wondered if Mr. Collins hadn't plotted this stunt ahead of time: Proclaim your incredulity, guessing you'll be objected to, while contriving to foster doubt in the minds of the jury about the validity of the transcripts.

◆ ◆ ◆

At some point I said, "I expect that what I'm recalling is embarrassing to the plaintiff. I know it is to me."

◆ ◆ ◆

At another point Mr. Collins said, "Mr. Baer, Dr. Marlowe proposed that after repeated retellings of so-called traumatic childhood memories, facts can change, accuracy can get corrupted, the input of others can slip into the recall."

"That's an easy one, Mr. Collins. My mother and my sister are the only two people I ever told about the transcripts."

41

Mr. Collins said, "No more questions, your honor," and my testimony was over. The judge adjourned the trial till the following morning. (What a short day!)

Feeling noble and indispensable and in need of a drink of water, I bounded out of the witness box and strode between the attorney tables (where the Rabbi and my mother were standing up at their tandem tables and rolling their necks in tandem)—past Naomi in the gallery (she had in fact been able to get off work)—and out into the lobby where a couple of people were smoking next to an ashtray the size of a conga drum.

I felt a tug on my sleeve. I turned. I stepped back. "*Mrs. Landy*. I didn't recognize you."

"It's the sunglasses," she said. "I've been here since morning." It wasn't just the sunglasses. She was as sharp-boned and handsome as ever, but the ruffles at the front of her blouse were gray when they should've been white and her hair looked slept on. "I saw your sister," she said. "Isn't she looking lovely."

"She's married now."

"Oh no, too young. I hope she loves the creature."

"She's still inside. I'm looking for water."

"I want to tell you something. Let your mother know I told you. Just listen a second."

"Well see, I gotta go."

"My husband's never wrong."

"Ah."

"I know I made it hard for him on the stand the other day, by introducing those photos, but believe me. My husband is never wrong. I want your mother to know that. Won't you tell her that for me?"

"I don't understand."

"Though technically speaking, he's not my husband anymore. Did you notice how exhausted he looks? It's positively tragic."

"I'm pretty thirsty, Mrs. Landy."

"And let's keep the origins of those photos a secret. *Entre nous* as they say."

"Okay. I mean, I already figured."

"When's the last time you had a haircut?"

"It's been a while."

"You could use a haircut."

"Yes. Thanks."

"Come by the house. I'll get Tonya to cut you."

42

I cut classes again the following morning and took the bus back to Jersey and the Mackinac County Courts. It was my mother's turn in the dock. I couldn't resist. I wore an Orioles cap down low on my head and sat in a corner way in the back because I didn't want her to see me. Naomi joined me a few minutes later with a kerchief on her head and inanely rouged cheeks.

The same old lady from the previous morning, with the ludicrous wig and her glasses on a chain, performed the swearing-in. My mother took an actressy stance as she straightened her back and stuck out her breasts (squeezed into a backwards sweater) like Lana Turner in *Madame X*.

"I swear to God, so help me," she said.

She wore solemn brownish lipstick and lavender eyeshadow, the combination of which made her look like you couldn't trust her.

Ms. Fonseca said, "Mrs. Baer, tell the court what happened over the course of your alleged sexual relationship with the defendant."

"Ahem. At first it was a thrill. I was wild with excitement. I fell instantly in love with him. Like I'd swallowed a potion. But it was scary as well. Scary as hell. I was scared we'd get caught. I was scared the congregation would see what we were up to. I was *hoping* they would see, if I can be perfectly honest about it. I'm under oath, am I not?"

All I felt was sorry for her at this point, not embarrassed like I'd get as a kid. I was attuned to the hurt and deluded yearning. She was desperate to be loved, to not feel empty, to linger forever in her blind and deaf and ultimately exhausting exhibitionism.

◆ ◆ ◆

Then I heard her say, "He gave me a new kind of feeling about myself, and I wanted to share that with the world—shout it from the pews—but of course, I didn't. *Quelle scandale.* Yet everyone could see it on me. I made sure about that. Making googoo eyes from my seat in the temple. Keeping him in his office so he walked in late to services."

◆ ◆ ◆

Ms. Fonseca said, "Did the defendant explain that you'd be part of his doctoral practicum and that the sessions would be recorded?"

"Yes."

"What was your response?"

"Reluctance."

"Why?"

"We were having an affair and he wanted me as a patient. I wouldn't call that kosher in anybody's kitchen. But I was anxious to keep a hold on him. I was pathetic. I was hopeless. And after I worked through my reluctance, which in the end was pretty flimsy, it felt like a miracle. I had him to myself. Every morning. Seven a.m. That's when he scheduled me. I'm up early anyway. And all my wishes and dreams and hopes had come true. What could be more exciting?"

Yeah, seven in the morning. When it was far less likely that anyone from temple would see her coming and going. That's how his mind worked.

◆ ◆ ◆

"What precipitated the end of your relationship?"

"The defendant started seeing other women. He told me so himself. He *showed* me so himself. He was a free and lusty spirit, he said. A polyamorous pervert. His words, not mine. And so he asked me to participate. In threesomes. And foursomes. And sometimes even fivesomes. In, you know, in orgies. Can I get a drink of water?"

The lady with her glasses on a chain around her neck brought her a glass of water.

❖ ❖ ❖

A little while later my mother said, "And they all started showing up at temple. All of the women. Never the men. There weren't many men. But that was the joke of it. All the women he put his spell on. The women he'd have me fondle under their turtlenecks. The women from the orgies which he held in the temple social hall or the Knights of Columbus. Yes, he'd rent venues. I'd look among the pews and there they'd be. His hypnotized crazies. With their jaws hanging open. Then one day it hit me. I was looking in a mirror. Mirrors all around me. These women were me. And I was these women. No better, no worse. I was thunderstruck. I was mortified."

I was thunderstruck.

I was mortified.

No wonder my mother hadn't wanted us in the courtroom. Orgies, turtlenecks, women, *men*. I pictured all those sad-sack hypnotized divorcées scattered around the sanctuary and scattered around our dining room table, eating potato chips and smoking—I pictured them with their tops off—moles and bones and asymmetric boobies.

And what about the men at those grubby events? How many? Who were they? Did Rabbi Landy put his hands inside their turtlenecks too? Their underpants even? Did he suck their hairy dicks? And how much money were they expected to pay for these reprehensible privileges?

And that's not even accounting for the lesbian fondles.

❖ ❖ ❖

"I went to see Rick," my mother was saying, with a glance at the judge. "I told him how I felt. That it was outrageous what he was doing. That he was spitting on these women. That he was spitting on me. I lost it, your honor. I yelled at him. I slapped him. I screamed. I kicked. I cried. I cursed. Then he threw me out of his house. Called me an ingrate. Called me a whore. We haven't spoken a word to each other since."

❖ ❖ ❖

"What is your major complaint with the defendant?"

"You don't engage in sexual contact with a patient. Period."

"All right, Mrs. Baer. I won't prolong this."

43

Naomi and I spent the lunch break at Blue Heaven Burgers on Potawatomi Road. We'd picked Blue Heaven because it was six long blocks from the courthouse, which made it unlikely our mother would show up there for her own lunch. We had skipped out of the courthouse with our heads down.

"I just bought these," she said, tickling an earlobe. "What do you think?"

"Elegant."

They were small unremarkable pierced pearl earrings that didn't look any different from the ones she usually wore.

"The others were getting old," she said. "I debated buying teensy rubies, but I think it makes sense to pay rent this month." She gave a hurried glance at the menu. "What are you getting?"

"Luncheon special. What else is there?"

"Agreed. Nothing else." She swept aside our menus. "So."

"So what?"

"Have you recovered from your nightmare on the witness stand yesterday?"

"Oh yes, big load off, that's for sure."

"Like I said, you were smashing. Nothing seemed to rattle you. Were you on Quaaludes? Or was it Strawberry Quik?"

"Maxwell House. Gallons of it. I hadn't slept the night before." I didn't explain that Avi was the reason for my sleeplessness. Who knows what kind of overfamiliar sister insinuations she'd've foisted on me about Avi's epic intoxication and the shock of the handjob—well, I wouldn't have mentioned that.

"The defense had nothing on you," she said. "Their arguments were so much soggy chipped beef on Wonder Bread toast. I'm proud of you, Andy."

The waiter appeared and took our orders—including two Tabs—and picked up the menus.

"Oh, and a couple of waters," Naomi said.

"Got it."

The waiter was cute, with Poindexter glasses, extra-long hair and a skimpy apron.

"I like the bowtie," I said. It was mega-big with polka dots.

The waiter yanked it away from his neck—it was attached with elastic, like a prop in a clown act, "Somebody told me they're in fashion again," and scampered away.

Naomi smiled until the smile froze over. "Rather predictable performance from Mrs. Baer this morning, wouldn't you say? Needy divorcées, synagogue orgies, rabbinical sex abuse. Ho-fucking-hum."

She was trying to act blasé about the sordidness of the testimony—just the fact that she waited till now to bring it up—and I'd waited too, aiming for a similar air of just-not-caring—because, close as we were, this was an awkward pass for a sister and brother. Our mother's orgies. Honestly!

I said, "You think we fooled her with our disguises?" Naomi had taken her kerchief off but she still glowed with rouge and I still had the cap on.

"She was playing to the judge. She never looked beyond him." She was fiddling with the sugar shaker.

I was fiddling with a fork. I said, "It's weird how she natters on and on, without any feeling."

Naomi said, "It's what the psychiatrist was saying on the stand the other day. You strip out the emotion when you dip into the past. Especially when the past is littered with trauma."

"But however it turns out," I said, "whatever the final outcome, the main thing is, she made the story public. He's locked in the stocks in the village square and everybody's laughing."

"I still don't think you get it, honey. She will not be avenged until that prick is convicted. He hasn't suffered one iota for the destruction he's caused, the emotional turmoil, the marital discord, the violence and intimidation."

"But they're going to find him innocent. I know it. I can feel it."

"Maybe yes, maybe no. Still—kudos to you, kid, for talking about the transcripts. You swore on a fucking bible. So much concrete incriminatory first-person evidence. That could totally tip the balance."

"I was terrified on the stand, you know."

"What else would you be?" She had put down the sugar shaker and was fidgeting, now, with the imitation sapphire ring that our father had given her for her eighth or ninth birthday. "It's only natural. Mom was scared too. I could hear it in her voice." She talked about the importance of fear and the importance of overcoming it—the fear she felt on her wedding day and her fear when our father abandoned the family.

Then, returning to the present, she said, "But as I was saying. Your testimony could help her. Perhaps she can win this. You did her a kindness. In the end you were nice to her. It might surprise you to learn this, but I've always been nothing but kind to her, I've always been looking out for her. I may have hated her guts, but I never despised her."

The waiter zoomed in with our luncheon plates and finessed a double landing. "Here we go. Two Blue Heaven specials. And sodas and waters in just one—here." He had the glasses on a separate tray and plunked them down between us—one, two, three, four—and pulled on the ends of his bowtie and went.

"What a cutie," I said. I touched the burger, then the pickle, just to move the food a little. "You have to admit Rabbi Landy brought some excitement into her colorless existence."

"No one should pay a price that high for a couple of months of happiness."

"They were at it for longer than a couple of months."

"In this kind of sitch the woman is only happy for a couple of months. After that it's all torture."

"How do you know all this?"

"*Days of Our Lives.*"

I laughed. "And what about you? Where does your so-called *happiness* come from? It certainly doesn't come from *her*. And I'm not talking about what happened when you fell for Nate."

"Well to be honest, Andy." She chomped on a couple of fries and I took a bite of my burger. "I had *you*. You always looked up to me. From a very early age. That gave me a certain confidence. Which is the launching pad to happiness. And come on, you know, I am not *that happy*. Mom, on the other hand, had no one. No father, no mother, no brother, no sis. And for quite a while now, no husband either. It's actually pretty sad."

"It is," I said, with maybe a third of the burger stuffed in my face.

"I know you don't believe that, but it is. I know you still resent her, with your leftover righteous outrage, but one of these days you'll outgrow it. My guess is you're halfway there."

44

It was the final leg of the trial.

Mr. Collins said, "Mrs. Baer, can you tell the court how many children you have?"

"Children? None. My kids are all grown. You should be asking me how many adults I have. I don't see what my fully grown offspring have to do with this proceeding."

"Let me put it this way then. How many *minor* children do you have?"

"One."

"How old is the child?"

"Fifteen," she perjured. "But I consider him grown."

"Can you tell us the child's name?"

"Tobias."

"And where does the child reside?"

"Excuse me, but what business is that of the court's? Why is he even asking me that?"

I hadn't spoken to Toby lately, what with the buzz of the trial and my schoolwork mounting, so I didn't know how to read my mother's hedging. Had Toby gone ahead with his plan to live with Shepsy? I couldn't imagine. Maybe he had. And why would Mr. Collins be bringing this up? And right from the start of his cross-examination? Maybe he was thinking that if my mother was awful enough to cede custody of her kid, the jury would see her as awful enough to hatch plots against the rabbi. Something like that. Pretty convoluted. But I never got to know.

Because Ms. Fonseca piped up. "Objection, your honor. This entire topic is irrelevant to the proceedings. I move that all references to the plaintiff's children, adult or otherwise, be stricken from the record."

The judge said, "Sustained."

I wondered how Mr. Collins knew to ask about Toby. Was there an open case with child welfare? Had Shepsy's mother gotten involved? Had Toby himself made a call to Mr. Collins? I never found out.

◆ ◆ ◆

Mr. Collins said, "In what ways do you believe you were damaged by your alleged affair with the defendant?"

"It wasn't the affair that damaged me," my mother said. "The affair was marvelous. The affair was great. I already explained that. It was the therapy that pulled me under. When he made me his patient, everything changed."

"*Made* you his patient? Didn't you have a say in the matter?"

"Yes. Sure. I knew what I was doing. But I was out of my mind with desire for him. I felt I had no choice. The concept of choice never entered my thinking. Rabbi Rick offered help and I needed help desperately. So I agreed to be his patient. The timing was perfect."

"*Perr*fect?" Mr. Collins repeated, with a smarmy stress on the *per*. "*Perr*fect for what?"

"My plan."

Another smarmy stress: "Your *plannnn*?"

"To make him mine. The rabbi I mean. To make the defendant mine forever. My plan all along. You know how it goes. You find yourself so fixated on a fella, on a person, on a lover, that nothing else matters. Your entire life gets vacuumed up into it. So much so that you'll do anything in your power to get him to be with you and stay with you and tell you he loves you forever and ever. That's how I was. How desperate I was. Like Marilyn Monroe singing 'Happy Birthday, Mr. President.' Completely caught up. Like something out of the opera. And let me be honest." Here's where my mother flummoxed us in the courtroom, Ms. Fonseca included. "He didn't *make* me his patient. I *strong-armed* him into making me his patient. You won't find these details in the transcripts Andy talked about. I *begged* him to use me as his guinea pig patient for the completion of his doctoral training. I wanted to be the focus of this essential phase of his studies."

I looked across the room at Kitty Fonseca. Her lips were shaped around an unformed word because she didn't know what to object to. Her forehead and chin were wrinkled with distress.

"When I began my course of treatment with him," my mother told the court, "I felt like I'd hit the jackpot."

◆ ◆ ◆

"Weren't you ever concerned, Mrs. Baer, about the effect this kind of behavior might have on your children?"

My mother looked stumped and possibly trapped. If she were a porcupine, she might have stood up her quills.

Before she could reply, however, Ms. Fonseca said, "Objection. Irrelevant," and the judge sustained her.

◆ ◆ ◆

Later Mr. Collins said, "It doesn't sound like anything changed after you became the defendant's patient. You were having the time of your life before you became his patient, and you were having the time of your life after you became his patient."

Ms. Fonseca said, "I object, your honor. Counsel contends to know the plaintiff's thoughts so well that he can ventriloquize them."

"Sustained," the judge said. "Jurors will disregard counsel's last statement."

Mr. Collins said, "In what ways do you believe you were damaged by the alleged affair? I don't believe you answered that question."

"In countless ways. But in only one way that made any difference. The defendant betrayed me."

"Excuse me, Mrs. Baer. But you don't sound betrayed. You don't sound destroyed or damaged or suffering."

"I'm on medication." (I hadn't known this.) "It dulls my responses. I was not on medication before I met the defendant."

"No more questions."

◆ ◆ ◆

There was one last witness, Toni Di Prima, sporting a dowdy brown dress and a couple of mulberry bags under her eyes. The bailiff swore her in and she explained to the court about how Rabbi converted her from Catholic-school Catholic to conservative Jew and how he welcomed her into the flock and included her in all sorts of organized sessions concerning community and womanhood and faith and sensitivity.

Mr. Collins said, "Now Ms. Di Prima. Kindly tell us what sort of involvement, if any, you had with the transcription of the tape recordings of the defendant's psychotherapy sessions with the plaintiff, Mrs. Baer."

"Well, Bea, see, the defendant and I—"

"The plaintiff, Ms. Di Prima."

"Right, right, sorry, the plaintiff. Pretty confusing. She'd been hired by Rabbi Landy to listen to the tapes and turn them into typescripts. The tapes of their sessions. Part of his schoolwork. The plaintiff started typing them, all by her lonesome, but it was tedious work." She pronounced it tee-jiss. "And she was getting pretty tired, kind of exhausted, rather overwhelmed, because the rabbi had a deadline, it was a piece of his final exam, and of course he couldn't type, so he asked me to help her. He paid pretty nicely. Two-fifty an hour. And sometimes we'd be up all night, listening to the tapes, stopping the tapes, typing, listening, stopping, typing—back and forth. It could get a mite monotonous. We'd get punch-drunk after a while. Not drunk-drunk, never. Neither of us drank. But after a couple of nights of this, Bea, the plaintiff, would say, 'Let's have a little fun with this. I'm so boring in this section. Let's make me more of a wiseass. Let's make me more of a sexy siren. Let's pretend I cracked some jokes here.'"

I tuned out the rest of whatever she was saying.

Verbatim. What a joke. How could I have been such a sap, to treat the transcripts as scripture? Lawyer Collins was right. There'd been some kind of doctoring.

During cross-examination, Ms. Fonseca asked about group therapy with the defendant but Toni stuck to her story that there was never any hanky-panky on the rabbi's watch. And when asked about her feelings toward the plaintiff during the period, Toni Di Prima said she worshiped Bea then and continued to worship her to this day.

45

After Toni Di Prima stepped down, the lawyers delivered their obvious closing statements (gross malpractice vs. delusional manipulation) and the judge delivered his instructions to the jury:

"It is your duty to determine the facts from the evidence only. Neither sympathy nor prejudice should influence your deliberations. Do not proclaim your opinions too loudly, so that your fellow jurors may deliberate without any undue influence—"

I muzzled a sneeze and whispered to Naomi, "Let's skedaddle. Before it's too late."

Naomi whispered, "Right."

We slithered out of the courtroom and onto the street and snuck behind the building to wait for our mother to drive away from the premises. Maybe half an hour later we stuffed our disguises into my backpack and hopped a cab that was idled in front of the jailhouse toward our mother's garden apartment complex.

"Remember," Naomi said, tissuing rouge off her cheeks. "We came in on the bus."

"I remember. 'We're here to distract you until the jury reaches a verdict.'" The cab went over a pothole. "Oof."

The driver said, "Sorry."

"How much is this ride going to cost us?" I whispered.

"Shah. I told you. I got you covered." Naomi made five times more money than I did.

"And so we just happen to show up like this? Knowing exactly when the testimony's over and exactly when she needs us to hold her hand and make her coffee?"

"She's got a lot on her mind. Leave it to me. She'll buy it."

She bought it.

She said she was glad to see us though she didn't seem it. Her apartment was dingier and messier than usual. She sat at the table. She stared at nothing. She welcomed the coffee. She chain-smoked and muttered in a disconcerting monotone. "I feel awful about it. I've lost all confidence. I thought this would change me. But look at what happened. I shouldn't have sued him. I don't trust the jury. We should have circled the wagons. We should have shredded Toni Di Prima. We knew she was coming. We should have foreseen it. And why did I say I *begged* him to be his guinea pig? What the hell is wrong with me?"

I said, "You may not be aware of it, Ma, but you sabotaged things when you handed that to the jury."

"Who asked you?" my mother said. "You weren't even there." She got up from the chair. "I'm taking a bath."

Naomi said, "I thought you needed to decompress."

"Not with *him* at the table." She left the room. "A good long soak is all the decompression I need." She stamped down the hall and slammed the bathroom door.

I continued more quietly. "All that talk about her plan. What a stupid mistake. And how she strong-armed the rabbi. She ruined it for herself. And fatally, I think."

"Keep it down," Naomi said.

I tried to be quieter. "She sabotaged her chances when she prattled about that stuff, and it may have been on purpose."

"What do you mean?"

"We studied it in class. In Abnormal Psychology." I heard the rush of bathtub water from the other side of the wall. "It's a phenomenon of the neurotic personality, a primary theme in psychoanalysis. You can be driven by unconscious motives to work against your own best interests, even your very happiness. In Mom's case, I think her hope is that the rabbi will be found Not Guilty—in the end that's what she wants—and there's a likelihood she'll get her wish because he brainwashed her so thoroughly that the only way she can live with herself is to ruin it for herself."

Naomi said, "And what kind of grade did you get in this class?"

"It's okay if you don't believe me."

"If she's really such a fuck-up, how do you explain her bringing the lawsuit in the first place? How do you explain the courage it took her? So she could screw it all up and help him get off? Do you think she's some kind of nincompoop?"

"She's still in love with him," I said.

Naomi said, "Stop."

"That's her sole motivation. Her endless maniacal unconditional love for Rabbi. And she doesn't even wonder for a moment," I said, "why she ever got involved with him. This royal mess of a whackjob. What attracted her to him. Psychologically speaking. And what it says about her self-esteem and her lack of self-esteem and her unacknowledged motives."

"Come on, Andy. Lighten up. You sound like you had half your brain taken out."

"All I'm suggesting," I said, "is that it might help her to get into therapy."

"It was therapy with that bastard that caused all the trouble in the first place."

"Therapy with that bastard was by definition worthless. It would benefit her to work with someone competent. I mean, she doesn't even take two minutes out of her pointless life for some quiet self-reflection."

"How do you know?"

"I know her pretty well."

"And who are you to lecture anyone anyway?" Naomi said. "Look at you. Completely uninterested in relationships, in love. Always mooning over some clueless galoot who doesn't even know who you are. You're worse than she is. At least she gets some action. No one with any brains would bother to listen to your quote-unquote insights when they come from such a numbskull. So maybe she's still in love with him. So what? The only thing you're in love with is the sound of your own opinions."

I heard the bathtub spigots twisted shut with a couple of squeaks.

"You're just jealous," I said.

"No I'm not and you know it."

◆ ◆ ◆

Later, after we all calmed down, after Kitty Fonseca called to say that the jury wouldn't be back with a verdict until at least the following morning, I asked my mother to drive us to the bus stop closest to the Turnpike so we could catch the express and return to the city fast, before the rush hour hit.

"By the way," I said from the backseat of her '64 Falcon. "What was that business on the stand about Toby? When the defense attorney asked you where he was living these days?"

"Oh that," my mother said, going straight instead of right onto Monticello Street. "He's just crashing at a friend's house for a couple of nights. I have no idea why they were worried about that. Or how they found out about it. That was all a big nothing." She was taking the roundabout detour past the rabbi's house.

"Where the hell are you going?" Naomi said from the front. "We have a bus to catch."

◆ ◆ ◆

Turned out Toby had in fact moved in with the Spencers.

◆ ◆ ◆

Another two years passed.

46

THE MACKINAC COURIER

April 12, 1977

MONTEVIDEO RABBI SENTENCED TO 2 YEARS FOR ABUSING CONGREGANTS WHILE POSING AS THERAPIST

MACKINAC - Rabbi Richard Landy of Montevideo, who posed as a psychoanalytic therapist despite his lack of training in the field, was convicted of gross malpractice and sexual abuse of four female patients whom he was treating between 1969 and 1974. He was sentenced to two years in prison and ordered to pay damages of an undisclosed amount to the claimants.

The four claimants were Mrs. Myrna Shapiro, Mrs. Gladys Gottesman, Mrs. Samantha Lipschitz and Miss Tosca Wunderlich, all of Mackinac County and all former congregants of Temple Shir Shalom in Montevideo, where Landy was employed as rabbi until his resignation in 1973.

During the two-week trial, the women testified that Landy, 50, had pressured them during therapeutic sessions to remove their blouses and, in some cases, their panties, after which he touched them sexually. One patient said that Landy engaged in masturbation and oral sex with her. Another said that he "badmouthed her husband" and urged her to have extramarital sex with what he called a "surrogate lover," meaning himself. A third patient claimed that she was coerced into having sexual relations with female patients in his group therapy sessions. All four women testified that the rabbi encouraged them to attend his religious services at Temple Shir Shalom as a spiritual complement to their treatment.

The prosecution claimed that Landy used newspaper want ads, business cards and word of mouth to promote himself as an analytic psychotherapist, even though he was not licensed to practice in that capacity. Landy claimed he had a master's degree in psychotherapy from Unami University in Chester, but school officials had no record of his matriculation. His bachelor's degree in philosophy from Iolanthe University of Arizona isn't recognized by New Jersey's psychotherapeutic licensing board, and Iolanthe has been under investigation for financial fraud. In some identifying documents, Landy also claimed to have earned a PhD in psychoanalytic theory from Fairmont State University in West Virginia, but an inquiry revealed that no such degree is offered from that institution.

Landy earned his rabbinical ordination from the New York Rabbinical Seminary in New York in 1954.

On Wednesday, after handing down the two-year sentence, the longest term allowed for such crimes under New Jersey law, Judge Marvin G. Kaplan said, "Each of the complainants sought your help for mental anguish and instead wound up being further tormented."

The four women joined forces earlier this year to file complaints with New Jersey's Consumer Affairs Department asserting that Landy had repeatedly coerced them to engage in unwanted sexual activity. Their complaints resulted in official investigations that eventually allowed the matter to proceed to trial.

On the witness stand, Landy denied any wrongdoing.

A similar suit was brought against Landy by a single litigant two years ago, Ms. Beatrice Baer, and ended with a deadlocked jury. Alberta Junghans, a Beechwood lawyer who specializes in psychological malpractice suits, said that group prosecutions are typically more successful than those brought by single litigants.

47

The news was anticlimactic.

My mother had moved on, about six months earlier, to a follow-up boyfriend, an *actual* boyfriend, dress salesman Barty Garfein (they'd met at a singles dance in Harrington Heights) who was divorced with three boys (they lived with their mother upstate in Shanny Valley) and an office in the Garment Center. He was a big, smiley, cigar-obsessed *tummeler* with a racetrack habit, a horny sense of humor and a muskrat toupée. I'd seen him a few times, at Passover for instance, and actually kind of liked him (he was exactly who he was, no hidden rabbinical motives or misogyny hit lists) although Naomi spoke to him rudely. Naomi said it was the same exact treatment our mother had gotten from Rabbi ("He treats her like his personal love slave") but I disagreed. This relationship was out in the open at least, and included steakhouse dinners and three-day weekends in the Bahamas and Vegas (where they saw Streisand perform *twice in one night*, including the added-on late show, at splendiferous Caesars Palace). But despite the adventure and the-sky's-the-limit spending, my mother played it wrong. That was the sad part. She would wait around for hours, a chain-smoking lovesick maniac, for Barty's promised phone calls, and throw on a raincoat over her nightgown (desperately familiar gesture) so she could fly to him faster when the call finally came. And after that Passover seder he came to at my mother's, she sat at his feet, like a powder-faced geisha, when he repaired to the living room to light up a stogie—flagrant and shameless before her three appalled children. Plus she started wearing *hotpants* (yikes)—red, satin, 42nd-Street-hooker wear—just because he asked her to. Even after all the suffering Rabbi Landy had put her through, she hadn't learned much beyond staying away from rabbis. She had an ironclad exclusive lifetime contract with barking top-dog alpha-male types who lived for her adulation. Well, somebody's adulation.

She had a ball with Barty Garfein in any case. But as Naomi once said, in this kind of sitch the woman is only happy for a couple of months.

Oh, and she never felt any guilt for letting Toby live with the Spencers.

◆ ◆ ◆

I was in my last semester of college, meanwhile, happily recovered from my fruitless obsession with Chris Maragliano (the attachment evaporated as soon as I confessed my love to his face, and he responded with a sweet-natured Thank you, I'm flattered, but it isn't the same for me) and enjoying Manhattan gay life on and off campus which included lots of brief affairs and mindless intoxication. Yes, Naomi had shaken me up when she told me I was a cold-hearted wiseguy who didn't know shit about relationships and love, but she was my sister, and I was used to thinking "What the hell does she know?" whenever she mounted one of her high-horse attacks, so I went on my way rejoicing.

(With a bit of a hitch, I admit, in the rejoicing.)

Fear of life after college was dogging me most of all, but there were still lots of youthful pleasures to be had in the interim, including the monthly gay dances at Columbia's Earl Hall which were famous beyond the campus, especially with Gotham's cosmopolitan chicken hawks, $2 to get in (a dollar with student ID).

Gay People at Columbia sponsored the dance, and as a regular with the org, I created flyers for the event that we plastered all over Morningside Heights and the Upper West Side and on lampposts down in the Village near the bars. The last flyer I drew was for the April dance, the ultimate of the spring semester and the ultimate of my undergrad tenure. I used a fine-point marker to depict a curly-haired blond in very short shorts wearing a backward cap and a fetching grin, his thumb stuck out, hoping for a hitch. David Robinson, the GPC president, said he thought I'd have no trouble getting a job as an executive assistant panderer on Madison Avenue after we graduated.

That last-of-the-season GPC dance was a splashy all-male lollapalooza (Columbia wasn't co-ed yet) with banks of colored lights and amps as big as bank vaults. The weather was beautiful, prematurely sultry, even long after sundown, and the windows and doors to the fire escapes were open to let the night in. I had a lot of friends through GPC, and we loved to dance as a group under the grand domed ceiling of the second-floor auditorium with its fancy steps in the front leading up to fluted columns.

Because of some scheduling mishap, the Jewish Campus Society was hosting an Oneg Shabbat (with its grape juice and mondel bread) on the first floor of Earl that night, directly beneath the deafening disco.

"Dancing Queen." "Don't Leave Me This Way." "Get Up and Boogie."

I'm sure we were a pain in the ass to members of the Jewish Campus Society as they sing-sang their innocent tunes about the Sabbath bride and the Lord of the universe.

It wasn't long into the evening, while David Robinson and I were dancing to "That's the Way I Like It," that I noticed a group of shadows, in dresses and suits, at the top of the fire escape. The music was too loud to make out their voices, and the fire escape too dark to make out their faces, so we just kept dancing. Let them gawk all they wanted at the gay boys shaking it up with the other gay boys.

Then I realized they must be members of the Jewish Campus Society who had wandered up the fire escape to see what was causing the racket.

A man-shadow pointed a finger into the crowd and spoke so loud that I heard him over the music: "Yep. That's Andy." He took a step into the room and I could see it was Avi, in a light-colored suit with a super-fat tie and a yarmulke high on his uncombed fluffed-up wolfman hair.

I mouthed to David, "Excuse me a minute."

David nodded in time to the rhythmic brass of the Sunshine Band and shimmied away, to another spot on the dancefloor, joining a new assortment of shake-shake-shakers.

Meanwhile, the intruders from the JCS had scampered away like possums down the fire escape, leaving only Avi.

I went right over. "What brings you to the gay dance, Avi? Didn't you graduate a year ago?"

It seemed like he couldn't hear me over the music. He grabbed me by the wrist and pulled me out to the fire escape balcony.

"Come down with me," I heard him say.

"What are you doing?"

He smiled. "Please."

He had the grip of a champion arm wrestler. I followed him reluctantly down the trembly steps, past the brightly lit window on the story below (maybe a dozen boring members of the JCS in their synagogue finest) and onto the grass in front of Earl Hall. Avi let go and hurried ahead, faster than me, toward the steps spilling down from Low Library.

There was no one on the steps. The lights were damped down. The music trailed off.

"Sit," he said.

We sat at the top of one of the flights—so many extravagantly inessential steps—and extended our legs across the granite gradations. Avi's polyester suit must've felt like a thermal heat pouch in the evening's tropical swelter, whereas I was dressed right, in shorts and a T-shirt.

"Great to see you," he said.

I smiled. "You too." My eardrums hurt, like there was a washing machine in my head.

"Quite a bombshell about my father," he said, sliding the yarmulke off his head and slipping it into a pocket.

"Oh. Yeah. Right. That."

"I bet your mother's happy." He undid his tie, as wide as a spatula, and pulleyed it off his neck.

I said, "It wasn't her lawsuit. So, I mean. You know."

"Sure. Of course." He took off his jacket.

I laughed a little because it looked like he was instigating a sit-down strip—yarmulke, tie, jacket—when he was only trying to make himself comfortable.

"What's funny?" he said.

"Nothing."

His *Shobbis* shirt was drenched with sweat. He tugged on the collar, cleared his throat and put his jacket on a step and his tie on the jacket.

"So?" I said. I wasn't used to seeing him awkward. "What's this all about? You made me flat-leave a friend on the dance floor, you know."

"David Robinson. Nice guy. I'm in a calculus class with him."

"I thought you graduated already."

"I took a leave of absence. Couple semesters. Try and straighten things out. I'm only just graduating now, like you."

I was intrigued but didn't show it. I was reluctant to feel any softness. We had a history together and it was mostly annoying. "So uh, what did you want to talk about?"

"My father for starters. I never knew he could be such a crybaby. He's acting like a wimp."

"Of course he is. He's going to jail."

"He isn't your typical convict personality."

"Maybe not typical. But he's got the personality."

I was on my guard—with what I thought was good reason—but something was already softening me. The summery air. Avi's efforts. The relentless lure of a wide-open future. "Your mother's the one I feel sorriest for."

"Yeah, poor *Eemah*. Such a colossal humiliation. But you know *her*. The original ice queen. Very little penetrates."

"Ah."

"Well."

"Well."

"Ah."

The weather was so warm, there should have been crickets, but it wasn't the season. All I picked up on were the syncopated thuds from the dance hall behind us and the proximity of Avi, who emitted wafts of heat.

I said, "Why are you being nice to me?"

His eyebrows came together, like greater-than and less-than symbols. I said, "We haven't been in touch since that awful night at the Lair."

"It wasn't that awful."

"It was for me."

He said, "I'm sorry, Andy. I was so liquored up."

The truth is it wasn't that awful, not really, if I was honest with myself. But I had the power to make him feel guilty and I liked that.

Meanwhile, I heard the spiraling whine of an ambulance siren which slowly dissolved into the Mister Softee jingle.

"I've been thinking about that night," he said. "About *you* that night."

"What's there to think? I made sure you got to your dorm, that's all."

He said, "That definitely wasn't *all*," as if this were something for us to banter about.

But I stayed quiet.

"Apart from that," he said, retracting a smirk, "you pulled off my shoes. You put me to bed. You took excellent care of me."

I said, "I had never seen anyone as plastered as that. Not even in *The Lost Weekend*."

"One of my all-time favorite pictures by the way. Especially the scene where he's trudging up Third Avenue, desperate for a whiskey."

I wasn't in the mood for vintage-movie small talk. "I think you understand I never liked you," I said.

I gave him credit. He didn't flinch. He even leaned in closer. "Yeah, but I always liked *you*."

"Me? Come on. That's hard to believe…"

"I was thinking I might find you at the dance tonight. I was hoping I would."

"…extremely hard to believe. And how do you even remember that night, when you were so ridiculously blotto?"

"I don't know. I just do."

"Cataclysmically blotto."

"You were kind to me. That stayed with me. Especially after I'd behaved like such a dick. I'm sorry I exposed myself in the men's room that night."

"You did a little bit more than expose yourself."

"No. I know. I realize. I'm sorry."

"You scared the bejesus out of me."

"I know it. I *know*. I said I was sorry."

The lyric fragment "love to hear it, got to hear it, turn the beat around" came trailing out of Earl Hall's windows and over the steps through the vibrating haze. It was eerie that only the fragment trailed and not the whole song.

"You never let me bully you," Avi said. "Going back to when we were kids. You always stood your ground with me. Most people didn't know how to do that. Most people *still* don't know how to do that. Fucking weenies."

I'd never thought of it as standing my ground. I'd just try really hard to bushwack through my fear of him, so I could maneuver around him at a kiddush after services and angle for a cookie without collapsing from fright. But it sounded like he never saw the effort it took. All he saw was the moxie.

Huh.

Lucky.

"By the way," he said. "I've given up drinking."

"Really."

"For the record," he said, "I'm sober."

It seemed like the truth. It didn't feel like acting. Something about him. It was hard to say what. The melting eyes. The rueful tone. Could assholes as big as he was handle tenderness and regret? I didn't think so. I didn't know what to think. Could he be lying about the sobriety?

"I went down the shore," he said, "some isolated beach town for a couple of weeks. To see if I could survive without a drink for a couple of weeks. I was lucky. I survived. But in the end. Well. I really don't know. I honestly don't. In any case. I was hoping I'd run into you."

"You said."

"Because I wanted to see if you'd—" He cleared his throat again. "—if you'd go to the movies with me."

"What do you mean? "

"A movie. In a movie theater. Maybe *Demon Seed*? Or *Smokey and the Bandit*?"

"Wait. Seriously? Those are my choices?"

"I had a feeling you wouldn't be interested. That's okay. I get it. Not a problem. In the least." He scanned the deserted symmetry of campus and rubbed his fuzzy facial scraggle.

"Avi, come on, you aren't even gay."

"Not everyone's out of the closet, Andy."

"Wait. So you mean you've never been tempted to toddle down to the Village on a Saturday night with a baseball bat?"

He sighed. "I know I've got baggage."

"Like the lost and found at LaGuardia Airport."

"I don't own a bat."

"Then a broomstick. Or a piano leg."

"I'm sorry I was ever mean to you, Andy. I genuinely am."

I didn't know how to respond to that. My read on him was blurry, wobbling. Yet he was up to his fifth "I'm sorry" of the evening and that struck me as pretty radical.

"I'm not my father," he said, "in any event. My father never apologizes."

I stretched my legs longer till they spanned four steps below us. "I'll have to think about this. I'll have to sleep on it. After a very long nap."

"No, I get it. I'm not going anywhere. I'm staying here in the city. I'm taking another year off. I got a part-time job at the Museum of Natural History, writing labels for the display cases. Then I'm thinking I'll go to law school. And if that's too ambitious, I can always drive a truck."

"I bet that's lonely."

He looked at me from two perspectives with a tilt of the head. "You know, your eyes are quite nice."

"I'm sure I wouldn't know."

"They are. Trust me."

I cracked my knuckles. I looked down the steps. "What about my knees?"

Avi guffawed.

Then a plaintive high-school pang of a voice came swirling out of the dance hall. *"Ooh baby I love your way."*

"Hey, that's not a dance song," Avi said.

"Yes it is. They spin a ballad now and then so we can all enjoy a slow dance."

More of the lyric drifted in. *"I wanna tell you I love your way."* Then drifted back out.

"Peter Frampton," he said. "I own the album."

"And as you'll discover once you're settled at the museum," I said, "it is the habit of the indigenous homosexualis, after gathering with his fellows at the watering hole, to slow-dance on occasion. So they can touch each other."

He put his hand on my knee. "Just touch?" But he was shy about it, so he took it away and snickered unappealingly.

Heat lightning sent a zigzag down from the sky, directly over the library.

"Did you see that?" he said.

I nodded. It was thunderless.

Another zigzag flashed above Philosophy.

"Whoa," he said.

"Beautiful." It seemed as if the lightning was calling the city to attention—a plea for a different mindset in the face of so much beauty. "Yet I still don't get where you're coming from, Avi. I mean, if it affected you so much when I took care of you that night, why did you wait this long to find me?"

"I don't know. Is it important to know that? What I know is I always respected you. I was always extra careful not to mimic you or put you down. Nothing derogatory or gay-bashy."

"You called me a dandelion. One of the last times I saw you. I'm not making that up."

"I don't remember that, jeez. But if you say so, I believe you. Again, I'm sorry. In my defense, I might've been punning. Andy? Dandy? Pretty lame, I guess."

"Totally lame. And inconsiderate."

"But whatever it was, I never thought your gayness was gross or disgusting. Not one bit. And let me add this. If you find I'm still an aggressive dickhead, I've got news for you. That isn't going to change. It's not like all the sudden I was magically transformed by some attitude hocus-pocus. I'm positive I wasn't. I'm still the same jerk I always was. I'm just a jerk without a drink. And I'm ready to come out. And I'd like you to go to the movies with me."

Acknowledgments

I'm grateful to Ian Henzel, of Rattling Good Yarns Press, for publishing this book and for guiding me through revisions that opened me up to deeper meaning and sexier plotting. My wonderful partner Mike Rendino helped me rethink the thrust of the story by getting me to imagine it more thoroughly and make the narrator less of a schlemazel. Formative teachers made me feel like I was a writer as early as 1964, including Miss Maragno of the tangerine lipstick, Mr. Schwartz and Scott Sommer. Rabbis Chernick and Poleyoff turned me on to the cryptic concision of the Talmud, which paved the way to critical thinking, joke telling and psychoanalysis. My longtime psychoanalyst Ellen Daniels led me out of the "Kiss Me I'm a Pancake" school of literature by getting me in touch with deeper hurts and better love. Kathleen Warnock and Rob Byrnes made me feel like $1.5 million per reading by letting me grandstand in public. My mother was a big reader so there were always books in the house. Sometimes I'd wake up and she'd be sitting in the same spot at the dining room table that she'd been sitting in when I went to bed, having read a Laura Z. Hobson or a Margaret Truman or a Philip Roth through the night. It was novelists like Roth and Dickens and William Peter Blatty, Alison Lurie, E. M. Forster and Chaim Potok who got me to value novels more than any other art form. And it was John Gardner who taught me what made those books effective: the casting forward and the eschewing of victimhood. Forster (him again) influenced me with his thoughts on round characters (think Elizabeth Bennet in "Pride and Prejudice") vs. flat characters (Elizabeth's mother). Professor Donadio instructed me in the joys of structural analysis and characters acting out of character. I'm grateful to early readers Felice Picano, Blair Fell, Oren Rudavsky, Sean Harvey, James Magruder and Stephen Greco. They excited me about the future. And my brother Steven always looked up to me as a writer. Well, almost always. (He was the one who named that literary school of willful obfuscation "Kiss Me I'm a Pancake" which I ascribed to before the therapist went to work on me.) Thanks also to Alison Jarvis, Beth Farb, Bruce Austern, Gerard Cabrera, Jacki Marino, Jed Marcus, Jeff Klein, Jen Levin, Jess Greenbaum, Kate Rounds, Lance Evans, Linda Appel, Marlene Rubens, Peggy Hickey, Peter Bingham, Robert Konigsberg and Tom Ott for schlepping to the readings. With friends like that, who needs politics?

About the Author

Dan Meltz was raised in the low-rent reaches of Jersey, 16 minutes from Times Square. He's lived in New York City for fifty years. His stories have appeared in *CrossConnect*, *Columbia Review* and the *Jewish Writing Project*. His poems have appeared in *American Poetry Review*, *Best New Poets 2012*, *Jewish Quarterly*, *Mudfish*, *Salamander*, *upstreet* and lots of other journals. He is a retired technical writer and teacher of Deaf young people. He has a B.A. from Columbia (no honors) with a major in English. His book of poems, "It Wasn't Easy to Reach You," was published by Trail to Table in 2025. "Rabbis of the Garden State" is his first novel. His longtime partner Mike Rendino is an award-winning playwright.